LET'S SPLIT UP

BILL WOOD

Scholastic

Published in the UK by Scholastic, 2024
1 London Bridge, London, SE1 9BG
Scholastic Ireland, 89E Lagan Road, Dublin Industrial Estate,
Glasnevin, Dublin, D11 HP5F

ISBN 978 07023 3852 6

A CIP catalogue record for this book
is available from the British Library.

Printed and bound in Great Britain by
Clays Ltd, Elcograf S.p.A.
Paper made from wood grown in sustainable forests
and other controlled sources.

7 9 10 8

www.scholastic.co.uk

For those who find comfort in the mystery.

PROLOGUE

2001

"I don't think this is safe."

"No shit, Shelley," Brad replies under his breath as he shoves his backpack through a gap in the metal fence. It's unclear whether the metal had worn away over time or whether the hole's been purposely cut. But they don't have time to fool around. Can't risk being caught. Not this close to graduation. "I'll go through first, OK?"

Shelley nods, giving him a reluctant go-ahead. Her hands tremble, but Brad *must* see what's on the other side. This could be his big break. He finishes high school next summer and colleges aren't exactly calling him up. He just needs a local station to see his show and the rest will be history. All this time developing *Truly Haunted* will be worth it. Get the famous Carrington Ghoul on camera and the TV studios will come running. Right?

In a perfect world, yes. But Sanera, California … is far from perfect.

Slowly, Brad slips his head through the opening, then snakes his body in after, trying not to scratch himself on the rusty metal. He makes it through unscathed, bar a few nicks on his jeans. He'll deal with his mom's wrath later.

He grabs his bag and brushes the dirt from it. Luckily, it's already dark brown, so the stains aren't too visible. At least he can hide *that* from his mom.

"OK, your turn," he calls to Shelley, without glancing at her. His focus is on the camcorder he's pulled from the depths of the backpack. This show needs to be the best of the best. It demands stakes. Production values. Editing. Showmanship. This won't be another shitty ghost-hunting show, like on MTV. This will be *the* ghost-hunting show.

It has to be.

"Thanks a lot, doofus." Brad pulls his attention back to her. She's brushing down his letterman jacket, which has fallen out of his backpack and is now covered in mud. She looks cute.

"I'm sorry," he says, reaching for her hand. "Thanks for doing this. It will be worth it, I promise."

She stares up at him for a moment, clearly contemplating her life's decisions, but eventually gives an annoyed smirk. "You're such an idiot."

"I am," he replies. There's no point in arguing with Shelley and, besides, she's right. Brad is kind of lost in life. He's on the football team but not good enough for a college scholarship. He doesn't particularly like his teammates and he's flunking school. It goes on. He's gone through high school as the golden boy, but now that it's coming to an end he's running out of options. No one is going to care he was the star quarterback when his hairline begins to recede.

He hauls Shelley to her feet but misjudges how light she is and she lands against his chest.

"Sorry about all the mud," he says.

She laughs. "What, this?" She motions at her now filthy jeans. Her smile is wide but Brad can tell it's slightly forced. As though inside she wants to cry. He knows how much she likes those jeans. He'll pay to get them cleaned, of course. He made her come with him so it's only fair.

He leans into her dirt-smudged face and kisses her. They stay there for a few moments, leaving words unspoken and unravelling the tension, before he slowly pulls away.

"Let's get this over and done with, yeah?"

They trek up the seemingly never-ending narrow driveway to Carrington Manor. It's long abandoned, although Brad knows that some kids used to come up here to party every so often. However, it's a Tuesday night so he and Shelley should be alone. It's not exactly the prime time to get high with your friends.

As they close in on the manor, the shrubbery that

conceals it from the gated entrance becomes less and less dense, exposing the true nature of the building. It's massive; Brad can't even tell how far it goes back. It's a Victorian-style build, though he only knows this because of his extensive research. Plus, it looks like it was ripped right out of some gothic horror movie.

"It's beautiful," Shelley says, her eyes fixed on the black building that somehow cuts through the darkness. "In a creepy way."

Brad snorts. "Yeah, the boarded-up windows kind of kill the charm a little bit—"

"Do you think there's … rats?" Shelley's voice is suddenly panicked.

"No, of course not!" There are without a doubt going to be rats. "There's no way rats could survive out here." They definitely can.

Shelley's shoulders relax. "OK, good." But she still looks cautious.

Eventually, they halt a few feet from the front steps. Brad looks around. "This should be a good first shot, right? With the house and a bit of the sky in the back?"

He hands Shelley the camcorder and she flips it on. For a moment, she fiddles with the settings, deletes some test footage, then adjusts the brightness. As soon as she angles the camera towards Brad, her face lights up. "It looks amazing!"

"Really?"

"Yeah, super professional," she replies. "The lighting is actually great."

Brad releases a sigh. He can't afford for this to be a half-assed job. "I think we're ready then."

"You know what you're gonna say?"

Brad nods. Of course he does – he's been practising all week. He swipes a hand through his brown hair, slicking it back as usual, making sure it's camera-ready, then pulls a few strands over his forehead – his signature style. Well, John Travolta's signature style in *Grease*. But it's Brad's at the moment. He unbuttons his jacket, revealing a stark white tee with his show's logo, *Truly Haunted*.

"I'll do my intro and then we'll make our way into the house," he says. "Keep the camera running all the time. We can edit stuff out if we need to."

"Got it," Shelley says, almost excitedly. At first, Brad had to beg her to come to these places with him, but now Shelley seems to enjoy it. Plus, she would do anything if it meant she might be able to include it on her ever-growing résumé. Unlike Brad, Shelley has five college offers in the bag. Two of them Ivy League schools. She seems to have already forgotten about the mud. "Ready to go?"

"Yep," he replies.

Shelley checks the shot again, counts down and finally shouts, "Action!"

Brad clears his throat and begins. "A cursed manor. An age-old curse. And a murderous ghoul… Join us while we explore Carrington Manor and discover the secrets that lie inside its walls. I'm Bradley Campbell, and you're watching *Truly Haunted*."

Shelley slowly pans the camera towards the house, and, like magic, lightning strikes, illuminating the manor in a ghostly glow. It's scarily well timed. TV gold. Stations would be clowns to pass this up.

Brad can't hide his excitement. It's perfect. The *perfect* shot.

Shelley pans back to Brad in a smooth arc, keeping it as steady as possible. Brad hasn't been able to afford a stabilizer yet.

"It seems the manor is calling us," Brad says ominously. His next words come with a fittingly sinister smile. Rehearsed, of course. "Let's not keep it waiting."

Brad slowly climbs the front steps, Shelley walking alongside as he talks. "Carrington Manor has stood for over one hundred years but no one seems to know who built it or when. In fact, the locals say it just appeared one day. One minute there was open land, and the next … a curious manor."

The truth stretches when he weaves his words, but the sentiment is there. There's no actual reports that the manor just *appeared* one day – he's not even sure where he read that – but it sure makes one hell of a story. *Good television*.

Brad can see the story is even creeping Shelley out a

bit, so he shoots her a fast smile. He can edit it out later. It seems to help slightly, as her expression settles from deathly dread to mild worry.

"There have been multiple sightings over the years of a figure that lurks in the halls of this very manor: the ghost of its owner, Robert Carrington. A shadowy figure seen at the topmost window of this manor, dressed in Carrington's dark suit, a scarf hiding his scars. A figure glowing with an unearthly light. At one point, the manor was a hotspot for teens, but eventually something scared them away. Believe these sightings, or don't, but the accounts all align—"

Grand thunder disrupts his words; the camera goes unsteady for a short moment.

"Well, he didn't like that," Brad says with a nervous chuckle. "Let's go back to the beginning. Carrington Manor was owned by Robert Carrington, the biggest landowner in the state. He had spent many years upstate but in 1918 he returned with his wife and children to Sanera to take up residence in his new home, which had stood empty for the past two decades. However, he soon made himself unpopular among the townsfolk with his haughty, superior manner and high rents. Carrington lost his wife and children to illness and his bitterness towards the locals increased. One Halloween night, in 1926, a fire broke out at the manor and Robert perished. No one knows how the fire started but, as the crowds gathered, *everyone* heard his pained wails. His screams for help.

Some say servants and locals tried to help – others say they abandoned the arrogant landowner to his death.

"Believing he had been abandoned, in his dying moments Robert is said to have cursed the manor – a curse many heard screamed from the upper window as the flames consumed him. He swore to haunt the house for the rest of time and punish those who had turned their backs, their descendants and all who live in Sanera. The locals now call him … the Carrington Ghoul."

Brad has practised this in the mirror countless times. Nevertheless, a shiver runs down his spine – so much so he has to rub his arm free of the goosebumps. It seems the manor has that effect.

"And now," he says, "I think it's time we found out the truth for ourselves, don't you?"

Reaching the top step, they come to a standstill. Boarded windows have rotted, exposing the dark innards of the house. They can see shadows of covered-up furniture.

"You OK?" Brad asks Shelley.

Another forced smile. "You told that story a little too well. It was really scary."

"That's what we're going for. Camera still running?"

"It is."

There's an odd expression on her face. "What's wrong?" he asks.

"Oh." She quickly smiles. "Nothing. Just … do you think there really is a ghost?"

Brad didn't expect that. To be honest, he hadn't even considered it. He definitely believes ghosts exist, but whether the Carrington Ghoul does … he doesn't know. There have been sightings – that's all. But then … isn't that how every horror movie begins? It takes the right moment, the right curious person, for the villain to strike.

"Look," he says softly, taking Shelley's free hand in his. "I've got you; I always do."

Shelley bites her lip before shaking her body free of the thought. "Yeah, I know."

"Let's go." Instantly, Brad flips back into character. "We're now entering Carrington Manor…"

The door is large, wooden and rotting. If only he had gloves. He reaches for the handle; it clicks open straight away. Too easy. He didn't expect it to be locked, but he *did* expect some sort of resistance. After all, the manor has been deserted for years. But then again, he's not the only kid who's poked around in here.

"And just like that … we're in." Brad nods at the camera and takes his first step into the house. The wooden floor creaks beneath his feet; the sound echoes through the entire entryway. It *is* a bit scary, but all he can think about is how atmospheric it will be on camera. The thought gives him butterflies.

He continues. "After the house fire in which Robert Carrington died, the house was abandoned. So we *should* be able to see the manor as it was, all those years ago. Try and piece together what happened on that night. How about we get some light in here?"

Now that they're inside, it seems darker than it did from the porch.

"Damn," Brad mutters. "We should have brought candles. It would have been way more creepy than torchlight."

"Look," whispers Shelley, and she points towards a candelabra on the wall, still holding candles.

Brad grabs one of the long thin candles, and lights it with the lighter he has permanently stored in his back pocket. The warm glow flickers in the cold interior of the manor. It's a sight that needs to be seen to be believed. *And it will be seen*, Brad thinks.

He holds the candle up to the walls, dispersing the light source to the paintings that line the walls. An astonished laugh escapes Brad's lips. He's read about this portrait, but it's another thing seeing it.

"Here we have a portrait of Robert Carrington and his family. As I mentioned, his wife and children tragically died from tuberculosis three years before the fire – a common cause of death at the time. Carrington was always a reclusive and cold figure, but after their deaths, he became hostile, and a menace to the town. He was even said to have threatened certain townspeople with a butcher's blade."

Despite it being a family portrait, Brad can only focus

on Robert's overbearing presence. His pale face is forever immortalized, bearing a pinched, frowning expression and glaring black eyes. He wears a dark three-piece suit and appears to loom out of the frame, his wife and children seeming to shrink into the background. It's most likely a trick of his mind but Brad is sure that Robert's eyes glance towards him.

Brad and Shelley continue on through the house, the floorboards creaking. At first, the jarring sound is uncomfortable on the ear, but it soon becomes bearable enough. Brad looks around, trying to see if there's anything else to film, but it's just old furniture and portraits.

It's obvious if there was anything of worth here, it was taken a long time ago. Suddenly Brad doubts himself. He's come here to find something extraordinary, to get himself noticed. He's riding on this, so what if they find nothing? What if…

"God, how can we make this actually *good*?" Brad blurts out.

"It *is* good," Shelley contests. She keeps the camera on Brad because if there is a ghost, it'll come when they least expect it. "Babe, we haven't even looked upstairs. Isn't that where he—"

"—died," he finishes, cheering up. Shelley is right. If there's something worth finding, it'll be upstairs. Right where it all ended.

*

As they make their way to the next floor, they're met with a line of large Turkish-style rugs that have been laid along the hallway, dampening the creaking noises. They're seemingly new. On the landing, several doors meet their gaze, some shut, others ajar. They pass them all, until Brad reaches the large floor-to-ceiling window that overlooks the entire front drive and beyond. He can just about see the part of the fence they snuck through from here.

He turns to the camera. "This is the exact location where Robert Carrington was last seen alive. It is presumed he awoke to the fire and rushed out of his bedroom, here." He points at a door nearby, adjacent to the bay window. "From the burns on the stairs, we can only guess that the fire had spread fast enough to cut him off, here." Brad's finger points towards the charred floor where no rug lies; he taps his foot quite hard on it.

The camera shakes as Shelley jumps. "Careful," she hisses. "This place is ancient. I don't want the floor to give way."

"It's fine," Brad tells her. Actually, he'd expected the manor to be in worse condition than this. Apart from the charred floor and dust, the house seems untouched – weirdly so.

"Let's make our way to Robert's bedroom—"

A haunting groan spreads across the landing, causing Shelley to gasp and look around, sending the camera away from Brad. Brad bites his lip. He has a show to film.

"Shell, it was nothing. Old houses make noises all the time." But he's uncertain himself. That did not sound like any noise a *house* could make.

Eventually, Shelley pans back to Brad. He steps towards the closest door, knowing it was Robert's bedroom from his extensive research. He'd found a floor plan at Sanera's public library. It's wild how much random shit they have there. He spent ages poring over the plan and knows the house back to front. His whole heart is in this. It's *the* Sanera ghost story. Every kid, person, adult and pet has an opinion on what happened here. This *will* be big.

The door is ajar. Which is weird, if Robert rushed out on the night of the fire. But the thought is a silly one. Of course people have been here since then. Kids, squatters have all been inside. There's no way they haven't been up here. Especially to the Carrington Ghoul's bedroom. It's like a Sanera hot spot. Or should that be … cold spot?

"This is the bedroom of the late Robert Carrington," he says, with a hand on the doorknob. It's icy on his palm when he pushes it. But, even though the door is ajar, it doesn't budge.

Which makes no sense.

A nervous laugh slips from Brad as he tries the door again, now with more force. How is it stuck? It's like something is blocking it.

Brad turns back to the camera. "Well, it seems Robert doesn't want us in here… Let's explore the other rooms."

13

Behind the camera, he sees Shelley's eyes widen.

But he doesn't understand why.

He doesn't—

Shelley steps back, terror in her blue eyes.

"Shelley?" Brad says, confused. "What's up?"

Nothing comes out when she tries to answer, fear clogging her words. She just points to him … no—

Behind him.

Slowly, Brad turns. He finally sees.

No.

The door is now open. A spectral figure stands in the doorway, its entire face veiled by a thick scarf, just two ghostly eyes visible. Instantly, Brad knows who it is. The dark singed suit hanging off its frame. He's seen it before. From many nights of research. From the reports he's read and the newspaper articles—

The legends are true. The Carrington Ghoul is real.

He barely processes this before the figure takes a slow step forward. Startled, Brad stumbles, falls to the ground, dropping the candle.

Shelley pulls Brad to his feet. Shaking, they face the figure.

The ghoul stands before the bedroom. For a moment, Brad is too stunned to move. Robert Carrington is right there, solid – yet Brad can see the scorch marks on his suit, feel the menace. The camera captures it all. Even the icy glow.

In spite of his terror, Brad is glad Shelley is getting this.

The figure doesn't move, but somehow its stillness is more frightening and, suddenly, Brad has had enough. He doesn't know if this is a prank or something else, but he's done.

"Fuck this," Brad mutters, and he promptly turns, yanking Shelley with him. They stumble their way down the hallway, past all the doors, all in thick darkness.

"What is going on?" Shelley screams. "Is this bullshit actually real?"

"I don't know," is all Brad can answer. Because he *doesn't* know. But right now the Carrington Ghoul looks very much real and—

"*STOP!*" Shelley yells, skidding to a halt. It takes a moment for Brad to realize why, but when he does, he freezes.

They have finally reached the staircase, but the figure of Robert Carrington is standing there, somehow. How is that possible?

Just a joke, Brad thinks. A prank. It has to be. Because if it's real…

Then that means the curse is real. It all is.

"What do you want?" Shelley cries. The figure is silent. "We – we'll leave you alone," she begs. "We won't tell anyone you're here!"

Brad can't speak. *Just a joke*, he thinks. *Just a*—

The apparition steps towards them and they both falter backwards, falling over their feet. Shelley is screaming.

Maybe someone will hear them, Brad thinks. But he knows they won't. They're miles from anyone who could help.

"Come on, man," Brad says, like he's negotiating. "Please, we're just kids. We're sorry for disturbing you. We'll leave. Please."

The figure takes another step. It's then that Brad spots a glimmer in its hand. A knife. No. Robert's infamous butcher's blade.

They turn and run. But the figure is faster. Now they're all the way back to the front window, and that's when Brad smells it.

Smoke, as well as gasoline, trickling through their senses.

He sees it then too. The candle he dropped. The nearest rug is ablaze and it's spreading quickly, scarily quickly.

The fire creates a barrier between them and the ghoul. They're stuck – *trapped* against the window.

The ghoul stops. And then … he speaks.

"You will die the same way I did."

The voice is rough, like it's coated in soot from the fire. But it echoes in the hall. It's a horrible sound. Deathly.

"Please," sobs Shelley. "Please, let us go."

The fire roars louder and harder and faster. Their voices are soon lost to the blaze. Brad pulls Shelley into his firm grasp and plants a kiss on her forehead. Only now does she drop the camera. It falls to the floor with a thud.

"It'll be OK," Brad whispers to her, but it's useless. She can't hear him any more over the raging flames. He glances back through the red and orange but the figure is gone. They're alone in the blaze. Dimly, Brad is aware of the smoke, choking his lungs. He falls to his knees. It invades his senses. The stench of death. He is aware of the pain – but it doesn't matter any more. It's useless to fight.

He closes his eyes.

Just like Robert Carrington did all those years ago.

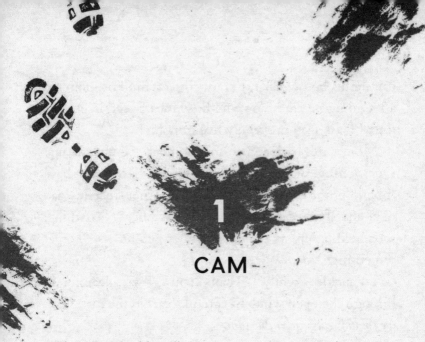

1

CAM

"Oh, Cam! Hold up!"

Mom's voice echoes across the entire front school yard. Well, it feels like it at least. Suddenly everyone's eyes are now on me. Sanera High is always watching and waiting for someone's parent to embarrass them. Even if it is just with a simple greeting.

I close the car door behind me and shoot Mom a less-than-impressed smile. Immediately I feel bad and morph it into a more appreciative one. "Yeah?"

"Don't forget I'm away on that work trip tonight," she says, half hanging out of the window, unaware her white blouse is scarily close to some dirt on the car door. "It'll only be the night. But do you want me to call Jonesy's mom and see if you can stay—"

"No," I say quickly. Jonesy wouldn't appreciate anyone

calling his house. That, I know for certain. His mom has a lot going on right now and he's embarrassed by it. "It's fine. I'll ask him in literally five minutes."

Mom stares back at me for a moment. Contemplating. Questioning. Before quickly moving on. She doesn't have time to probe too deeply into my life – not since my dad died and she became the sole breadwinner. Next thing, she's holding up my track bag with raised brows. "Forget something?"

I chuckle slightly. "Thank you," I say, leaning in through the open window, careful to avoid the dirt. *Man, we should really clean this thing.*

"Let me know what you decide to do, please."

"I will."

"And don't forget to eat—"

"Mom!" I bite. Not maliciously, but to interrupt her before I'm late to class. Otherwise, we'll be here all morning. She always feels guilty before she goes away – I don't know why. It's not her fault that it's just us. There's going to be times when I'm home alone. I've gotten used to it now. Well, I've had to.

She sighs. "OK, fine. Say hello to Jonesy and Amber from me… Love you."

I smile, grab my bag and head towards the front entrance. I hear music nearby. My eyes scan the area and find some kids with a boom box, inconspicuously smoking something they probably shouldn't be on school grounds.

But hey, I don't judge. It'll probably be legal someday. It's not for me though – I need a clean head for track.

I find myself bobbing my head to "You Get What You Give" when I finally hear the familiar jumpy exhaust of Mom's car pull away. Or, rather, Dad's car. Even after being fixed, her car still makes that dreadful noise. It doesn't exactly fit with her job as a hotshot marketing executive. But no, she won't get a new one. *Too many memories*, she always says.

I know what she means. And I feel exactly the same. Mom has Dad's old car. And I have his old *old* car. They'll be with us until they're heaps of unmoving junk on wheels.

Once the rumbles distance themselves, I waste no time in peeling off my track jacket. Mom loves me wearing it – me, not so much. I enjoy track and all, and I know I'm good, but I don't feel the need to boast about it everywhere I go like the other *jocks* – Kenny and Brad and the other footballers. Track is relatively normal. High school football is another beast entirely.

But that's Sanera High for you. It's a lot. Why a small town like this has such a ridiculously large school is beyond me. Sure, it's the *only* school in Sanera, but there's not a whole lot of kids either.

The red-brick exterior and blocky design remind me of every school in the movies. Like a prison but with more windows.

I head inside the main hall, where everyone is clustered

into their cliques. Jocks, cheerleaders, geeks, stoners, mathletes, all the stereotypes. On paper, I'd fit in with the jocks, but in reality … no. I'll stick with people who don't revolve their entire personality around the sport they compete in.

My best friends, Amber and Jonesy.

I look around for our homeroom. We've been back at school for a month or so and I still struggle to find it. It's a maze in here. Every room, hallway, turning, passage – they look the same. Then the bell rings … and suddenly all hell breaks loose.

The pleasant music from the boom box quickly cuts off and I'm pushed aside in the flurry of people. My back hits the wall and I take cover by the lockers.

Thankfully, it doesn't take too long for the human traffic to die down and I make a run for it. I'm already late. One minute it's a wall of noise, and the next you could probably hear a pin drop.

I run through the halls, stressed now, when—

"You should be in homeroom," a high-pitched yet masculine voice calls out to me, stopping me in my tracks. I stumble and almost fall but catch myself before I face-plant. Slowly, I turn to the origin of the voice to find Mr Graham … my homeroom teacher. A stern expression is on his face, accompanied by crossed arms. Teacher code for "less than impressed".

So should you, I want to say, but instead settle on

something a little less accusatory. It's not like Mr Graham to be *so* strict. "Just on my way there now."

A grin breaks across his face. "Cam, I'm kidding."

"Sorry?"

"You're late by sixty seconds, don't worry. If you're late, then so am I!"

I force out a laugh. Mr Graham thinks he's hilarious; the rest of us disagree. But that's Mr Graham for you. He means well. I follow him to class in silence as he chatters on about how bad the finale was of some Tudors documentary he watched last night, my eyes fixed on the back of his grey-and-brown tweed suit until we reach the room. Mr Graham teaches history and totally dresses the part.

"It was completely historically inaccurate," he finishes, flinging open the door. "Factually all over the place—" He coughs, loud and uncontrollably, which quickly fades into a low clearing of his throat. "Apologies, my allergies are awful this time of the year…"

I spot Amber and Jonesy across the room and wave.

"Sorry I'm late, class," Mr Graham announces, as I slip past him. "I trust you're all preparing for the day ahead and not taking advantage of my absence." He frowns at Kesia Bates on the front row who's casually knitting a scarf even though we live in California. She puts her needles down.

I find my way to the back left corner, squeezing through the filled desks to where Jonesy and Amber are huddled. Jonesy has his usual dark grey hoodie hanging off his slim build, and his brown curls perfectly frame his similarly coloured eyes. Amber, on the other hand, is decked out to the nines. She's had her braids done since yesterday. They now crest halfway down her back and are interspersed with red and brown. The pop of colour matches the red of her jacket.

"Nice of you to finally show up," Amber comments.

"Hi," I say as I take my seat in front of Jonesy. My gaze meets his. "Hi, bro."

Jonesy smiles and I'm sure his cheeks redden slightly. "Hey." His words crack slightly as he speaks. It makes my chest pang. Why, I'm not quite ready to think about yet.

I move on. Quickly. "Mom had a million instructions before she left on her trip. You know how she gets. So, did I miss anything?"

"I heard there's a new girl starting." Amber always has the news. Where she gets this news, I don't know. I think she has a third eye or something.

"There's never new people," I reply.

"*I* was new," Amber replies.

I blink. "Five years ago."

She sighs. "Whatever. It'll be nice to have somebody new around. I'm bored of seeing the same people all the time."

"Wow, love you too," Jonesy says. "Wait – *it'll be nice to have somebody new around*?" He juts his head forward. "You mean, we're going to take her in?"

Amber laughs. "I'm not proposing that we adopt her, but I know how scary it can be starting a new school. In Sanera. *And* in senior year? That's rough. Let's just see what she's like, OK? If she's nice, there's no harm in showing her around."

She's right. But it'll be strange integrating someone into the gang after it being us three for so long. Sure, we have our own friends outside the group and all, but our gang is different. It's like a little family.

"You're right," I finally chime in and turn to Jonesy. "Right, Jones?"

Jonesy looks at me, then Amber, reluctant and reserved. When it comes to people, he's not as forward as us. Seems shy, but once you get to know him – a whole new person.

He groans before ultimately giving in. "Well, it's not like I can say no."

Amber bares her pearly teeth and tugs at his sleeve excitedly. "I wonder what she'll be like. Wait, let's guess her name – Rachel." There's a certainty to her tone, like she already knows. But then again, that's Amber. So confident in everything that she does. Fearless.

Jonesy thinks and scratches his temple. "Veronica."

She turns to me. I "uhm" for a second before settling on "Daphne".

Amber scoffs. "She's a teenager, not a middle-ager."

"You asked us to guess!"

The door creaks open, interrupting my words.

Everyone's head shoots towards the noise. It's a sea of blonde and brown and at the end of it: the new girl, a deer in headlights. Can you blame her, facing sixty eyes?

"Miss Allen!" Mr Graham says, attempting to save her. He rises from his desk and ushers her into the room. "Welcome to Sanera but more specifically 21A. As you can see, we're all delighted to meet a new student! We don't get many!"

There's a pause in which Mr Graham waits for the girl to respond. When she just stares, he carries on. "I trust you have your schedule for the week?"

She nods.

"Then you know that I am also your history teacher. It's lovely to meet you." Silence. Mr Graham adjusts his gaze elsewhere. "Would anyone care to show Miss Allen around today?"

"I'll do it," Clive Loomis mumbles under his breath, and we all roll our eyes.

He's a creep. When I say Sanera has its stereotypes … it's true, even down to the douchebags. There's a few of them. I'm unsure if I can count them on two hands. But everything leads back to that football team. Figures.

"We will," Amber calls out. Her kind expression seems to work because the new girl looks grateful.

"Excellent," Mr Graham says. "Please show our new

student a warm Sanera High welcome!" He raises his hands into the air in some celebratory … pose. It doesn't quite work with the tweed.

No one says anything, but you have to give him points for trying. The new girl should feel lucky it isn't Miss Phelps introducing her. Or, even worse, Mrs Strode.

"Hi," the girl offers as she approaches. Timid. "I'm Buffy."

"Darn," is the first thing I think to say.

Buffy's eyes widen. "Sorry?"

"Oh. No, we were trying to guess your name before you got here."

Amber chuckles. "Safe to say we were all way off. I don't think any of us expected a vampire slayer in our class."

"Well, I've never heard *that* before," Buffy sarcastically replies. She's blonde, and pretty too. A dimple appears in her cheek, teasing at a smile. "Where shall I—"

"Here," Amber says, removing her jacket from the seat in front. "I'm Amber."

"Cam."

Jonesy raises his hand. "Jonesy."

Amber scoots in her chair until she's sitting close to Buffy. "So, how do you like Sanera so far?"

Buffy shrugs. "I've only been here for a few days so I can't say I hate it—"

"Yet," I finish.

"Cam!" Amber cries. She turns to Buffy and smiles reassuringly. "He's kidding."

"I *am* kidding," I say, meeting Buffy's gaze, throwing in a small wink that I'm pretty sure Amber misses. Thankfully. Amber is one of those *good* people. She doesn't like to talk shit about anyone or anything, even our dullsville hometown. "School is … school."

"My mom said this is a good high school. Best in Sanera."

I snort. "This is the *only* high school in Sanera. You go here or you don't get anywhere. But I'm guessing you know that already?"

Buffy doesn't immediately respond, but she doesn't need to. Obviously, she *didn't* know that. I wonder why she's here in Sanera in the first place. It's not exactly the hotspot destination.

Amber hurries on eagerly. "Cam's only playing… It's not bad. It's like any other high school, really. For every annoying teacher, you get three nice ones." She nudges Jonesy. "Tell her."

Jonesy finally pitches in. "There are some decent ones. Mr Graham, for instance. So long as you laugh at his … attempts at jokes, he's not bad. Classic nerdy history teacher who also runs the school musicals. Full of tricks."

Buffy smiles. "I feel like I'm going to get lost every period. My last school was nowhere near as big as this place."

"I would say you'll get used to it, but I got lost myself this morning," I admit.

"Cam is very hopeless though," Jonesy declares.

"That I can attest to," Amber adds. "The school is a big ol' maze but once you know your way around, you're set. Where did you transfer from?"

"Palatio High in Connecticut."

Amber's brows raise. "Oh wow … not close at all." Her eyes sweep over Buffy's outfit. Every single layer of it. "First time in California?"

Buffy looks down at herself. "What, is it obvious?"

For the first time, properly, I take Buffy in and yeah, it's not the most logical attire for Sanera, or California for that matter. Long-sleeved tee, jeans and a denim jacket. She'll get it eventually.

"I love your shirt," she says to Amber. Instinctively, all our eyes go to her yellow tee. It's bright and bold. Just like Amber.

"Thanks. My mom's a tailor so this is courtesy of her. What brings you to Sanera, anyway?"

"My mom got a new job she couldn't pass up, so we moved almost overnight. A fresh start." Her words seem oddly wooden – rehearsed, almost, I think. But she's nervous. Maybe she'll loosen up a bit as the day goes on.

The rest of homeroom goes like that. Mostly small talk, a bit stilted, but it's still nice. And surprisingly, as the time goes on, it *does* start to feel less awkward. Except to

Jonesy, maybe, who is clearly still reserving judgement. I'm sure he'll express his opinions later though. Who knows? Maybe Amber's right and a new face in the gang would be a good thing.

When the bell finally goes, the whole class stands up at once and I can see Buffy panic again.

"Where's your first class?" Amber asks, her words barely audible over the cacophony of chair scrapes, zippers and teenagers.

Buffy studies her schedule for a long moment, before timidly reciting, "Bio in 45B."

Amber's eyes light up. "We're in the same class! Mrs Strode."

I see Buffy's posture loosen. "Is she nice?"

"Super chill."

As we file out, I notice Mr Graham is speaking on his brick-sized cell phone. It's old as hell. "Hello, how can I…" His voice tails off. An expression crosses his face that I can only describe as one of absolute shock. "You can't be serious," he murmurs.

I nudge Jonesy and jerk my head towards the teacher. Amber and Buffy are too far ahead to notice, but Jonesy's eyes narrow in curiosity. Mr Graham listens for a moment, then nods, hangs up and slumps back into his chair. Hand on face, he sighs through his fingers. His face is ashen.

He stares blankly into space until he eventually catches us gawking. He promptly sits up and straightens his suit jacket, forcing a smile. "Come on, guys, off to class. Nothing to see here."

It's clear it's not *nothing*. "Maybe he got dumped," Jonesy whispers.

I snort. "Mr Graham wears jackets with elbow patches. He doesn't have a love life," I whisper back.

We head to first period, and forget all about it.

2

JONESY

"Ayo," a loud voice says, forcing my nose out of my history textbook. It startles me a little, but after a quick glance I find that it's only Cam. He finishes track about now.

"What brings you here?" he asks, as he crests the row of bleachers I'm perched on. His face is flushed from the exercise and his knees are grazed. Not that I'm looking. His messy blonde hair is almost brown now that it's drenched in sweat. Yet, somehow, he still looks good.

"Free period," I reply and close the textbook, then motion to his knees. They look sore. "Bad fall?"

Cam frowns before realizing what I'm referring to. "Oh, that's nothing. I tripped on the track. The guys aren't letting me live it down."

I smile at him. *The guys*. It reminds me how different

we are. Cam's a jock – as much as he likes to fight it. I'm very much … *not a jock.* "That's not like you."

"How so?" Cam says, just before opening his water bottle and pouring the remnants of the liquid over his head. With one hand, he swipes his locks out of his face and lets his eyes flutter open again.

I wonder if he had things on his mind and that's why he fell. I wonder what they were. I wonder … "You don't normally trip," I finally answer.

He blinks. "And you don't normally ask so many questions." A hefty sigh escapes him as he takes a seat next to me. I can practically feel the heat radiating off him. "Did I miss the memo that the bleachers were the new study spot?"

Now it's my turn to blink. "It's nice," is all that comes to mind. Nice? *Why, Jonesy? Why?*

Since when am I so nervous around my best friend?

"I thought you had come to watch me," he says. His head is low; his eyes on his hands as he fidgets with his fingers. Some things never change. Whenever he's nervous, anxious, thinking, Cam fidgets. It's his tic.

"I didn't even know you were out here," I say, truthfully. "The library was packed so I relocated. I thought the football team practised here and you guys were in the gym."

"Coach randomly cancelled football practice," he explains. "So we thought we'd take their spot and make the best of the weather."

It takes a second to process his words but, when I do, I'm slightly confused. Football … cancelled? This is the *Sanera football team*. The school is obsessed with sport. It pours money into the team. They don't cancel practice for *anything*.

"Cancelled football practice?" Even repeating the phrase aloud sounds weird. "Since when does Sanera *cancel football practice*?"

Cam shrugs. "Today, I guess."

"Don't you find that odd?"

"A little," he says. "But things happen."

He's right, obviously. Cam doesn't ask too many questions. But something feels off.

"Jones –" Cam nudges me, his warm shoulder bumping my own – "you're overthinking it. Besides, we have more pressing matters." He raises his brows at me, widening his blue eyes.

My chest tightens. "And what would those be?"

Instead of answering, he holds his finger up.

"Wha—"

"Three, two, and—"

The school bell rings.

"Lunch," he says with a pleased smile. "Look, I gotta go get cleaned up. I'll meet you in the cafeteria, yeah?" Cam's already on his feet, walking away, looking back over his shoulder at me.

I nod. "Be quick."

"I will."

*

Amber throws her hand up in the crowd, signalling our table. I'm not sure why. We sit on the same table every day. Everyone does. Before high school, my mom told me that high school was "nothing like the movies". And maybe that's true for other places, but here? It's literally Rydell High. Even down to the singing Australian, Margot. She's nice.

I throw my bag down, just as Cam appears and does the same. He's changed from his track gear to his T-shirt and jeans. "That *was* quick," I say.

"I keep my word." Cam nods at Amber. "How was Carlton?"

"Fine. She said my English paper was suboptimal. Buffy was there. We've had a few classes together now." Her words come sporadically, through sips of her soda. "I said to sit with us." She dares us to disagree with her eyes. "Which I hope is OK. I know we don't usually. But I like being helpful. I like her."

"Do you … *like* her?" asks Cam.

Amber rolls her eyes. "Why did I ever tell y'all I'm bi? No, nothing like *that*. I think she's sweet. As we've already discussed, I know how it feels to move schools. I want to help make the transition a little easier for Buffy and I don't need you two scaring her off!" She puts down her drink. "Especially you, Jonesy."

My head flies up. "Hey. What did I do?"

"I know what you're like. Grow up," is all she replies.

I spot Buffy traipse into the cafeteria, eyes scanning the room for a seat. The most anxiety-inducing thing on your first day. Do you sit alone, or do you try and find the one person you know? It's a nightmare.

Instinctively, all our hands go up in unison; her worried gaze eventually lands on us. I see relief spread across her face and she takes a step forward – then stops.

Kenny Lloyd, star cornerback and infamous douche, has stepped into her path. It clearly takes her by surprise because she nearly drops her food. He leans in and whispers something to her. As he does, I see her expression – completely unenthused. Then she leans a bit closer to Kenny and whispers something in his ear.

To my surprise, Kenny's mouth falls open, almost in shock. He backs away, his pride between his legs. I watch his oversized letterman jacket get smaller in the distance until he's only a memory in the cafeteria.

"Serves him right," Amber mutters and Cam and I nod.

"Hi, everyone," Buffy quietly offers as she reaches us, hovering uncertainly, like she didn't just destroy the most annoying kid in school.

"You clearly had the privilege of meeting Kenny." Amber yanks her bag from the adjacent seat. "Here, sit. You remember Jonesy and Cam." She motions to us from the other side of the table. Both of us take breaks from our food to mutter our hellos. "So, what did Kenny have to say for himself?"

Buffy takes her seat, placing her lunch tray on the table and her backpack on the floor. "Nothing I haven't heard before."

Cam and I eat in silence while Amber chatters on. When she pauses, Buffy leans forward and smiles at me and Cam. "You two are very conversational."

Amber snorts. Cam too. I look up cautiously, surprised by her sudden confidence. She seemed so shy this morning. Is this what a few hours in Sanera does to a person?

"All right, new girl," Cam says, pushing his tray aside. "Let's talk."

Buffy smirks. "What would you like to talk about, Cam?"

He shrugs. "Up to you."

To my surprise, Buffy laughs. "I had a feeling you'd say that. True to type."

My brows raise. She's known Cam for all of ten minutes. "What do you mean by that?" I ask, curious.

"It's high school. Everyone fits in somewhere, everyone has their *role*."

Amber chimes in. "You're making it sound like we're in some teen movie."

Buffy takes a sip of her drink, and continues. "Sure, movies are exaggerated to all hell. But there's some truth in there too."

"OK," Cam says. He splays out, his leg peeking out from the side of the table. "If I'm *true to type*, what role do I play in all this?"

For a moment, Buffy stays silent, gazing at Cam. I expect her to say something bland and flattering, about how hot he is and how that means he must be popular. Instead, she says, "Well, your hair is wet, which tells me you've come from the showers. Which means you must do some sort of sport, and your grazed knee tells me it's probably track."

My eyes widen. Who is this girl?

Cam grins as he retracts his leg back under the table. "I could've grazed my leg in football, baseball, you name it."

She shakes her head. "Not like that. That's some sort of burn from like … rubber. Also I overheard some very upset guys talking about how football practice was cancelled today."

Cam scoffs. "Fine, I do track. What else?"

Buffy smiles at her correct assumption but she doesn't seem surprised by it. "You're the *joker* of the group, that's clear. Easy-going. Nothing gets to you. Or does it?"

Cam glances between me and Amber because that's him down to a T. It's creepy. How does Buffy know this stuff?

"What about me?" Amber asks.

Buffy turns her searching gaze on Amber. "You strike me as an empath, quick to help those in need, if you will. Like how you were the first to volunteer to help me this morning," Buffy recites, like she's reading it from a guidebook. "Well, the first to volunteer with good intentions. I imagine you're also the glue of the group. I think these two do what you tell them, because they know you're usually right."

Amber sits back, clearly impressed. "Damn, Buffy."

Without asking, Buffy turns to me, eyes locking on mine. She takes a little longer with me than the others. I wonder if I'm too hard to crack but I'm quickly proven wrong. "Jonesy is the brains. Reserved, cautious, but not shy when you get to know him." She bites her lip. "You like things set in stone and unchanging. You're not sure how you feel about newcomers—"

"OK," I interrupt. Not sure I need the character analysis. But I do stare back at her. "And what about you?"

Buffy smiles. "I'm perceptive."

3

AMBER

"Nice work," I say, trying to move on, feeling the tension, especially from Jonesy. Buffy is clearly not his cup of tea. But it's early days. I don't think Jonesy is used to someone who might possibly be as smart as him. "How's your first day going so far?"

"A lot better than I thought it would go, honestly," says Buffy. "I'm sure it would've been a different story if you guys hadn't helped me out."

I'm pleased to hear that. It's scary stepping into a new school, especially alone. Some people have great experiences, but then there are horror stories – cue every single slasher movie ever.

"How long have you all been friends for, anyway?" Buffy finally picks up her burger and awaits an answer.

"I joined here like five years ago," I reply. "These bozos

took me in, against my will, and they never let go."

"You could've made us sound a smidge less possessive," Cam says, mouth full. But he's just playing. He knows what I mean. Friendships normally fade; ours hasn't. I don't know what I would've done if it had. The memories we've made in half a decade could fuel a lifetime. It's rare you stay friends with the people you make at the start of school.

I turn back to Buffy. "What was your old school like?"

She takes a bite and chews. "It was fine."

"You must miss your frie—"

The school intercom chimes and the entire cafeteria falls silent. Almost eerily – it's like the dead of night.

The boys and I eye each other. It's an odd time for a school announcement. They usually take place in the morning. It's well known that Principal Higgins normally goes out for lunch. In fact, in all my five years here, we've *never* had an announcement in the middle of the day. Something is up.

"*Hello, Sanera,*" echoes across the entire room.

Instantly, I know I am right. Something is *definitely* up. The tone, the timbre. It's haunting. Sombre.

"*I am aware this is a most unusual time for a school announcement, but I have pressing news I must inform you all of.*"

Whispers fill the room.

Speculations.

Thoughts.

Theories.

41

The boys and I exchange more puzzled looks. The whispers around us turn to mumbles. I wish they'd be quiet for a minute. This sounds serious.

"*There is no easy way to say this. But it is with great sadness that I have to inform you of the death of two of our own. Two Sanera High students were, tragically, found dead last night.*"

My blood runs cold.

Two students?

Dead?

What the...

"*After speaking with the Plains County sheriff's office and confirming that their families have been informed, I can reveal the identity of the victims. The first is Shelley Jones.*"

Someone lets out a cry.

Shelley Jones? Bubbly Shelley Jones, the cheerleader? *This isn't happening.*

"*And the second is Bradley Campbell.*"

I swear every single person in the room gasps. And then everyone starts talking, shouting.

Brad and Shelley are dead. The football star and the cheerleader. The "it" couple. Hot, perfect. Brad – sure, he was a little jock-y sometimes but still a nice guy. And Shelley? I speak to her every day in gym. I've even tutored her before, when she was worried her math grades were taking a dip – math is my thing. Not that she needed it, but she was obsessed with improving her grade average before college. Shelley had plans. She had college offers. And now…

Dead.

Gone.

Never coming back.

The voice continues. *"I am unable to disclose any more information at this time but the sheriff's office will give updates when they have them. You are all dismissed for the rest of the day. Please, go home and try to recover from this terrible news. Your parents and caregivers will be informed and on-site counselling will be available. That is all."*

There is a short moment of static over the speakers and then it goes quiet. The entire cafeteria – the entire school, presumably – is in shock. I can tell people around me are talking but I can't hear the words. It's like the room is a movie and someone has pressed mute.

Eventually, I realize that Buffy is talking to me, or at least trying to. "Are you OK?" she says.

I want to state the obvious and scream at her that *of course I'm not OK*, but I don't. This is her first day, and two students are dead.

Instead, I nod and stand up. More people quickly do the same. They were all waiting for someone to do it first.

My feet are fast on the sticky floor as I exit the cafeteria. People stream past me. There are already bustling crowds in the corridors, trying to escape the confines of Sanera.

There's a sudden heavy feeling in the air. It's surreal. I can almost *feel* the sadness around me, tightening at my throat, clambering down my windpipe. It's palpable. I've never felt anything quite like it. But then again, it's not every day the two most popular kids in school end up dead.

But how? What happened to them? We don't know anything. Not yet, at least.

I take deep breaths, trying to calm down. *It must have been an accident*, I think. We're in Sanera, not some big ol' city. Nothing happens here. It's a boring place with boring people.

Or at least … I thought it was.

A slight sense of relief washes over me as I fall through the front doors. The lukewarm air is not exactly the fresh air I need, but it'll have to do.

"What the actual…" I say hopelessly, stopping on a nearby patch of grass.

Jonesy shakes his head. "It's … unbelievable," he offers. "I knew something was off earlier today."

I look over. "What happened earlier?"

Jonesy scratches the back of his head. "Well. First there's the fact that football practice was cancelled, which I thought was strange."

I nod. *I guess that is strange.* Sanera doesn't cancel any sporting activity if they can help it.

"And then there's the fact that Mr Graham got a call

and he looked shocked. That must have been the principal telling him what had happened. That was in homeroom. Why did they wait so long to let everyone know?"

"Some sort of accident," I say helplessly.

Buffy speaks up. "Principal Higgins didn't say how they died. Which makes me wonder."

"If it was a crime?" Cam adds.

She half shrugs and half nods. A brisk wind comes out of nowhere. Buffy quickly pulls her jacket from her bag and dangles it over her shoulders.

"Come on," I snap. "A *crime*? Let's not talk like that, please."

It's all too much. Two people are dead. *Dead*. The word doesn't even sound real. Death is something that affects the older generation. *Kids aren't supposed to die.* Especially not those two. Brad and Shelley were star pupils. Well, that's not quite right – Shelley was a star cheerleader and mathlete. She managed to balance the two. Everything she touched turned to gold. Brad, on the other hand, seemed to be scraping by in most classes. But he was a jock, so set for life. Their lives are – were – perfect. Full ride scholarships to the best colleges in the country. Right?

Brad had some random ghost-hunting show, I remember now. He held regular showings at his house because he was so excited for people to watch it. We all used to poke fun at it, but actually it was quite sweet. It made him more than *just a jock*.

"I'm gonna head home like Higgins said," I say abruptly. "My parents will be worried."

They all nod, understanding. Buffy steps forward and hands me a piece of paper. She's clearly had it ready for most of the day because her number is scribbled on it.

"If you need anything." There's a hesitant smile but I can't smile back. Can't be helpful and caring and positive Amber right now. *Sorry, Buffy.*

I nod my thanks, say my short goodbyes, and set off by myself. It only takes a few steps for me to pull my Walkman out of my bag because my mind won't stop spiralling. I realize I only packed one minidisc with me and it's full of eighties stuff, but it'll have to do.

I press play and the comforting sound of "Funkytown" fills my ears. It's hardly the most opportune time for such an upbeat and groovy song, but I need something to take my mind off whatever just happened. And if it's funk, so be it.

I decide to let myself get lost in the sounds. Until I'm home at least.

A fragrant smell greets me when I finally close the front door behind me. Head pounding, I throw my bag to the floor. My legs give way. My back slides down the door frame until I'm slumped on the ground. A meagre sob tries to escape but I push it back as soon as I hear footsteps closing in.

"Amber, is that you?" Mom's voice calls out from the other room. I don't have time to reply before she appears at the kitchen door. Her hair's tied back loosely and she's wearing her apron, the same one she's had since I was a kid. Her cheerful expression changes when she spots me on the floor.

"What happened?" she asks, her tone immediately steeped in worry.

She hasn't heard? I'd have thought every parent would've been notified, or at least she'd have seen it on the news. Our school isn't super competent though. They're probably still composing the email.

"Turn the TV on," is all I can think, or bear, to say. It must be on the local news now. I need to see it for myself. Part of me wants everything that happened today to be a figment of my imagination. But I have a bad feeling it's all too real.

Mom stares at me, then hurries into the living room. I stand with trembling legs and follow, only now noticing my heartbeat. It feels like my heart is slamming back and forth in my chest, faster than the pace of my feet hitting the wooden floor. I put my hand on my chest to try and calm it.

When I reach the living room, Mom flicks on the TV and immediately flashes of blue and red fill the dusky room. A large house fills the entire screen and instantly I can tell it's Carrington Manor. Droves of people and vehicles surround the property. It's a whirlwind of sounds and colours, except for the house. The house is black, looming. Every time I've passed it when leaving town, it's hard not to get a chill, especially with all the tragedy that surrounds the place. But how it's connected to Brad and Shelley, I have no idea.

"What am I looking at?" Mom's eyes dart to me for answers. I gesture to her to turn the sound up.

A news reporter with a slick suit and red hair stands in front of the building, speaking into a mic. "For those just joining us now, the reports are true. The charred remains of two teenagers have been recovered from Sanera's infamous Carrington Manor, which has been abandoned for decades."

What were Brad and Shelley doing at Carrington Manor?

The news reporter motions to the building behind him. The house looks cold, like the life has been sucked out of it. "The sheriff's office, police and firefighters were called to the property just after two a.m. when locals awoke to what they described as 'the smell of death'."

Countless questions flood my mind.

Brad and Shelley died in a house fire?

Did they start it? Two kids messing around in an abandoned building. Kids snuck in there sometimes. Accidents happen, right? Old buildings are dangerous, anything could have happened. My thoughts spiral as I try to make sense of this.

"As of an hour ago, the victims have been identified as Sanera High students Bradley Campbell and Shelley Jones."

Mom gasps.

Photos of Brad and Shelley appear briefly on the screen. It's their yearbook photos – good-looking, great teeth, great smiles. The images are presented in black and white, which must be customary when someone dies. Photos that were once a celebration of completing a year of school are now tainted. They'll forever be their *death* pictures. God, I barely knew Shelley really, but I feel terrible.

I can't even imagine how their friends, their family feel. Nobody deserves this.

"This tragic event comes almost seventy-five years after Robert Carrington – the manor's original owner – died, also in a mysterious house fire—"

The reporter breaks off as something grabs his attention. He calls out, "*Sheriff! Sheriff!*"

The camera shifts and Sheriff Rogers, the county's head of law enforcement, appears on screen. He looks flustered. The reporter moves in, mic in hand. "Can you tell us anything more about what happened here this morning?"

The sheriff bites his lip, clearly deciding what to say, what to disclose, and what to omit. I've only ever seen him on the news, warning kids not to graffiti or wishing people happy holidays, or line dancing. The last one was a weird fundraiser thing – not relevant. I lean forward.

"It is a tragic day for the people of Sanera," he says. "To lose anybody is a blow to our community, but Bradley and Shelley were integral to this town."

The reporter doesn't move the mic away. "Of course. Sheriff, can you tell us anything more about the fire – was this an accident?"

A long pause. Sheriff Rogers glances at the reporter, then back to the manor, before settling on the camera.

"Investigations are still under way but I can almost certainly say that there has been no foul play here. A metal candlestick was found at the scene. This appears to be a tragic accident – a fire that broke out when these two young people were exploring the house. They found themselves trapped."

"But it's a coincidence, isn't it? That Robert Carrington died in the same way."

The sheriff bristles. "Robert Carrington?"

"Yes. The ghoul—"

"Let's not jump to *senseless* conclusions," Sheriff Rogers interrupts. The dark thick moustache on his lip twitches. "Ghost stories are just that – stories. Instead, let us pray for the victims' families and help them through such a trying time. That is all."

And then he's gone, walking back up the long path to the manor. But the reporter isn't satisfied. It wasn't juicy enough, it wasn't a good enough headline, clearly. He turns back to the camera.

"That was an exclusive, directly from Plain County Sheriff Rogers, dismissing the tragic events of this morning as an accident. But one can't help but wonder. For years, Robert Carrington's ghost has been said to haunt the manor, waiting for the right moment to exact his revenge for his fiery death. And now, two children have met the same terrible fate…"

I groan. "What the—"

"Don't you dare even finish that sentence Amber Janelle Grayson," Mom hollers. Even under stress, manners are important to her.

I huff. "They're seriously trying to throw in a stupid town legend theory?" My voice rises. "Kids are dead! Don't they have any respect?"

Arms wrap around me, but I wriggle out of Mom's grasp, intent on the screen. I'm caught in a tangle of fear, anger and curiosity. It's one thing to believe in the Carrington legend but it's another to broadcast your belief on live television when people are grieving.

The reporter turns towards the house, and then eerily glances back to the camera.

"It makes you wonder, huh? Let's hope there are no more *tragic accidents*. My name is Rick Field and you've been—"

The TV goes black as Mom clicks the remote. And the room falls into an uncomfortable silence.

"You don't need to be watching that right now," she

mutters, pulling me into her shoulder. "Ghosts and ghouls, honestly!"

I groan. Ghosts and ghouls. Are not real. "That's what we get for moving to a town where nothing happens. They run with the wild theories."

"I bet people are believing it too." Mom squeezes my hand so I shut my eyes as I relish the familiar closeness. The comfort, after today, is needed. "How was school, honey?"

I can't help but laugh. "Before or after I found out my classmates had died?" Mom waits. "It was fine," I finally admit. "A new girl started—"

"And?" Mom probes me for more information.

"… I was getting there," I reply.

Mom raises her hand, mimics zipping her lips shut, and lowers it again. It makes me smile, just a little bit.

"Her name's Buffy. She's nice. I had a few classes with her so I've been showing her around, introducing her to people, trying to be helpful."

I look over to Mom. She's frowning. "What kind of parent names their child *Buffy*?" she says in disgust.

"Mom!" I end up chuckling though.

"We don't often get new families in Sanera," Mom muses.

I shrug. "She moved here from Connecticut, with her mom for a job. That's all I really know."

"A job … in Sanera?"

Now that I think of it, that doesn't make a whole lot

52

of sense. Sanera is tiny. What job could there possibly be here? Sure, there are *jobs*, but something special enough to relocate for? Cam's mom is having to commute out of town just to get a chance at a promotion. Something seems off.

Mom pats my arm. "Well, it'll be good for you to make some *girl* friends." She makes sure to emphasize the gap between the words. Oh, Christian parents…

"I thought you liked Jonesy and Cam," I say.

"I do!" Her voice goes slightly higher. "But you know how set in his ways your father is."

"Of course."

Mom removes her hand from mine and brings it to my cheek. It's warm, comforting. Needed. A little awkward. "Your father won't be home for a while. Why don't we watch a movie?"

The rest of the afternoon and evening is spent on the couch, unmoving for hours. After I force her to watch *Charlie's Angels*, Mom falls asleep, her head on my shoulder, and I don't have the heart to wake her. I manage to slip away sometime after nine.

I go to check the front door but as I reach it, it opens. I yelp and stumble back. "Honey?"

Just Dad. My hand finds a place on the left side of my chest. "You scared me."

Dad closes the door behind him. He's in his work

attire. He's a lawyer. A dark tan check suit with matching waistcoat. He has a whole stash of them he cycles through.

"Honey. I heard about those poor kids. How are you feeling?"

"I'm fine," I reply, and cross my arms. I'm not sure how many more times I can repeat myself and go over it again. "Mom's asleep on the couch … I'm gonna head to bed."

"OK, honey. Goodnight."

I offer a smile and then head to my room. In a matter of seconds, familiar scents and colours meet my senses.

I'm great at sleep. Give me a bed, blankets and at least three pillows and I'm set. In no time, I'm nodding off, my mind surrendering to dreamland, when my phone pings obnoxiously loudly. I'd forgotten to put it on silent. Of course. With a grunt, I flip the switch on my night light and peer at the mobile in a warm yellow glow.

It's a text from Cam, which is odd this late. I feel a flicker of unease. I click on the message.

Jonesy's in 20?

I glance towards my bedroom door. I don't know why; it's not like I can see my parents from here. Mom's passed out downstairs, and Dad's probably joined her. They won't notice me sneaking out.

Am I seriously contemplating this?

If I'm caught, I'm grounded for life – longer than life. It would give Dad ammunition to stop me from seeing Jonesy and Cam. He's always thought it weird that I was friends with two guys. *Boys and girls can be friends, Dad!*

Screw it. I want to see my friends after the weirdest day of my life. I thought burrowing away at home would be the best thing for me, but now … the idea of lying in bed alone with my thoughts sounds like the worst possible idea. I text back.

You're on.

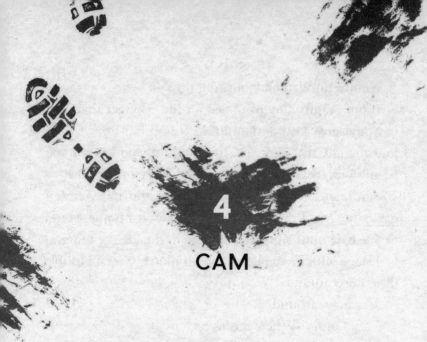

4

CAM

"She's coming," I say, as Amber's text comes through. I thought she might be asleep, because Amber likes an early night. Part of me secretly hoped it would be just me and Jonesy because – well, never mind.

She's most likely almost here. My gaze drifts from the phone and over to Jonesy, who's preoccupied with Macey, his dog. It wouldn't surprise me if he didn't even hear me. Apparently belly rubs take all his attention.

"Jones." Nothing. I cross the room and plant myself next to him.

My sudden presence seems to finally get his attention, though he still doesn't look at me. "I did hear you, by the way."

"Is that so?"

He nods. "Wanted to see how agitated you'd get." He goes back to stroking Macey.

"I didn't get agitated," I snap.

"Enough that you felt the need to come over and sit next to me." There's a chuckle brewing behind his words, I can feel it. He's only messing with me. Or is it something else?

"Maybe I just wanted to sit down."

"Right here?" he asks, then motions to the multiple other seats around. "Wouldn't any of those suffice?"

I glance around at his basement room, in all its seventies glory. When Jonesy's mom and dad separated, they let him decorate the room however he wanted. And he chose this. It's very cool, I admit. Even if it does look like the Mystery Machine threw up in here. Quirky, like Jonesy.

A laugh escapes my lips. "I can move if you want me to." I let my gaze meet Jonesy's. Macey has already got the memo and jumped off his lap. In my peripheral I can see her trotting off to her bed.

"Do you want to move?"

What is happening? What is this? Are we flirting? No. Right? Because Jonesy and I are old friends and we don't flirt. Do we? This past few weeks or so, I'm no longer sure. Sending off college applications has put everything into perspective. Next year, we'll be gone – well, Jonesy definitely will be. Me, I'll be lucky to get into somewhere that isn't Sanera Community College. That goodbye is on the horizon and it's shaking everything up.

"Not particularly," I reply, still unsure of everything. Which isn't like me. These new feelings are confusing.

Jonesy lowers his head. He's flushing, I can see. "Look," he says, "I don't know how to say this but—"

The basement door opens, interrupting us from whatever *that* was. Maybe it was for the best. Familiar voices sound from the top of the stairs, then before I know it, Amber is in the room.

But she's not alone.

"Buffy," Jonesy says. He doesn't hide the surprise in his tone. I'm surprised too. "You're here."

Before she has time to answer, Amber jumps in. "Sorry, I should've asked—"

"You didn't ask?" Buffy instinctively steps backwards, looking embarrassed. It's not that's she's unwelcome. It's just we've known her for a total of half a day.

"It's fine," Jonesy says, although I can tell from his tone that it isn't. *Sure, bring this complete stranger into my home.* He stands up from the couch, his hand briefly brushing mine. Our eyes meet for a split second. "Welcome to our little hangout, Buffy."

She gives a tentative smile, looking around at her surroundings. There's no overhead lighting down here, only lamps and candles, to really *enhance the vibes*... Jonesy's words, not mine.

"It's so rad," she says. "I love—"

Before she can finish her sentence, a certain adult puppy jumps up at her, and in seconds she's one with the shaggy carpet, being licked. Thankfully, she's giggling and not screaming. Amber tries to help, but it doesn't work.

"Macey, come on, girl," she whisper-shouts. She needn't bother – Jonesy's mom won't hear. She's most likely conked out in her room. Amber's hand grasps Buffy's and slowly pulls her to her feet.

"What breed is she?" Buffy asks, once she's taken a breath. She bends down to fuss the pup a little more. She's swiftly pushed on to her back as soon as she does, and the belly rubs commence.

"Staffordshire bull terrier." Jonesy smiles as he watches. "British breed. I'm British, before you ask."

Buffy's brows crease. "You don't sound it."

"We moved here so long ago that I've almost completely lost the accent," he explains. I remember his accent back then. When Jonesy first moved here, it was like being best friends with Oliver Twist. *Memories.* "We brought Macey back after our last visit a few years ago."

"She's gorgeous."

After that, the conversation seems to dwindle and we all head to the couches. Amber takes a seat between me and

Jonesy, while Buffy takes one of the armchairs.

"I'm guessing y'all saw the news earlier?" Amber asks, her head resting on her hand. I know what news she's referring to, of course. Like there's any other news today.

Buffy nods. "That reporter – Rick something. Trying to pin their deaths on a ghost? That's messed up."

"Ghoul," I say, my finger up in protest.

"*Ghoul*," Buffy corrects herself. "Who believes that crap?"

"Carrington Manor and its resident *ghoul* is a big thing around here," I explain. "It's like Sanera's urban legend. Every town has one, and this is ours. Some people believe it more than others. Carrington Manor certainly *looks* haunted."

"Have you seen it?" Buffy asks.

"The ghoul or the house?"

Buffy rolls her eyes. "The house!"

I smile. "We all have. It sits on this big hill on the edge of town. Twenty minutes away, give or take."

"Some kids sneak in," Amber says. Then adds, "Not us though."

Buffy's eyes widen a little. "They sneak in? Why?"

Cam snorts. "Why do *you* think teenagers would want to sneak into an abandoned building where they wouldn't get caught?"

Buffy's mouth forms an "O" and the sound that leaves

it is similar. "Do you think that's what Brad and Shelley were…" Her voice trails off.

"I don't think so," Jonesy says.

Amber nods. "Brad had this ghost-hunting show that he'd been trying to get off the ground. I wouldn't be surprised if the visit was something to do with that. He couldn't pass up the chance to investigate Sanera's very own ghoul."

"So they were at the manor to film his show," Buffy says. "Then they started an accidental fire. I wonder how."

"They dropped a candle, faulty wires … the list goes on," Jonesy says.

Buffy shakes her head, looking unconvinced. "Well, faulty wires makes no sense. The house is old as hell – did it even have wiring?"

Jonesy shrugs. "By the twenties, around half of the homes in the US had electric power."

"But you don't know that Carrington Manor was in that half," Buffy combats. "I highly doubt that Sanera was on the grid back then, don't you? Even if it was, old-ass Carrington probably wouldn't be the first on their priority list."

I grin at Jonesy as he frowns. He's used to being the smartest in the room. As much as he's trying to hide it, there's a tinge of jealousy on his features. Just a tinge.

Amber shrugs. "She has a point."

"Then it was a candle," I say. "They took a candle around the house with them and it fell or something." As soon as the words leave my lips, even I'm not convinced by them. It must have taken a while for the fire to take hold. Why didn't Brad and Shelley just … leave?

I catch Jonesy studying my face. "What are we suggesting right now? That this *wasn't* an accident?"

"We're not suggesting anything," I say. "We don't know anything. And we don't want to, right?"

Amber nods. "Leave it to the people who know what they're doing."

Buffy nods slowly and looks off, as though pondering something. I don't know what to make of her yet.

"Let's see if there's an update." Jonesy reaches forward and grabs the TV remote. I see the light of the television in his eyes before the sound promptly follows. There's a bunch of static at first – thanks to Jonesy's abysmal connection – but then talking ensues. A familiar voice.

Staring back at me is the red-headed reporter from earlier. *Rick Field*. Smug little man. He looks thrilled to have something to cover that isn't local sports games.

The reporter is still at Carrington Manor but the crowd has gone. Only one news van remains, as well as a few police cars. I focus on Rick Field. The words are jumbled at first, then form themselves into sentences.

"… Tragic accident – or something of a more supernatural nature? I don't know about you, but a candle being found at the scene is not enough to rule out foul play. The circumstances of the deaths are uncannily similar to the way that Robert Carrington died. It makes you wonder, doesn't it?" The reporter steps closer to the camera; the whole time the manor looms behind him. It's menacing. "Sheriff Rogers will hold a press conference tomorrow afternoon to answer any pressing questions revolving around the incident at Carrington Manor. But until then I'm Rick Field and this is—"

The screen goes black once again.

"Dickwad," Amber says, TV remote in hand. She must've snatched it from Jonesy. "He's just trying to make himself relevant by pushing this ghoul theory. Sanera isn't exactly buzzing with TV-worthy news so this is his one opportunity to fill his pockets. Everything will be explained tomorrow and everyone can stop trying to come up with stupid-ass theories."

She's right. As always. I glance at my watch. "You girls know it's almost midnight? Well, eleven thirty."

Instantly, Amber stands. "I should probably head off if I want to ever see you losers again." Ah, yes. Her dad loves us. Not.

"I'm going to say goodnight too," Buffy adds, getting to her feet. "And – and I just want to say thank you for everything today. I know it's been freaking weird, but you people being so nice – well, it means a lot."

Amber and I smile, but I have to nudge Jonesy to do the

same. He's still uncertain about Buffy, I can tell. And if I'm honest, so am I. But I'm not going to be mean to her face.

"You're welcome," Amber says. "It's not been an ideal first day but I'm glad we've managed to help. We'll see you in the morning."

"When everything will be explained," I say, in the most sarcastic tone I can muster.

Amber doesn't rise to the dig. "That's right. Make sure you lock up."

And then they're gone and, once again, it's just me and Jonesy alone. But if I thought our strange maybe-flirtation would continue, I'm wrong. He's sitting right the other end of the couch.

Maybe it's for the best.

For both of us.

5

JONESY

School is weird today.

Brad and Shelley were friends with basically everyone, so a ton are missing today. The halls don't seem as busy, the classes aren't as full. I don't even know if my parents know about what happened. When I got home from school yesterday, Mom was already two bottles deep and my dad was not there. Obviously.

Mom's been the same since Dad left a year or so ago. Since before then, even. Her drinking was the reason their relationship fell apart, and her addiction has only gotten worse. He tried – we both tried – to get her help but she didn't think she *had* a problem. Not much one can do when the alcoholic doesn't want help.

At first, I was supposed to live with Dad. He tried hard to persuade me. But in the end, I couldn't justify it. Not just leaving Mom, but Sanera too. And Cam. And Amber. I told Dad I'd rethink after graduation, which isn't so far off now. Time flies. I still can't believe he left though. He left me, even if he tried to take me with him. He left me.

I shake my head free of the thoughts. School should be an escape from home life, and thankfully it usually is. I love school. Weird, I know. I just happen to be good at it.

Although, today, it's not an escape from anything. Carrington Manor is all everyone can talk about. And I mean *everyone*. Even the teachers are clearly distracted. Mr Graham's cardigan is buttoned up all wrong and he gets confused halfway through taking attendance. A good five minutes is then wasted by him trying to rectify his fashion faux pas.

Classes are mostly gossip sessions while the teachers feebly try and keep order. We get a lecture about trespassing and another about fire safety. We're told not to speak to any press. Amber and Cam (and Buffy, who I guess is now part of the group) don't share any classes with me today, so I barely speak to anyone until lunch.

When the clock does finally strike midday, I'm out of that classroom as fast as humanly possible. I practically shoot through the halls and reach the cafeteria before anyone else. The pick of the room is mine ... but not really. Like I said, everyone has their unofficial, official assigned seating.

As I sit down at our table, it gets me thinking: what

are we? I don't think our group really has a name. We're not popular. But we're not unpopular. We're the ones who get forgotten about because we're not the scholarship football players, or the cheerleaders. Not science geeks, and not in band. Amber signed up for cheerleading try-outs once but chickened out at the last minute. I don't blame her. Those cheerleaders can be brutal. Shelley was the nicest out of all of them, now that I think of it.

I look around. I'm expecting it to be quieter today, but it's *really* quiet. Minutes pass and the room doesn't fill. Nobody enters bar a few freshmen. *What is going on?*

Cautiously, I grab my bag and approach the exit. I toy with the idea of asking the handful of other students in there what's going on but they look as clueless as me. Did lunch already happen or something?

As soon as I reach the double doors, I spot flurries of people leaving school, talking excitedly. I hurry after them. When I finally step outside, I find what looks like the entire student body. It's a zoo out here.

I stand on the steps, scanning the crowd for my group. I come up empty-handed. I see the sheriff, perched on a makeshift podium that I recognize as a stage block from the auditorium. Usually, he'd be wearing his trademark light-coloured hat outside, but not today. Instead, his bald patch is on display for the whole of Sanera to see. Around him are a line of reporters all with mics, and cameramen to boot. That's when I spot the rows of news vans lining the school parking lot. At least ten of them. They're holding a news conference ... at the school?

"Hello, hello, is this thing on?" Sheriff Rogers' voice cuts through the chatter. "Thank you for joining me today this Thursday afternoon. We do not usually hold press conferences. But this situation is unprecedented in Sanera and I felt it was important to address certain rumours that have been flying round. I would like to take the opportunity first to say that, as initially reported, we can confirm that the tragic deaths of Bradley Campbell and Shelley Jones were accidental. There is no foul play suspected in this case."

Muffled questions come from the front row of reporters but they're too far away for me to make anything out. The sheriff ignores them and continues.

"Now, as I say, it has come to my attention that many individuals are casting the blame on to ... supernatural methods, shall we say."

"Was it the ghoul?" a student yells.

"Tell us the truth!"

Because my parents aren't from Sanera, I never grew up believing in the Carrington legend. But I know that it's a serious deal here. Now I think of it, on my way to school today, a few stores were closed. Is that because people believe the Carrington Ghoul is running rampant? Is that why hardly anyone is in school? Seriously. What happened to logic?

The sheriff raises his voice. "Let me remind you that the community is grieving. These fantastical theories are only hurting the family and friends of Bradley and Shelley more."

His tone is scolding. I can tell he wants to yell, "Shame on you." And he'd have every right to. It's ridiculous. Let the victims rest. Let their families attempt to process in peace. I stare out at the crowd again and finally find my friends, and Buffy, huddled right in the centre. They haven't seen me yet; they're too engrossed in what's going on.

"Sheriff, let's cut to the chase." A voice makes itself known over the crowd, loud enough that even I can hear it from back here. The red-headed reporter from yesterday. Rick Field, if I remember correctly. "I'm going to say what everyone here is thinking. Are you really refusing to investigate a possible connection between the case of Robert Carrington and the two teenagers? Natural causes or not, it's uncanny. Supernatural even."

As soon as the words leave his mouth, the crowd goes silent.

Sheriff Rogers scratches his head and opens his mouth, before closing it. He repeats this process a few times before finally answering the pending question. "As stated before, there is no suspicion of foul play—"

"It surely can't be a coincidence," Rick interrupts smoothly. "The deaths of Bradley Campbell and Shelley

Jones are almost identical to that of Robert Carrington seventy-five years ago. An unexplained, fast-spreading fire that killed the victims almost instantly. In his dying moments, it is rumoured that Robert Carrington swore his revenge on the people of Sanera. One cannot rule out the possibility of the legend finally coming to fruition. We all may be in danger!"

Sheriff Rogers splutters on his podium. "Nonsense! You said it yourself. *Rumoured*. Everything you say is rumours and theories and legends. My job as sheriff of this county is to keep you all safe. If I thought you were in danger, I would say so!" He takes a deep breath and smooths his moustache. "Brad and Shelley died as a result of a tragic accident. Now, that's all I'll say on the matter. Please, trust the professionals on this." He stops and stares at the crowd who are again silent. "Thank you for listening."

As soon as he steps off the stage, everybody erupts. People are indignant, scared, I can tell – and the sheriff has done nothing to calm the rumours. Eventually, though, the sea of people begins to disperse and I push through to find my friends. It isn't long until I spot the top of Cam's blonde head.

"There you are!" he calls out, his eyes meeting mine. "Where were you?"

I raise my brows. "I missed the memo. *Clearly*. But I saw it all."

Amber nods. "Wild. That Rick Field has some nerve, still pushing this ghoul angle."

"I'm not sure the sheriff will shake the curse story. Not in a small town like this," says Cam.

He's completely correct, I think. Nothing happens in Sanera, so when something remotely interesting or tragic *does* happen, the rumours spread like wildfire. I mean, the last big crime was the convenience store robbery … ten years ago. It's not every day (or year) that people die in haunted mansions. I can't see people dropping this one any time soon.

Buffy speaks up quietly. "The ghost stuff is ridiculous," she says. "But Rick Field is right about one thing. You can't deny the similarities between the cases … right?"

All three of us look at each other, unable to come up with a response. The deaths of Robert Carrington and Brad and Shelley *are* eerily similar. But if Sheriff Rogers says there's nothing to worry about, we have to trust him. He wouldn't do anything to put us in harm's way.

"I think we need to get out of here," Amber says. "The ice cream parlour is calling my name."

"I'm in," Buffy says quickly.

"But we have school," I say.

"C'mon, man." Cam nudges me then places his face close to mine. "Live a little!"

I stare back at him. *C'mon, man. Live a little!*

The words hit me like a truck. Do I not live? Am I not

fun? I look over my shoulder at the double doors that are swaying back and forth as kids re-enter the school. I'll only miss a free period and double history. And math. They're my best subjects. I'll be fine. It'll be fine. Everything is fine.

So why do I feel like I'm going to regret this?

6

AMBER

We end up skipping the last four periods, which I can tell majorly stresses Jonesy out. It's a short walk to the ice cream parlour and in no time we're all in a window booth with milkshakes. Judging by the foot traffic in town, we're not the only people to ditch today. Everyone is too distracted to stay in school. But some stores are shut. It seems the rumour feels too close for some people.

Cam and Jonesy are next to each other, eyeing each other oddly every few minutes. I wish they'd work it out already. There's something there and they need to grow up and act on it. At the end of the day, though, it's not my place to *speculate* so I will impatiently wait.

Our conversation starts off normal, if you can even say that. General school stuff, video games, movies. But then, gradually, it transitions back to real life. It's hard not to talk about what happened. Everything seems to link back to it. As soon as school comes up, so does Brad and Shelley. As soon as horror movies come up, so does the Carrington Ghoul. It's inescapable.

"So, I understand the legend of the ghoul," Buffy says and places her hands on the table. "But why did Robert Carrington swear to haunt everyone? Because they couldn't get the fire put out fast enough?"

"Long story," I say.

"Tell me."

I'm surprised no one has told her yet but I guess she's barely had a free minute before the town turned upside down.

"Robert Carrington wasn't the *only* person to die in the manor," Cam explains. "Three years before, his entire family got sick from tuberculosis. He sent for doctors but they refused to go for fear of it spreading, so … they passed away."

Buffy's eyes widen.

"Robert had never been the warmest person by all accounts but, after that, he became … disgruntled. He blamed the locals for what had happened. He owned most of the land round here and pushed the rents up. He was not the nicest person to be around. Even threatened people with a butcher's knife, apparently."

Jonesy speaks up. "Then things got worse. Soon he wasn't just charging high rents. He started evicting everyone without warning and a ton of people were left homeless."

"Wow. He really hated the people of Sanera."

"They hated him back. And then there was the fire…"

"My God." Buffy sits back in the booth. She stays there for a moment with her thoughts before suddenly leaping forward again. "Wait, does that mean…"

Jonesy nods. "Right! Was the fire really an accident? Or was it revenge? It's all speculation. *If they can't have a home, neither can he…*"

Buffy's mouth falls open. "Well, he definitely has reason to haunt us, if that's the case."

Jonesy snorts. "Sure. But then again, ghosts don't exist."

Buffy shrugs. "Have you ever seen one?"

"No, because they … don't exist."

"There are legitimate, recorded sightings. Unexplained phenomena. Aren't you the tiniest bit curious?" Buffy eyes Jonesy, the sceptic. I wonder whether she really believes in the supernatural or whether she's just enjoying testing Jonesy. He scowls. Maybe this is what happens when you meet someone on the same IQ level as you.

I don't know how I feel about the supernatural myself. I need to see something to believe it.

Jonesy, however, holds firm to his stance. "There's a rational explanation for any so-called supernatural phenomenum. There are no such things as ghosts."

"Ghouls," Cam corrects, and Jonesy rolls his eyes.

But Buffy isn't done. "I think we should just consider—"

She stops suddenly, her eyes fixed on something outside. "Isn't that the reporter from before?"

"Rick Field?" I lean forward to get a better glimpse. I spot Julianne Moore red hair just down the street. "It sure is." I look over to see Buffy's on her feet, throwing on her jacket. "Where are you going?"

"I'm going to go speak to him," she responds, like it's a perfectly normal thing to do.

"And why would you do that?"

"She thinks the ghoul is real," Jonesy says. He sips his milkshake, unenthused. "She and Rick Field are going to play ghostbusters."

"That's not what I'm saying. It's not that I believe in the ghoul, necessarily. I *do* believe something fishy is going on. There are too many similarities between the deaths for it to be completely coincidental." And before we can comment, she's walking out of the store.

"I'm going too," I say, pushing my chair back.

"I don't want to miss this either," Cam adds. We both glance at Jonesy. He shakes his head.

"Suit yourself," Cam says.

We catch up with Buffy as she corners Rick on the sidewalk. He's clearly taken aback by our sudden presence.

"Can I help you?" he asks. The contrast between his pale skin, red hair and green eyes creates a striking and disconnected appearance.

"You're the reporter covering the Carrington Manor deaths, right?" Buffy asks. "You came to our school today."

Rick nods slightly. "What's it to you?"

"I'm curious about what you were saying – about a possible link between these deaths and that of Robert Carrington. Care to say more?"

He snorts, grins a little. Small dimples appear alongside his orangey freckles for a moment until he speaks again. "I mean, look at the evidence. Same exact circumstances. Same freaking spot, right by the bay window. Same fire that spreads at almost unbelievable speed. I believe in coincidences, but this… There's *no way* it was an accident."

I step forward. "Sheriff Rogers said—"

Rick Field guffaws right in my face. "*Sheriff Rogers.*" He imitates me. "Sheriff Rogers couldn't solve his way out of a paper bag."

"Why do you say that?" I ask.

"Look around, kid. What crimes has he solved? It's Sanera for goodness' sake. Nothing happens here so why would he be fit to solve the death of two children?" His voice has risen. People gawk as they walk past, causing him to lower it again. "Just think for yourself, instead of listening to people who have no idea what they're doing."

"But why jump to ghouls?" Cam responds quickly. "Why not something more … rational?"

Rick gives him a knowing look. "Which would be

what?" He clearly doesn't want to say it for himself for whatever reason.

I swallow. Because if it wasn't an accident and it wasn't a ghoul, *something more rational* would mean…

"Murder," Buffy whispers.

Silence falls over us all. Are we really suggesting Brad and Shelley were murdered? How have we jumped from a town legend to this?

Rick gives a slow nod. "I can't say that, of course. I don't have any proof and I've got my career to think of. But something seems fishy to me. We have to wait for the autopsy… Hopefully there'll be something that finally kicks that incompetent sheriff into gear."

A shiver runs straight through me. Autopsy. Holy shit. All of a sudden this all feels a whole lot more real. And it's a lot easier for me to believe than the aforementioned spectral theory. All of a sudden I kind of wish we were back to *that*.

Rick glances at his watch. "Look, I've got to go. You kids stay safe." And just as quickly as he appeared, he vanishes into an alleyway, his computer bag swinging in tow. That man is a mystery and I'm not sure I entirely trust him or his motives. I think he only cares about ratings. But he has definitely opened our eyes.

"My God," Cam says first. It's probably the only reaction to that. "*Murder?*"

"Aren't you glad we spoke to him now?" Buffy asks.

I shake my head. "Not really, no," I answer honestly.

I glance down at the goosebumps across my forearms. "Why would someone *want* to hurt Brad and Shelley?"

"I don't know," Buffy says, then, with an odd expression, glances between me and Cam. "You're not going to like this—"

"Then no," I bite. "Don't say it."

"Hear me out!"

"I want to hear," says Cam. I glare at him but he just shrugs. "What? I'm nosy."

I sigh. "Fine... What won't we like?"

"I think Rick's right. There's more here than meets the eye. I don't think the deaths were an accident. I don't buy the ghoul but I'm sure there's something connecting the deaths. Someone went to great lengths to kill Brad and Shelley in the same way that Robert Carrington died. To make the curse come alive. Brad and Shelley were athletes, right?"

"Yeah," says Cam. "So?"

"So let's say they drop a candle and the rug catches fire. They can't outrun it? Smash a window? Try to escape? Unless something – or someone – was stopping them."

Cam and I look at each other.

Buffy goes on, her fair hair jaggedly dancing as she makes exaggerated hand motions. "Maybe – just maybe – we could do some research into Carrington. Maybe we can find something that links what's happening now with ... back then."

"We know everything about the ghoul," I say. "Everyone does."

Buffy shakes her head. "You know rumours, gossip, stories. I'm talking about facts. There's got to be more – in the records in the library. Information, articles, anything that's been stored away and forgotten about. There might be a reason that Brad and Shelley were targeted." I catch the urgent note in Buffy's voice. *She wants this*, I think. Why? What's in it for her?

"You're getting ahead of yourself," I say gently. "The deaths could be – and probably are – purely coincidental."

Buffy falls silent. Then, after a blink, she says, in a calmer voice, "You're probably right. I think it wouldn't hurt to look into it. The sheriff isn't going to. And if we come up empty-handed … well, I'll have had a crash course in Sanera history." She smiles. "What do you think? Are you in?"

A long moment passes without us answering her. There's no harm in it, sure. But what if we *do* find something? That almost scares me more.

I think about Shelley and Brad. They deserve answers. I sigh. "I guess it won't hurt to look." Buffy's face lights up and Cam nods. I spot Jonesy leaving the ice cream parlour. I motion in his direction. "Now you just have to convince *him*."

7

CAM

We repeat the same school routine as yesterday. We stick around for the morning and then, at lunch, we ditch. It's not like me – or any of us really, especially Jonesy, who is the hardest to convince. I manage to sway him eventually. This time though, as we pass through town, instead of heading to the ice cream parlour, we carry on down the street until we reach one of the oldest buildings in Sanera.

If Buffy is serious about us researching Carrington Manor, there's only one place to go.

The library.

This place has been here for more than a hundred years and if there's going to be any forgotten information on Carrington, it'll be here.

Its doors are wide open and pinned to the wall with two aged chairs. A lot of kids are ditching today but none of them are here. It's empty – bar the older woman sitting behind the desk. Part of me is surprised it's still open. Even more stores have shut their doors as the stupid rumours erode people's common sense. It's like everyone suddenly forgot the Carrington legend wasn't a ghost story we'd tell each other at sleepovers.

My eyes dance around the walls, finding bookcase after bookcase. "I haven't been here in years," I whisper.

"I can tell," Amber says.

"And this is why you're on track for straight Bs," Jonesy mutters. "Except math."

Amazingly, the librarian is the same lady I remember from when I was a kid. She always kicked me out for talking too loud. She had white hair all those years ago too. It's like she's been ripped from my childhood and placed into 2001. A light pink cardigan rests atop her frail frame, lightly perched on her shoulders and over a similarly pale blouse.

Her face lights up when she spots us.

"Hello, kids," she says, peering up from her book, her voice croaky. I can just about see the tip of her wire-framed glasses over the old leather-bound volume. "What are you here for? School project?"

It's a good enough excuse. And *we* didn't have to come up with it. But then again, do we really need an excuse? It's not against the law to do some research.

Amber speaks up first. "We're researching Carrington."

The librarian's face wrinkles into something less friendly. I can't tell what her expression is though. Concerned? Curious? Annoyed that a bunch of teens are looking into such a touchy subject?

"Very timely, given the recent tragic events." She stands and points. "If you follow aisle B to the end, you'll find the town history and local interest section."

I smile at her but her focus is on Buffy. Her eyes drift up and down her frame, scanning her—

"You know, I may forget names, but never a face. And I've never met you, have I dear?" she says softly. "I'm Mrs Adler." Her mouth creeps into a smile. I'm sure she didn't mean it to come off so … scary.

With a hand raised into a short wave, Buffy replies. "Buffy. Nice to meet you. I just moved here from Connecticut."

"New in Sanera! Goodness, it's rare we get anyone moving here. It's normally the other way around."

"Yeah, me and my mom— Wait, why do people move away?"

Mrs Adler is right. People don't tend to stay in Sanera after school. It's a stepping stone; the locals try and get out as soon as possible. There are no opportunities, especially if your dream career is something other than the *norm*.

"Ah, you know what people are like," Mrs Adler replies. "Once they think they're too good for Sanera, they're gone. That's just the way of a small town, my dear.

Anyways … good luck with the research. Do let me know if you need any assistance."

I nod and start to drag Buffy off, but Mrs Adler isn't finished. In a louder, sterner voice, she calls out, "And don't be making a ruckus in my library!"

Ah, that's the librarian I remember. "Yes, ma'am."

We disappear into the ocean of shelves. "Well, she flipped her switch quickly."

"Yeah," Jonesy says, his eyes not leaving the shelves as we pass them by. "I always remember her being a bit weird." He gazes at the countless tomes as we walk past, his eyes transfixed like he's staring at the stars. He's in his element. Smart, cerebral Jonesy, always with his nose in a book. It's cute – it would be cuter if he wasn't acting so back and forth with me. Something shifted recently and I don't know how to fix it. There's a distance between us that wasn't there before. I'm not sure if I want it to go back to normal or…

Never mind. I need to focus. Researching Carrington Manor might have been Buffy's idea but I can't say I'm not curious. It's hard not to be after our run-in with Rick Field, esteemed douchebag journalist. But he might be completely wrong. I'm all for exposing the truth, but you also have to have your head screwed on.

All the same … maybe we'll find out something about the Carrington legend that no one else knew. Something grand and obvious, linking Robert's death with Brad and Shelley's. The thought sends my heart racing.

"These floors are creaky as hell," Buffy comments, purposely stomping harder. "You'd think they were hollow. *How* old is this place?"

"Older than anyone alive, I know that," Jonesy replies.

We reach our destination; my stomach drops. Mrs Adler did not mention how extensive the town's history is. There are hundreds of books, folders, boxes. It seems endless. How can a town as small as Sanera have this much history? Didn't we just establish how little goes on here?

Buffy drags her hand down one of the boxes. It's not damp, but it looks like it was at one point – it's covered in brownish stains. She peers at the label, which bears smudged ink and muddy smears.

"Whoever decided to keep logs of all this is a—"

"Asshole," Amber interrupts.

"I was going to say nerd," Buffy says, eyeing all the neatly categorized boxes. She shrugs. "But asshole works too."

We all share a laugh, which is nice. Teens having fun in the library, who knew? But it's short-lived as we take in the enormity of the task at hand. I eye the rustic mahogany shelves stuffed with folders. Sanera's agricultural history… Sanera's sewage work plans… *Beauty pageants?*

This place is going to get boring fast.

"God help us," Amber mutters under her breath.

"I don't think even he can help with this," I say.

Jonesy reaches up for the highest box on the shelf. The

bottom of his stomach makes an appearance, but I glance up and away. Nuh-uh. The box in his hands is what I meant to look at. For sure. I think it used to be black, but wear and tear has morphed it into a faded grey colour.

"Well, we better get a move on."

Saying the next three hours are a drag is an understatement. We sift through old newspaper clippings, town brochures, family trees, anything. We find articles about the ghoul of course – every few years one of the local magazines or newsletters announces a new sighting. But no one died as a result … and most of them were debunked anyway.

THE CARRINGTON GHOUL SPOTTED!

It was a teenager dressed up … on Halloween. There are a few like that, actually.

THE GHOUL RETURNS…

This one's from 1998 and clearly there's a resurgence of interest in the ghoul around that time because it's one of many sightings of a shrouded figure in the window at Carrington Manor. It must be why kids don't go there as much now. Kids like to act like they're all tough but … yeah. Easy headline, easy money. Although, the number of reports from that time does give me pause.

Could one of them really have been the ghoul? No. This is ridiculous. I'm wasting time. On to the reject pile they go.

We find information on the manor itself, and about Robert, but it's all pretty much stuff we already know. Except Buffy, of course. She sits wide-eyed as we fill in the gaps of her knowledge, especially the tragic deaths of his wife and children.

"I can't imagine losing my family and then living with that," she says. "Losing someone you love ... that's awful."

I swallow. Dad died a few years back and it's the worst. It always will be. I wonder suddenly about Buffy's dad. She hasn't mentioned him and I wonder if he's in the picture. *We don't really know anything about her*, I think.

"Do you think the original fire could've been a suicide?" Buffy asks. "Robert couldn't bear to go on without his family, so..." She tails off, looking round at us all.

I shrug. "It's a possibility. I guess."

Amber joins in. "Ask anybody, and they'll all have a differing opinion. Some people think it was an accident – a candle falling on the carpet. But most people think that the fire was started by the people he pissed off."

It makes the most sense. Hurt people hurt people.

"Wait," Buffy says. "You said Robert Carrington owned all the land round here. What happened to Robert's wealth when he died? His houses?"

In unison, we all look to Jonesy, because he seems to know more about everything than the rest of us.

He sighs and places the papers in his hands down. "There's a bit about it in his obituary. From what I can tell, Carrington had no living relatives so all his assets went to the state. Which was most of Sanera. The building we're currently in was one of his." He goes back to flicking through the box in front of him.

"I've lived here my entire life and I never knew that," I say.

Buffy looks around like she's seeing the room through new eyes. It's still a dusky and dingy library that hasn't been renovated in years but Mrs Adler does what she can with it.

"And Carrington Manor was abandoned?"

"Yep," I say confidently. "*That* I know."

"Why let it fall into disrepair? And what happened to Robert's money? And—"

"Hey," Jonesy says. "Focus. Last box…" He holds up the slightly mouldy cube and then sets it down. We all watch in anticipation as Jonesy's hands disappear into the box and come out holding a wad of stapled-together newspapers.

With fast fingers, he flicks through the pages and with every page his eyes widen more. "*Sanera Daily, October, November 1926*. These are – holy shit! – these are the newspapers from the months round the time of the fire."

"You're kidding," Amber says. Finally, after reading through planning permission forms and boring sewage documents, we've hit gold. A piece of information about that night. What we came for. We all crowd around Jonesy.

"So if Carrington died on October thirty-first, it'll be covered in the next day's paper," he says, rifling through. "Here we go. November's papers." He holds up the wad and gasps. "Wait."

We stare. The front page of the first paper is missing. Someone has torn out a whole page from the stapled-together wad, and I have a feeling I know what would have been on that front page – the report of the fire at Carrington Manor.

"Someone has been here…" Jonesy says slowly. He goes through the pile. "They're all missing sections, whole articles from that week. And I bet they're all reports to do with Carrington. I can't imagine anything else *that* interesting happened on a random October day in Sanera."

"Why would someone do that?" Buffy asks. "And is it something to do with the recent deaths?"

"The papers have clearly been here for a long time," I say. "The articles could've been cut out decades ago."

Buffy shakes her head. "Or not."

Jonesy peers closer at the pages to inspect the way the reports have been ripped out, dragging his finger across the tears. "Interesting," he mutters.

"Very interesting," says Amber. "Let's lay the facts out there. We have two kids dead in a place where Robert Carrington died in very similar circumstances, seventy-five years earlier. We have no proof if this is coincidental or not. And someone has torn all the articles about Robert's death out of the paper. Am I missing anything?"

Amber looks around at all of us as we sit in silence. "Cam's right. Hundreds if not thousands of people must have been through this box, seen the newspaper clippings. It would be silly to assume they were taken recently."

Buffy snatches up the wad of newspapers. "I'm going to go ask if Mrs Adler knows anything. She might have seen someone in this section going through the box…" Before we can move, she's trotting through the aisles until she's back at the front desk. We hurry after her.

"Someone has ripped articles out of these papers." Buffy holds out the pile accusingly to the poor woman.

Mrs Adler's face is a medley of stress and confusion. "I—"

"These are the newspapers from November 1926, the month after Robert Carrington died at the end of October that year. Any mention of that night is gone."

Buffy places − slams − the papers in front of the librarian. *A little overboard*, I think.

"My," Mrs Adler mutters. At first I think she's annoyed − *sure, come into my library for the first time ever and boss me around*. But then her expression changes. "You're right."

She inspects the pages further. Buffy's eyes don't leave Mrs Adler's frail hands. After a long moment of silence, she places the stapled wad down and lowers her glasses. They don't fall, instead hang from the thin chain round her neck.

"Well, I agree. Someone has definitely torn some articles out, but you knew that already."

"Any idea when?" Buffy asks eagerly.

"No. All I can say for certain is whoever took them must have done so in the past year. I did an inventory of the history section last year and remember going through the newspapers extensively. I would've remembered *this*."

I gulp. It doesn't prove anything, but it's still weird. I glance at Amber and she seems to be having a similar reaction – cautiously interested. Jonesy is looking thoughtful – standard – and Buffy is pink-cheeked with excitement.

Buffy says, "Do you know if anyone has been in the history section *recently*? As in, the last few days?"

"Nobody," Mrs Adler says. She gives a wry smile. "I don't know if you can tell, but the library isn't exactly bustling with people any more. The only visitors we get are here for general fiction and to study … both of which are right in my line of sight." She points ahead. "Nobody has been down there in the archives in a while."

Buffy doesn't hide her sigh. I shake my head at her. Better not to keep pushing.

Mrs Adler narrows her eyes. "What project is this for? I never asked."

"Oh, um … local history," I say quickly and stupidly. *Local history? Oh, yes that famous class.*

A disapproving "mhm" is shot our way before Mrs Adler climbs to her feet and takes back the papers. "Well, if that is all, I will thank you for bringing this to my attention. It's getting late, you kids should get home."

It seems we've been dismissed.

8

JONESY

I slump on to the couch before anyone else and am immediately attacked by Macey. Bring it on. Today has drained me, and on top of that, I think I have over ten paper cuts from hunting through the archives. So dog kisses will do.

"Well, it wasn't a total bust," Buffy says, taking the same seat as the other night. "We know someone stole articles about Carrington's death somewhat recently."

I roll my eyes. "Someone stole some newspaper articles somewhat recently? Let's go tell the sheriff because we have a lead." I'm not trying to be mean but she's riling me up. Macey finally gets bored of licking my face and settles on my lap. In a matter of seconds, she's snoring. If only I could fall asleep that quick.

"If nothing else, we can say we went to the library," Cam says. "Not many teenagers can say that."

He's leaning back in the couch, his arms resting along the top, splayed out. He definitely knows how to make himself at home. Although actually this *is* like his second home at this point. His mom is constantly out on work events and dinners. I guess it beats staying home alone.

Amber's phone rings and she's quick to pick it up. By her speed to answer, I can tell it's her parents. Her dad gets quite overprotective if she's forgotten to tell him where she is.

As soon as the phone reaches her ear, I can hear a muffled panicked voice at the other end of the line. She turns away as she listens. "Dad – slow down – what?" She looks at us. "Someone, turn the news on – Dad, it's OK. I'm at Jonesy's, I'm fine."

I reach forward and grab the remote control from the coffee table. In a blink, the dull screen comes to life and, in another, the picture returns. It's still on the local news channel from before and instantly I see the damned manor. I've seen it more these past two days than I have my whole life. The shot stays there for a few more beats, while red and blue lights flash against it. Then it cuts to Sheriff Rogers and another officer, who is speaking to the camera.

"Another press conference?" Buffy says. She leans forward. "Something is wrong."

I turn up the volume just as the other officer steps back and the sheriff steps up. His face is grave.

"Good evening, Sanera. Thank you for joining me at such short notice."

He gulps. In front of the entire town. My stomach drops. "What the fuck is going on?"

"As I said yesterday, it is my duty to keep you all safe. In light of recent discoveries, I am here to inform you that the deaths of Bradley Campbell and Shelley Jones are now being treated as murder."

Amber gasps. "Dad, I'll call you right back."

Buffy watches the screen, gaze intent.

Cam looks to me but I can only shrug. I know we suspected something might be wrong, but now hearing it on the news … it feels all too real. The goosebumps on my arms are testament to that.

The sheriff continues. "The autopsies have revealed some disturbing new information. Namely that the victims were found to have multiple stab wounds to their chest and stomach areas…" The sheriff's voice trembles slightly. "It is also clear that these lacerations were dealt post-mortem."

"Holy shit," Cam mutters, his eyes wide.

"If you have any information that can assist in bringing justice to our victims, the sheriff's office is open twenty-four hours. We will of course keep you updated. Please, stay safe. Stay indoors unless necessary. And keep calm. We'll solve this thing. There will be no further questions at this moment. I'll share more as I have it."

He backs away. At the conclusion of his words, Rick Field appears back on screen, like he always does. Already back in the spotlight.

He looks delighted.

"There we have it, folks. Sheriff Rogers has now declared the enquiry into the deaths of teenagers Bradley Campbell and Shelley Jones an active murder investigation. What did I tell ya? The culprit is clearly extremely dangerous. If you witness anything suspicious, do not put yourself in harm's way. Police will be patrolling the town so law enforcement will not be far…"

Rick's words trickle out as my brain seems to implode. The words I want to say are stuck at the back of my throat. It's like they're trapped.

This is no ghoul, I think. Lacerations — that means a person did this. A flesh-and-blood murderer. And *post-mortem* stab wounds? What kind of sick and twisted person does that? I'm no expert but I don't think a ghoul can wield knives. Then there's also the case of the fire. This person would've had to wait until the fire was out to … *deal* with the bodies, and that would risk being caught by emergency services. Why go to all the trouble?

"I'm going to call my mom," Buffy says first.

"I've got to go. My parents will kill me if I'm not home in five minutes," Amber adds, her voice panicked. I can imagine how worried they are right now. It reminds me that Mom is upstairs, unaware of any of this as far as

I know. I bite my tongue. Suddenly I really, really don't want to be alone.

I look up and find Cam staring right at me. Instantly we come to a mutual agreement. He doesn't want to go home alone. And I won't let him. We shouldn't be alone. He's always been the more *bro* one of us, but that doesn't matter right now.

The rumours are true.

Brad and Shelley were murdered.

And whoever did it is still out there.

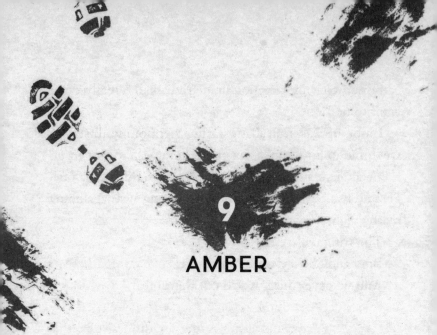

9

AMBER

Dad is waiting outside Jonesy's house when I open the door. His dark eyes somehow pierce through the dusky lighting. Just from the outline of his burly silhouette, I can see the tension fall from his body. I'm safe.

"Amber Janelle Grayson, I was about to call the police." His voice is loud and he brings it down a notch. "I was worried."

"I know," I say, and in a blink his arms are wrapped tightly around me. "I'm not going anywhere!"

Dad tuts. "Glad we can agree on that... Now we're going home—" He stops himself as he pulls away, looking over my shoulder. "You must be Buffy."

I realize Buffy is just behind me. She smiles nervously. "Nice to meet you, Mr Grayson." She hesitates, clearly not wanting to interrupt our *moment.*

"Is someone picking you up?" Dad asks. "We can walk you home."

Buffy shakes her head. "It's fine. My mom will be here any minute. But thank you for the offer."

"I'll see you at school," I say, and then I wonder. Will school even happen now? Has everything we ever knew changed for ever?

Dad pushes me inside our house, locks the door, and then steps back. "OK, *now* you're safe." Before I know it, his arms are locked around me again.

I notice the aroma. Just in time for dinner. Oh, this is going to be a long talk about safety and staying out of harm's way. Lucky me. Dad's not usually back in time for meals so, when he is, he doesn't shut up.

I slide my bag from my shoulder and plop it beside the front door – Dad frowns.

"I'll move it after dinner."

"Mhm, I've heard that before."

A small chuckle escapes my lips. I realize what the aroma is. *Casserole.* Mom's casserole is always mushy. I follow Dad into the kitchen and find Mom taking the food out of the oven. Instantly, a sense of warmth washes over me, somewhat drowning the dread sitting at the pit of my stomach. But not entirely. I don't think that's going to go anytime soon. How can it?

"Oh, sweetheart," Mom says, abandoning the dish to

engulf me. "We were so worried. Are you OK?"

That's all it takes to set me off. My eyes well at first and then gush. Tears fall from my eyes more easily than I thought possible.

"It's OK, honey," Mom whispers as she pats the back of my head. "We're here. We're here."

It's then I feel Dad's warmth engulf me as well. We're now standing in the middle of the kitchen, a clump of bodies, while the food gets cold.

After reheating the food, Dad insists we try and have a normal evening. Whatever that means. I'm not in the mood to argue. Before we eat, we say grace – I know, but according to my parents I have to accept it while I'm under their roof.

"It was nice to meet your new friend, Buffy," Dad says. "How is she settling in?"

I bite into my food first – too hungry – but I do finish chewing before I answer. There may be a murderous ghoul on the loose but I still have my table manners.

"Good, I think. She's maybe a bit … full on," I say.

Mom puts down her fork. "Full on? How?"

I blink. How do I explain that Buffy had us researching a murder case all week? "She insisted we go to the library today, which was … interesting."

Mom looks to Dad. "And that's a bad thing?"

"N-no," I stutter. "It's just – never mind." I give up

trying to craft a lie and shove a piece of chicken in my mouth. If I keep talking I'm accidentally going to say we were actually there to research Carrington Manor because Buffy insisted there might have been something fishy going on before we actually *knew* something fishy was going on. My parents would be delighted if I started poking around a murder investigation. *Breathe, Amber.*

Thankfully, Dad brushes past it. "Well, it must have been nice for Mrs Adler to have some young people in there for a change. Amazing how she keeps that place going. And Buffy seems like a lovely girl so I hope you are making her welcome. Sanera can be a big adjustment. We know how difficult it was for you when we moved from Chicago."

I nod. "We *are* making her welcome. Me and the boys."

And then the obligatory sigh comes. "Oh, *the boys.*"

"Dad!" I place my own fork down. "Jonesy and Cam are my friends. Of course they're going to help show Buffy around."

He ignores that. "You should invite her around for dinner sometime."

"Jonesy and Cam too?"

"No," is all he says. Which doesn't surprise me at all. Every time Dad has met the guys … it's always the most awkward interaction. It's why we always meet at Jonesy's. That way I can avoid the questions.

Which one is your boyfriend? Neither? You're just friends? Really?

Why are you only friends with boys?

Is there something you want to tell us?

It's relentless.

"Well, I'm glad you finally have a girl friend," Dad says approvingly, then tucks back into his food.

He's clearly done with the conversation and I'm glad. Like Mom, he makes sure to separate the *girl* from *friend*. I don't laugh aloud but I do internally. This is exactly why I haven't told him I like girls. He seems so scared of the fact I could possibly be a lesbian. I'm actually bisexual – not that it should matter to him. I'm still his daughter.

It seems it's Mom's turn to start a conversation. "So, honey," she says timidly. "What is town like right now? I haven't had a chance to get out today."

I shrug. "More stores were shut. People are scared – either of a killer or a ghoul. I have a feeling it's going to be even worse tomorrow. People are overreacting."

Mom and Dad look to each other.

"What?" I ask, unable to read their expressions. But I know I won't like it. Whatever it is, they both think it.

"We think we should all be careful," Mom says.

Dad nods. "You never know."

"Are you saying you believe in the ghoul?" I can't believe my ears right now.

"Oh, of course not," Mom insists. "Ghosts and ghouls! That's silly. But a killer – like Mr Field and the sheriff said – that's another matter. It's better to be safe than sorry. I think we should have a quiet, family time this weekend. Inside."

Again, I almost feel like laughing. My parents have always feared the worst and now, amazingly, they're justified in never letting me out again.

I finish my food. As soon as I'm done and an appropriate amount of time has passed listening to my parents talk about their day, I excuse myself. It's not too far-fetched to say I'm going to do homework, even if it is Friday night.

As soon as I step foot into my room, I lock the door behind me. Can't be too safe, like Mom always says.

I retrieve my phone from my pocket and call Cam, who I know is with Jonesy. Then I add Buffy on to the call. In no time, we're all talking over each other.

"Hey," I say, interrupting everyone. "… Hi." I don't know what to say.

Jonesy and Cam reply in unison. "Hey."

Finally Buffy offers a short greeting. "Hi there… Everyone get back OK?"

It's only been a few hours since we were all together but it feels like longer.

"I only just managed to get away from my parents," I say. "I don't think I'm being let out of the house this weekend." And in all honesty, I don't think I *want* to leave the house.

"Same here," Buffy adds. "Mom is terrified."

I feel bad for Buffy. She moves here, expecting a fresh start and hopefully a smooth-sailing senior year. Instead, she gets a murder investigation. She can't even feel safe in her own home.

"Cam, please tell me you're going to stay at Jonesy's?" He may have this fancy new security system but never trust electronics. Any horror movie can tell you that. Never trust anyone or *anything*, for that matter.

"For tonight," he assures me. "Mom won't be back until late so I didn't want to take the risk and, you know … be killed."

"Delightful," I say. "Why don't we—"

"Listen, I'm gonna have to go," Buffy announces abruptly. She sounds preoccupied. "Glad you're all safe. Take care this weekend. Thanks for looking after me. I'll see you on Monday." Then she disconnects from the call.

"That was strange," Jonesy says.

I nod. It was.

"I don't trust her," he adds, to which I roll my eyes.

"Why not?"

"Well, for one thing, why is she here? *No one* relocates from Connecticut to Sanera without good reason. *Amber, you're different.* And for another thing, isn't it weird how interested she is in this investigation?"

"She was right, wasn't she? Something was wrong."

Jonesy says stubbornly, "It's weird."

"She's fine. Intense, but fine. You're just being overly

cautious, Jones. I'm going to head off too. I'm exhausted."
I yawn. "Night, you two."

Jonesy and Cam offer their goodnights and then
I hang up.

My brain is frazzled. A double murder, in Sanera?
I hope the sheriff's office and the police are putting
everything into this. But all I can think about is what Rick
Field said. *Nothing happens here, so why would the sheriff be at
all fit to solve the death of two children?* I hate to admit it, but
he's right. The sheriff and our police are not equipped for
a case of this magnitude.

And if they don't solve this thing … if they don't find
the killer…

I don't want to finish that thought.

I shut my phone off and retreat to bed. Today has been
a day, to say the least – and something tells me things are
only going to get scarier.

10

JONESY

Cam's phone pings.

"Amber and Buffy are going in tomorrow," he says.

It's Sunday night and so many kids are ditching school, we had to check. If we're going in, we're going together.

"Thank God for that," I mutter, collapsing back into the couch. Macey is instantly at my feet, clearly sensing my stress. Dogs are clever like that, Macey probably more so than most. She knows to comfort me when Mom is being … Mom.

Cam and I fall into an uneasy silence. This weekend has been weird but then so have the past few weeks. Every time Cam and I are together too long, things are just … off. There's a tension there. Unless it's all in my head.

"Jonesy," Cam says at last, cutting through the silence.

His voice is gravelly after our day of absolutely nothing. "What's up?"

I look at him properly for the first time in what feels like weeks. Sure, I've looked at him, but not *really*. Not at his face for any longer than I've needed to because it makes it all more real.

The thing that I've been trying not to admit these past few weeks (or months or years) is this: I like Cam. I like him a lot and I don't want to deal with the consequences of that. If he doesn't feel the same, it'll make everything weird. Or weirder than it is already. That's not what I want for myself, or him, or Amber. She deserves friends that can be in the same room as each other.

"Jones, please talk to me," he presses. "I wasn't sure whether to mention it, but we haven't been *us* recently." That's one way to put it.

"Well, yeah," I say, in the most sarcastic tone I can muster. "Two kids died. A ghost is on the loose. People are—"

"You know what I mean," Cam interrupts. His voice is quiet, but it scares me. He sounds so serious, like I've never really heard him before.

"I'm sorry," is all I can think to say. *I'm sorry?*

"What could you possibly have to be sorry about?"

I want to form words and for them to have meaning, and give explanations and reasons, but nothing comes. My stupid brain won't work. I want to yell and scream that *I'm scared that I'm slightly in love with you and I have been for a while and I want to be together, but I'm terrified too.*

Before I can even think to utter another word, Cam is at my side. I only realize he's there by the sudden movement on the couch and the light brush of a hand on my thigh. It catches me off guard, but I don't bat his hand away.

"Jonesy, if I've done anything to make you…" He pulls his hand from my thigh almost instantly. "I'm sorry, I didn't mean to—"

"It's not that." My voice is breathy as I hold back the tears that I've suppressed for so damn long. "I don't…"

"Hey, hey." Gentle hands wipe at my tears as they trickle down my cheeks. "For the last time, what is this all about, Jones?"

"Cam," I say, pulling myself away. "What is … *this*?" My hands motion between me and him.

"This?"

I sigh. "Us! What are we doing?" The tremor in my voice is noticeable. "And please don't make a joke."

"I'm not."

"But you always do! That's you, Cam. Buffy knew, just by looking at you. You're the cool joker guy who does sports. I'm the anxious nerd. We're so different."

Cam shuffles in his seat, eyes fixed on me. "I think

being different is great. If everyone was the same the world would be ridiculously boring. Why do you care?"

"Because," I stress, "I… I like you."

Silence.

I decide I may as well keep going. "I have *liked* you for years and have always hidden it from you because I was too scared to say anything. But recently—"

"Jonesy." His voice is loud enough to stop me. He grabs my hands from in front of me and holds them tight in my lap. "Breathe, please."

My eyes dart to the ground then to his annoyingly perfect face. From his blue eyes to rigid jaw and back again. But now, there's understanding in those eyes. His pupils are dilated and he's blinking slow.

"Jonesy, me and you…" he says, like he's walking on eggshells, unsure of either what to say or how to say it. Maybe both. He holds up his hand and balls it into a fist. "We're like this. A rock. We've been friends since we met, right?"

I nod, wondering where he's going with this.

"I'm scared too," he admits.

Cam is meant to be the cocky, blasé one. He's not supposed to be scared. "You … are?"

"Are you kidding? Of course! You're intimidating!"

I laugh and he grins, before continuing. "Well, in a way. You're scary smart. But I like that. I like *you*. The way I think you like me. And hey, what's to say pushing this a little further is a bad thing? Natural progression is a *good* thing, like … ask evolution!"

I squint at his analogy. "I think you mean natural *selection*, but…"

He stares at me. "Way to burst my bubble."

"Sorr—"

His finger brushes my lips. "Do not even dare say sorry."

My breath falters and, in the most neutral tone possible, he continues. "I have pent-up feelings for my best friend. I think anyone would be terrified."

Cam has feelings for me. Cam. The words send a shock to my system. All this time I've been bottling my own feelings up, and for what? They haven't gone away. They've just been hidden. Forced away out of fear of what he might think. All this time, I thought they were unrequited – and now…

Now I know the truth.

And, along with the shock, comes something else. An ache. A wanting – a need, maybe.

"Are you serious?" I ask.

"Deadly."

I wince. "Don't."

Cam releases a short breath. "Poor wording on my part but the sentiment is real." He raises his brows at me. I can see his eyes better now. Big, blue and full. "If you feel the same, I would love to see where this goes."

"But what if…"

"No buts." A shrug rolls off his frame. "You don't get anywhere in life if you always worry about what can go wrong. Sure, if it doesn't work out, it could get weird between us. But…"

He stops himself.

I continue the thought for him. "But if it *does* work out…"

Our eyes meet and suddenly the room, and all its funky colour, fades away until it's just me and him. Ideally, this is how it'd be. Me and Cam, alone, without any of the outside world and their judgement.

"Exactly," he says, his voice low.

A small smile carves itself on to my face. Maybe this, me and Cam, is worth the risk. Maybe.

Cam's grin meets mine. Our faces are level and only a few inches away. I can feel his hot breath on me, and I assume he can feel mine and the nerves that come with the closeness. I've never done this before.

He leans closer but still not close enough to make contact. Instead, his eyes leave my lips and graze my eyes. He says two words and they make me melt.

"May I?"

11

AMBER

"Amber!"

I cement my feet into the grass as I hear Mom's voice. I spin round to find her standing at the front door, a dish towel in one hand and her car keys in the other.

"Are you sure you *have* to go in today?"

I throw my head back and stare up at the sky before lowering it again. "Mom, we talked about this."

"I know, but I still don't understand why school is so important right now." She takes a step out of the house but keeps the door ajar with her foot. "You said it yourself – everyone's on edge, classes are all over the place. Wouldn't you rather stay at home?"

I sigh, because part of me absolutely would rather stay at home. But all I could think about this weekend was the case and the missing newspaper reports and what Rick Field said and … I need to get out. I need to see my friends.

I know that Mom is scared the same way everyone else in this town is scared. Including me. But I can't stay hidden in my room for ever.

"I want to *try* and get back to normal," I say. "Besides, Buffy hasn't had one regular day since she moved here. I'd like to help give her that… If it's a drag, I'll come home, yeah?" I try to sound as breezy as possible, hoping she relents. I'm unsure of success until a close-lipped smile crests on her face.

"Fine," she submits. She lifts up her keys. "But at least let me drive you."

"I'm fine! I need the fresh air."

"Amber…"

I dash back to the front door and rest my hands on hers, lowering her car keys. "Mom, I love you and I will let you know when I get to school. And then I will send regular updates. OK?"

She sighs. "If I don't hear from you…"

"You will!" The words leave my mouth as I'm darting back down the driveway and on to the sidewalk. "Love you!"

"I love you too!"

I lift my hand to return her wave, then head off down

the street. I understand why she doesn't want me to go. But something dark is afoot in Sanera and I need to find out what.

"There you are," Cam says, as I round the corner on to the front school yard, right where Sheriff Rogers held his impromptu press conference. That already feels like weeks ago. Time flies when you find out shit has hit the fan.

Cam and Jonesy are perched on a rusted bench that was probably at one time painted. It's the sort of rust that sticks to your clothes and breaks off with the slightest touch. I don't know why they've chosen it. But it's the *way* they're sitting that strikes me. Close to each other and not as far away as possible, like they have been lately. Did they finally talk, like normal people? Have things changed between them – in a good way?

I join them but don't acknowledge it. They can tell me in their own time. "How was your weekend?"

It should be a simple answer, but by the looks on their faces they don't exactly know what to say.

Instead they settle on, "Fine."

"Right," I reply.

"Hello," a voice calls out that I recognize as Buffy's. I turn and wave. We haven't spoken since the other day – just a quick text exchange confirming we'd be in today. Her dark blonde hair is pinned back into a low ponytail;

she seems to have finally ditched her jacket as well. This October heat is the real deal. Instead she's in a white tee and low-cut dark denim jeans.

"Have I missed anything?" she asks as she takes a seat next to me. Immediately, a waft of her perfume hits me.

"Not at all—"

A loud crackle silences us all. It's harsh and grating, and a multitude of moans echo across the front yard.

"Hello, hello … is this on?"

Like clockwork, everyone's head turns to the sound. Already, a crowd has formed near the kid standing in front of the mic. I know him. Tall, dark hair, letterman jacket…

"Is that who I think it is?" Buffy whispers. "The creep from the canteen?"

"Kenny Lloyd," Cam replies. "Brad's best friend."

Buffy kneels on the bench so she can see more clearly. "What is he doing?"

"I think we're about to find out," Jonesy says.

Kenny taps the mic again, smooths back his hair and settles into a relaxed pose. "Hello, Sanera High." His voice is loud and confident. "If you – somehow – don't know me already, I am Kenny Lloyd. Cornerback on the Sanera Sabrebtooths – and Bradley Campbell's best friend."

If the school yard was quiet before…

I don't hear a breath, a shuffling, a cough, anything. Everyone is watching Kenny.

Kenny takes a deep breath. "There's something I want to say, something I want you all to hear. About Brad and Shelley's murder…"

There's another sound then – a cacophony of screeching tyres.

News vans. A shit ton of them come screeching to a halt beside the spot where everyone has gathered. I'm getting déjà vu. The sliding doors all fly open and a myriad of reporters bundle out of each van. It seems every single news station in the state is here. I'm pretty sure I spot some national stations too. And right in the centre of them is Rick Field. *Of course he is.*

My eyes float back to Kenny to find him facing the cameras with a satisfied smile. He called the press, it's clear. He's always been an attention seeker. Always trying to ride the high of being Bradley Campbell's best friend. Wherever Brad went, so did Kenny. I know he's doing this to look good. To make the murders about him.

"This is so typically Kenny," Cam says under his breath.

It's clear with whatever Kenny's about to say, he wants a bigger audience than just the student body. And with the number of cameras pointed directly at him, it seems he's getting his wish.

"As I was saying …" he says, although now he is noticeably a little less confident than before. Now that the television cameras are on him, he's slightly lost the cocky, smug edge he exuded before. Nervous.

"Brad and Shelley's murders were unjust, unfair, and darn right monstrous," he says loudly. "There is no ghoul. The suggestion that two kids have been killed by supernatural means is an absolute insult to their families. I am proud to call Brad's mother, Anne, my second mother and it has broken me to see her these past few days. No mother should ever go through what she is going through right now. Parents should be choosing colleges with their kids, not the fucking font for their headstones."

His words – and how sincere he sounds – startle me. Kenny was Brad's lapdog, but I didn't know Brad meant this much to him. And by the look of Cam's confused expression, he feels the same. He's told us plenty of locker-room stories about what a pig Kenny is. This passionate sincerity doesn't seem like Kenny. What is he playing at?

My gaze catches the back of Rick Field's head and a thought occurs to me. It makes me wonder if he's put Kenny up to this, put the idea into his head. This whole display makes great television and that's exactly what Rick wants.

He goes on. "So consider this a promise to Anne." He straightens up and looks over at everyone, especially the cameras. "To the freak who did this, count your days, because you will not get away with it. The police aren't doing their job. They've clearly missed something – the killer could still be there, for all they know! I'm going to

Carrington Manor, tonight, to search." Someone at the front starts cheering. "If anyone wants to help me catch this son of a—"

The microphone cuts out so the rest of his speech goes unheard, by us at least.

It seems the teachers have realized what's going on. A couple clamber on to the stage, urging him away. I spot Mrs Lauders, Ms McCreedy and Mr Graham. Gently they lead Kenny away, as the cameras whirr and flash. Mr Graham stays back and attempts to calm the crowd.

"Um, everyone, please calm down," he says, raising his timid voice above the shouts. "Kenny is clearly very upset, but getting angry won't help…" But it's no use. Everyone's too riled up.

"My God," Buffy mutters. "Talk about attention-seeking."

Cam's eyes follow Kenny as he's led away, still shouting indistinctly. "Kenny is a grandstander. One hundred per cent. But you heard him. He sounded genuinely angry… It's hard to fake that."

I stare off, Kenny's words replaying in my head. *To the freak who did this, count your days, because you will not get away with it… If anyone wants to help me catch this son of a—*

"Do you think he's serious?" I ask. "About going to the manor?"

"I think so," Buffy says. "He's going to tear Carrington Manor apart looking for clues. Or the killer."

"Won't the police still be there?"

Jonesy speaks up. "At this point in the investigation, they've probably got all the evidence there is – or everything they *think* there is, anyway. I imagine they just have a cop car surveilling the area."

Squinting, I glance at Jonesy. "How do you know that?"

Instantly, he blushes. "I watch a lot of *Crime Scene Investigation*." He shoves Cam when he nudges him. "What? It's good, OK! You learn a lot."

"OK," I say. "Well, hopefully Kenny will calm down. And I guess we wait and see if the police have found any evidence."

Kenny was sent home. The teachers try to pretend his little conference didn't happen, but it's been blasted all over the news.

I've had to call Mom multiple times to tell her I'm alive and well and not about to join a mob descending on Carrington Manor. She had a lot of questions about Kenny's speech, most of which I couldn't answer. No, I don't know why he thinks he's going to find something at the manor. That's what I said to her at least. But I do wonder. Is Kenny right? Have the police missed something? If Rick Field did put him up to this, maybe he's done some good for once.

We head back to Jonesy's after school. Buffy comes too. I guess she's become part of the gang already without us even realizing. I kick my shoes off and sink my feet into the soft carpet. Of course, Macey is with me.

"Soda?" Jonesy shouts from the other side of the room, where he has a mini fridge. He throws us all an ice-cold can, then addresses the small presence looking up at my drink. "Macey, you can't drink soda ... *no*. Wagging your tail extra hard doesn't change that."

I fall into the couch as Jonesy makes his way over to the rest of us.

"Everything I have she wants – she won't even eat her food if I don't pretend I want it first." He plops right next to me.

"Well, maybe you should take one for the team," Buffy says, trying not to laugh.

"Huh?"

Cam leans forward and widens his eyes. "Eat the dog food, man."

Jonesy snorts. "You're such children."

"You're making my brain melt," I say, but slowly my smile fades. I can't take my mind off what happened earlier. "Kenny clearly thinks there are clues to be found at Carrington Manor. We found out someone had taken the newspaper articles from the library. What should we do about it?"

Jonesy shrugs. "I was thinking ... nothing?"

Buffy throws her two cents in. "I think we should tell the reporter. Or the police."

"And what will they do?" I ask. "It's not a crime to take some newspaper clippings out of the library. Well, maybe it's a library crime, but that's all."

"I still think it might be connected—"

"Buffy," Jonesy says sharply. "Why are you so interested in all this? You didn't even know Brad and Shelley."

The room falls silent. I didn't expect that from Jonesy. He's never confrontational.

"Jones ..." I say, "leave her alone."

"It's OK," Buffy says. "You're right – I didn't know Brad and Shelley. I'm just scared, I guess. And when I'm scared, my way of coping is ... not coping. I throw myself into things completely." Her gaze falls on Jonesy. "But I shouldn't be dragging you all into it too. I'm sorry."

He hesitates. "No, *I'm* sorry," he says at last. "It's just—"

"Hey, everyone," Cam suddenly says.

Jonesy scowls. "I was in the middle of..."

"*Hey.*"

We fall silent and follow Cam's gaze to the TV, which has been on mute. He leans forward and turns it up. The sound is a blur at first and the picture is fuzzy but an aerial view of a house is on screen.

"Holy shit," Cam says, as we read the chyron on the bottom of the screen.

THE CARRINGTON GHOUL
STRIKES AGAIN.

It's like the air is sucked right out of my chest. No. This can't be happening. Not again. But this time, the image… It's not Carrington Manor. It's a built-up area. Somewhere in Sanera.

Cam leans forward, his mouth agape. "Wait. That's Kenny's house." His eyes don't leave the television as the aerial shot of the house transitions to a wide shot of the street. Herds of reporters hound the residence, even more than earlier. This has gone statewide, clearly.

What. Is. Going. On?

The screen cuts then to the news studio, the harsh cold lights a shock to my eyes. But I've never seen it like this. The background is full of staff running around, phones at their ears, clipboards in hand. Chaos. They clearly weren't ready for whatever has happened. Finally, the middle-aged newsreader at the centre of the frame looks up, and his sombre voice echoes through the television.

"We have breaking news. The mutilated body of a third Sanera High student was discovered at four p.m. today. The parents of the deceased contacted the Sanera police department soon after. We can confirm the body has been identified as seventeen-year-old Kenneth Lloyd."

Gasps sound from all of us. Even Macey senses something is off because she stops clawing at our feet and sits quietly, watching the screen. She then tucks herself into my legs.

"The horrific attack comes just hours after Lloyd made

122

a public threat to find the culprit behind the deaths of Bradley Campbell and Shelley Jones just last week. It seems his message was heard. At this time, the police are asking citizens with any information regarding these murders to come forward…"

"Fuck," is all I can think to say. What else *is* there to say?

"It's now also being reported that Mr Lloyd's stab wounds are similar, if not identical, to those of Bradley Campbell and Shelley Jones. Visceral."

All at once, everyone's phones blow up. Notification after notification. Then calls. It doesn't stop. I look down and see Dad's name flashing. I go to answer, but before I can press accept I see a familiar face is plastered on the TV screen. Sheriff Rogers looks the worse for wear.

"Thank you. Citizens of Sanera, this is a terrible shock for us all. In the wake of this third tragic death, a town-wide curfew is now in full effect. Between the hours of seven p.m. and six a.m., anyone under the age of twenty-one must remain inside for their safety. I will keep the people of Sanera updated with any developments. Thank you."

He then scurries off camera. *He looks scared*, I think. He most likely thought being sheriff in a county like ours would be a cakewalk. Until now. He's not equipped for the job. I'm sure more and more people are waking up to that. Rick Field was right all along.

I mute my phone and go to pull Macey closer for comfort but she's already retreated to Jonesy. She's on his lap, looking as frightened as I feel. I'll call my parents in a second, I just need to think this through, to actually let this sink in. We all look at each other, unsure of what to say, unsure of who will break the silence first.

"The sheriff doesn't know what he's doing," I say at last.

Cam nods. "I know," he says softly. "Three murders officially class this person as a serial killer, right?"

Unanimous nods.

"I think you're right," Buffy says. "The sheriff *doesn't* have a clue. Which means more deaths. Unless he gets some help."

I glance at her. "What do you mean by *help*?"

"Exactly how it sounds. He isn't going to solve this on his own."

Buffy fidgets, her hands clawing together on her lap. Nervous tic? "Look, I don't like it any more than you do. I have not had a single normal day since moving here. And at first, it was like I said – I wanted to research the case as a way of controlling how scared I am. But now … now, it's different. Now there's a real reason to try and help. Another kid has died. The killer isn't going away – not unless we do something to stop them."

I look at Cam, who is frowning at his lap. Then at Jonesy. His face is pale – paler than usual. When he speaks, the harsh tone from earlier is gone, but he's still not happy. "Buffy, what exactly can *we* do? We're teenagers. With no experience. No anything."

A pause. Then, "I think we need to go there," Buffy replies.

"Where?" Jonesy asks, but he already knows. We all do. There's nowhere else that could even be a possibility. "*Carrington Manor?* Are you out of your mind?"

Buffy gives a faint smile, exposing her pristine teeth. "Yeah, probably. But we've already established that the authority figures in this town are out of their depth. The police could easily have missed clues. Like the fire spreading so fast, right? We all agreed that Brad and Shelley should have been able to outrun a little candle fire. If we can find anything—"

"Again! We are teenagers!"

It silences Buffy for a second but it doesn't stop her. Instead she continues but with a softer tone. She's not letting this go. "Even more reason to go, if we're the … target demographic." Odd word choice. She looks around at us all, eyes wide and appealing. "Look, I just don't want anyone else to die."

It's ridiculous, I think. Two kids were killed in that house. And as much as I don't want to believe in the Carrington Ghoul, the rumours still echo in my head. Buffy can't expect us to agree to this. The others *won't* agree. Surely.

I look at them. Jonesy looks panicked, Cam thoughtful.

At last, Cam sighs. "I think she's right."

"Excuse me?" Jonesy says, his arms flying around as he

speaks. Given how reserved he usually is, this tells me he's scared. We all are.

"I don't want to go," Cam argues. "But this case needs to be solved and I have no faith in Sheriff Rogers to do his job. Hate to say it, but Rick Field was right. Someone is attempting to use this supernatural story to cover up murder."

Jonesy stutters. "W-well – surely, they'll call the FBI now."

"If they're interested. I'm sure there's thousands of cases that need their help. How do we know they'll choose this one?" Cam says. His hand falls on to Jonesy's. I'm unsure if he notices. But Jonesy does. His cheeks redden as soon as he's touched. "This killer is clearly moving fast. By the time help comes, who knows what might have happened?"

My stomach turns at the word *killer*. It's brutal and sounds horrible on Cam's lips. But it puts everything in perspective. Someone in Sanera is out there killing teenagers and nobody is doing anything to stop them.

Jonesy nods slowly. "Kenny wanted to solve this thing for whatever reason, and I … agree we should do something about it."

So Buffy and Cam are keen. Jonesy is persuadable. And me? What do I think?

I'm famous for always doing the right thing. Mom and Dad are always saying how sensible I am. Surely the right thing to do is step back and let law enforcement handle things. Stick to the curfew and keep my head down. But…

I want my sleepy, safe town back. And as much as I hate the idea of digging further, I hate the idea of there being a murderer on the loose even more. When life gives you lemons … break into a murder house. That's the expression, right?

"Amber? What do you think?" Buffy asks. She runs a hand through her hair and lets it fall back on to her shoulders.

"I think … I think we owe it to the victims to try and solve this thing," I say. "If the answers could be inside Carrington Manor, then we should go there."

Slowly, the others all nod. Jonesy looks reluctant, but I know he's with us.

Buffy lets out a breath. "Then it's settled. But I think we have to do this tonight. Evidence isn't going to sit around for ever. Someone killed Kenny to stop him searching. We need to strike while the iron's hot."

A silence falls – it's not uncomfortable. It's more … apprehensive. Cam grabs Jonesy's hand and squeezes it tight. Clearly, they're over hiding anything.

I think for a minute. I've seen plenty of horror movies. And I know how these things go. We need to be careful and smart. If we go into this unprepared, that's when we risk everything. Stay on our toes at all times. Never turn our backs.

I clear my throat. "Hey, everyone. If we're going into a haunted manor … we're going to need a plan."

12

AMBER

We'll be there in five.

I glance at Buffy's text. Shit. She sent it seven minutes ago. Cam is picking us all up and I'm late.

I close the bedroom door quietly. I can't wake my parents. Like clockwork, another text pops up. This time from Jonesy.

Here.

My heart drops a little but, still, I fire back a quick text to give me a minute. Typical that tonight of all nights Mom insisted on us having a family games night. "To help you de-stress," she'd said. I'd had to fight to not make a sarcastic comment, but anything to please them.

Dad had picked me up from Jonesy's rather than let me walk the five minutes. He ended up dropping Buffy home, too. He made sure to give me a scolding for not picking up his call right away. Of course, I didn't tell him that I saw it and muted it. I'd never be let out of the house again.

I guess we're really doing this – going to the manor tonight. It all becomes real as I throw an old denim jacket over my sweater for extra warmth, then grab a flashlight from the back of my dresser. It's been in there for as long as I can remember. Dad said it's vital for every room to have one in case of power outages. *Thank you, Dad. I hope you don't find out about this.*

With as much silent agility as I can muster, I clamber out of the open window and perch on the flat roof, turning back to close the window behind me, in case of killers. I may be putting my own life at risk but there's no way I'm putting my parents in the same situation.

Before I know it, I'm sliding down the porch and vaulting on to some grass. It's better than hitting concrete but it still hurts. I make note of the hidden key for the garage and wipe my forehead as I look round. Cam's car is parked a few houses over. He flashes his headlights to alert me to his presence.

I quickly make my way to the idling vehicle. Cam drives his dad's old '78 Charger. His mom has offered to upgrade it if she gets this promotion, but he says he doesn't want to. It's one thing that connects him to his dad after he died, so it's understandable. But one day it's going to break down and not turn on again.

I slip in the back. The entire gang are here. They're all wearing darker clothes, like we agreed, and carrying flashlights.

"Can I at least put my seatbelt on?" I say on the end of a breath, as Cam shoots off. His hair blows maniacally before he cranks the window up. "We're not in a car chase."

"I want to get away as quickly as possible. The less people see us, the better."

"Whatever… Y'all get away OK?" My words come out muffled as I focus more on getting my seatbelt on. When I look up, they're all nodding.

I know Jonesy would be fine getting away – bless him, no one would notice – but the others might have some trouble.

Cam nods. "Mom's busy working. She's got this important promotion," he responds. His voice is flat. *This should be good news*, I think. I make a mental note to circle back to this because he's not happy, clearly. His mom works hard, especially recently – but she usually pays close attention to Cam. Maybe he misses her.

Buffy says, beside me, "So, it appears we're the only ones who had to jump out of windows tonight."

I turn to her. I can't make out much, other than her

hair is up and out of her face. And that she's wearing black. Other than that, it's too dark in here to tell.

"Technically I *slid* out of my window," I correct. "Didn't want to bring Macey to protect us, Jones?" I'm trying to inject some humour into the tense atmosphere. Understandably, everyone is a little on edge. This is no place for a dog, but I would have still liked the doggy love. My parents never agreed to me getting a pet so I must live vicariously through Jonesy and enjoy Macey whenever I can.

He glances at me in the rear-view mirror. "I would not bring my beautiful angel to that place ... besides, she would probably roll on to her back if someone attacked us."

I laugh but it quickly turns into a muffled *something*. It's like a moment of realization. We're actually going to Carrington Manor. We have our plan, sure. But things could go awry at any second. We've agreed to flee at the first sign of danger — which I guess means we should be turning round right now.

But we don't.

13

CAM

The drive to Carrington isn't too long, especially with it being the dead of night. The roads are empty, thanks to the curfew. I think everyone who lives in Sanera has driven past Carrington Manor at least once in their life, whether it's out of curiosity or just passing. It's a little out of the main town but close enough. Twenty minutes max, but tonight I think we do it in fifteen. There's not a single soul on the roads.

I hold my breath as the house comes into view. The roof of the manor crests on the horizon and the moon illuminates it like the creepy-ass place it is. It sits upon the highest point in Sanera, guarded by tall metal fencing and a plethora of overgrown greenery. As we get closer, the house retreats behind the massive trees. It baffles me how it vanishes in almost an instant.

I spot a cop car stationed by the front driveway, so I don't park directly outside the gates. Instead, I drive past the building, just out of sight if anyone does a patrol. If someone's passing by, the car should go unnoticed. Key word: *should*. But this is our best bet. There's nowhere else to ditch it.

We climb out. I throw some moss and branches on to the hood of the car, but they don't really do much to hide it. "OK, I think that'll do," I say, patting the trunk. "Ready?"

No one answers, but we start walking anyway. There's a strange vibe in the air. Like something is watching us, waiting. I think we all feel it because we end up walking shoulder to shoulder until we reach the iron gates. My feet are heavy and I'm glad when we stop, some distance from the front gates and the police car. From what I can tell, the officer inside is fast asleep.

I pull my flashlight from my back pocket. Loads of kids have snuck into Carrington over the years and apparently there's a—

A hole in the fence. Slightly to the right of us.

"It's not very big," Jonesy says doubtfully.

"If Brad and Shelley got through…" I begin to say, but an idea enters my mind. "Give me a sec."

I quietly prise the skewed bar of the fence with the back of the flashlight. I keep going until the gap is, finally, slightly bigger.

"That's good enough for me," I say, as I begin to slither carefully through. I don't plan on contracting tetanus.

I'm also careful not to stand in the patch of mud on the other side of the fence. Buffy quickly follows, then Amber. When Jonesy attempts it, he loses his balance and falls knee-first into the mud.

I reach for his cold hands and pull him to his feet. He nods his thanks and quickly rubs at his jeans.

"I hate this plan already."

The walk up the hill takes longer than I think any of us expect. It seems to go on for ever. By the time we reach the top and the house, our fear has turned into annoyance. We're tired. And cold. Sanera may be warm in the day, but at night? Deathly. Or maybe it's the manor. It wouldn't surprise me if it's cursed with eternal winter or some shit. Wouldn't put it past Mr Robert Carrington at all.

"Remind me to never come here again," Amber says, bending over, her hands on her knees as she catches her breath. Buffy is the only one who isn't clutching for air from the trek upward. God, what do they teach them over in Connecticut? I do track and even I'm winded.

"You people ready for this?" Buffy's voice is stark and abrasive against the harrowing silence. It's haunting, almost like she's about to start reciting a ghost story.

Amber replies instantly. "Not at all."

"No," Jonesy adds firmly.

I hesitate, trying to think of some sarcastic, witty remark. But I've got nothing. I shake my head.

Buffy nods. When she speaks, her voice trembles. Nobody can mask their fear completely. "Good," she says. "I'd be concerned if you *were* ready."

We stand in a line, looking up at the front steps. Some are cracked and broken. The house must be fragile by now. It's withstood two house fires. What is this place made of?

My eyes linger for a moment more before I explore the exterior. The manor is painted black, mottled from the years of rot and mould. There's a myriad of windows across the entire front of the house but it's the one at the second floor that strikes me. It juts out into a crescent shape with a stained windowpane and—

My heart stops.

A figure stands in the window, looking directly at us. I see nothing else but darkness and glowing eyes.

I gasp and blink. When I open my eyes, it's like nothing was ever there. Surely I didn't make that up?

"Cam, you good?" Amber asks, her hand reaching for my back. She holds it there until I answer.

"I thought I saw something in the window up there."

Like meerkats, their necks all promptly snap upward. Then they look back at me with confused and almost disappointed looks on their faces. Of course they didn't see anything. Maybe I didn't either. This freaking house is making me imagine things.

"It was probably just a reflection of one of the trees," Jonesy offers, but he doesn't sound too sure. It could be an explanation though. Some of them are about the height of the manor. It happens all the time in the movies – the character gets scared of something outside the window, and it ends up being a tree branch tapping on the glass. It's textbook horror movie, right?

Only, sometimes, it's not a tree branch.

"Let's get this over with," I say, unconvinced.

Amber chuckles nervously. "I'm glad you're actually as scared as the rest of us."

"Why wouldn't I be?"

"Because you're *Cam*. You always bring the light to the situation."

Now I laugh too. "Fine. I refuse to be the first one to crack."

Buffy sighs. "Who is going to crack?"

"No comment." It'll be Jonesy, obviously. But I keep that to myself. And he might surprise us all; I don't want to jinx that. Sometimes in horror films, it's the good-looking nerdy worrier who saves the day.

Who will be the first to take a step forward? Silly question; it's me. Buffy may have been the one to initiate this plan but I don't want the new girl to take over completely.

The aged stone steps are silent beneath my feet. Absence

of sound is sometimes scarier than noise. Now is one of those times. As I walk up, the others follow, albeit slowly. Thank God. I don't think I could physically go any further without them behind me.

Now that I'm here, I understand why there are so many stories about this place. This shit is scary. All the visible windows are boarded, which I knew.

All except the one where I saw the figure.

No. Not a figure – a reflection from the tree, I tell myself.

My feet stop as I reach the door. Seeing the manor up close changes everything. The wooden boards are rotting, crumbling. Termites too, maybe. *Delightful*.

The door is not locked; I can tell that from where I stand. It's ajar. The sheriff probably thought the fence and stationed personnel were enough to keep the public out. Oh, and the murderous ghost.

After a deep exhale, I push the door gently. A long creak follows as the door dances on its hinges, followed by a bang as it swings fully open. I wince, praying that it didn't wake Mr Sleeping Cop. Thankfully, all is quiet.

Now, the entryway is exposed. I peer inside. It's the biggest house I've ever encountered, the moon illuminating it just enough to make out the inside. There are countless doors and entryways on the left and right, and a giant double staircase that leads up to the second floor. I wonder if there's a basement – not that I'm going anywhere near it. Amber and I have watched enough horror movies to know the basement is the last place to go if you want to live to see tomorrow. You don't even need to watch horror movies to know that.

I take my first cautious step into Carrington Manor. A wash of chill air envelops me. I can smell smoke. It catches at the back of my throat. It was the smoke and flame that killed Brad and Shelley, before they were stabbed. The thought of death swirling around my lungs makes me feel sick.

The others follow me in – and, as Amber crosses the threshold, the door slams behind us. We all jump out of our skins; a shriek leaves someone's lips. Jonesy's.

Amber turns and wrestles with the door handle. She manages to force the door open but it shuts again as soon as she lets go. "Just the wind," she assures us.

"In horror movies, it's *never* just the wind," Jonesy says under his breath.

I open my mouth to say *we're not in a horror movie*, but … we might just be. "That is exactly why we need to be sensible. We can't let our guards down, because in every horror film teenagers are dead meat."

Jonesy blinks. "Why would you say that … like, right now?"

"Cam's right. For once," Amber adds. She continues before I can argue with her sarcastic remark. "*Halloween. Friday the 13th. A Nightmare on Elm Street. Scream. I Know What You Did Last Summer*—"

"This is *not* helping."

Despite the circumstances, I find my lips pulling into a tight smile. God, why do I find him so cute? Jonesy isn't afraid to show his emotions, and I'm jealous of that.

"I could think of other places I'd like to be right now," Jonesy says.

"You think any of us *want* to be here?" Buffy combats.

"It was your idea." He's still not over it. Clearly.

Buffy lifts her chin. "Yeah, it was," she says. Her eyes are shining in the darkness. She brushes a flyaway hair from her face. "I want to find out what happened that night. I want justice to be done. But I don't like being here any more than you do."

We venture further inside the old manor and circle the room, looking into all the corners for anything out of the ordinary. Better to be safe than sorry.

There's nothing though – except dust and cobwebs. So much dust.

"Look who it is," Amber calls out. Her dark eyes are fixed on a large portrait, and I take my best bet on who it is. Four figures, but one stands out. I know the face, it's infamous now.

"His wife was way out of his league," Amber observes.

I stare at the looming painting. There's not a single smile but perhaps that's a product of the time. To make family portraits almost ghastly.

"We should get a move on," I say at last, definitely

not at all disturbed by the painting. There's an air of uncomfortableness that comes from it. Knowing every person in the painting is dead is creepy as hell.

"Wait, do you think we should have a lookout?" Jonesy asks.

It's not a bad idea. Someone to warn us if Mr Sleeping Cop or the sheriff decide to come knocking. Or … anyone else. I try not to think of who that could be but again every horror movie ever comes to mind. The masked figure. The monster under the bed. The child who had supposedly died at camp so his mom took revenge on the teenagers— Sorry … spoilers.

But wait. We can't split up. Rule number one of every horror movie ever: *do* not *split up*. And also don't have sex. But right now, that's less of a worry.

"Too dangerous," I say. "Too risky. We should stick together."

Amber is frowning. "I don't know," she says. "I don't want to get caught trespassing. My parents would kill me. A lookout might be good."

"We won't get in trouble for trespassing," I reply.

"Trespassing on a crime scene though?" Amber's words are unsure and now she's making me second-guess everything.

"OK, fine," I say. "But I'm the lookout. I'm not leaving any of you on your own."

"Cam," Jonesy says. "I meant I should do it." He looks

worried – but there's no way I'd let him volunteer instead of me.

"What happened to *don't split up*?" Buffy asks.

I blink. "I changed my mind. But if I die, you can't fight over who gets the car—"

"Nope," Jonesy interjects. "We are *not* talking like that."

I chuckle and walk the short distance back to the front door. The floorboards are a twisted symphony until I eventually stop by the boarded window beside the entrance. I give them all a cheerful salute but I'm sure they can see through my bravado. A look passes between Jonesy and me – a look that makes my chest ache. Without even saying a word, I can tell what he's saying to me. *Stay alive.*

We've been in Carrington Manor for three minutes and already our plan has gone out the window. So much for not splitting up. But we can still look for clues, for evidence, for anything.

I wave at them. "Go, before I change my mind."

14

JONESY

"Let's check this floor and then go upstairs," I say. We might be here for a while. There's got to be over twenty rooms just on this floor.

Who on earth needs this big a house?

Not that it did Robert Carrington much good.

"It's not in bad condition," says Amber. "For a haunted house that's been set on fire twice, I mean."

I frown, looking around. She's right. I'm not an expert in arson but I'd have thought the house would look more beaten up. The signs of the fire are few and far between. Everything – the old furniture, the portraits, the thick curtains – seems untouched by it, under the dust.

"Doesn't this seem off to you?" I finally say aloud.

"In what way?" Amber replies.

"Well, like you said, it doesn't look like a house that was set on fire a week ago." It doesn't add up.

"It's almost … supernatural," Buffy says.

"We're not going there again," is all I say to that. "There's always an explanation."

We walk on.

Buffy doesn't let up. "And what *is* the explanation here?"

"I don't know," I reply. "But whatever it is, it has nothing to do with a ghoul."

We search through a drawing room, kitchen, pantry and several smaller rooms. Finally we arrive in what must have been Carrington's study. I think it's the last room on this floor, but it wouldn't surprise me at all if there are hidden passages in this hellhole. Maybe we should be checking the bookcases for faux books or little latches.

I guide my flashlight around the room before stepping inside. Amber waits at the door.

The desk in the centre of the room catches my eye and in an instant I'm there, pulling open the drawers. They're all empty.

"Anything?" Amber calls.

"A bust." I'm about to walk away when something inside a drawer catches my eye. It's a clue if ever I've seen one. "Hold on."

I'm crouched over, flashlight as close as possible to the wood to make sure I'm seeing this right. Etched into the inside of the drawer, as though with the point of a compass or knife, is a word.

"*Library*," I read aloud. Wait… "Library?" I look up to find the girls staring back at me, waiting. "Did Carrington write this?"

"Could be," says Buffy. "Or someone else."

I think about it. *Someone else. But who?* "Maybe there's something hidden in the library? Which is where, do we think?"

"Maybe upstairs?"

"What could be in there though?" Buffy asks.

I stand up straight. "That's a good question."

We head back to the hall. We still have an entire upstairs to explore. Where the murders were committed. Yay… Hopefully, a library will be waiting for us with answers.

"Everything OK?" I whisper-shout to Cam as he enters my view.

He's perched by the windowsill, his gaze fixed outside. As much as I'm uncomfortable with him being alone, I'm slightly relieved I didn't get that job. I don't know what I'd do if someone actually appeared – probably freeze in horror. That would be no use to anyone. Whereas Cam … he'll know what to do. He always does. That's why I feel so safe with him.

He raises a thumb in response. Even though it was

a volunteer position, it's obvious he's a little peeved he doesn't get to do any exploring.

"Did you find anything?" he asks, his voice raised.

"Maybe…"

I can sense from here the curiosity on his face, which is backlit by the moonlight. It's almost like there's a heavenly aura that surrounds him. Or maybe it's only me who feels that way.

"We'll fill you in later. We're just checking upstairs."

I turn round to find Buffy already climbing up the grand steps. Amber and I have to put a stride in our step to catch up with her.

"Someone's eager," Amber says when we reach her side.

"I don't want to leave here empty-handed. We need *something*, even if it's small."

I nod. It sure would be a bummer if we risk our lives sneaking into a supposedly haunted crime scene and leave without anything to show for it.

"I'm still nervous about leaving Cam," Amber admits. "Should we get him?"

I know what she means – I feel uneasy about it too. But he'll be OK. "No, it's fine. Cam's a big boy."

"Didn't need to know that," Amber comments under her breath but it's not long before she's giggling at her own joke. Buffy tries to fight the urge, but she ends up guffawing too.

I can feel my cheeks heating. "You're children."

"Sorry," says Buffy. "I think we needed a laugh," she adds.

As quick as the tension was split, it stitches itself back up. Buffy, still in the lead, takes the final step on to the second floor. An uninterrupted line of coloured rugs leads straight down to the end of the hall – well, *almost*. The rug at the end by the bay window has been burned. It's either red or brown but it's hard to tell.

The second floor is more of what I expected from Carrington Manor. The evidence of a house fire is more apparent, from the stench of burning and the soot-coated banisters. Both fires started up here, right by Carrington's bedroom, according to the news reports.

Thankfully, as we walk, the remaining rugs muffle the creaky floorboards. We travel further down the hall and a foreign smell hits my senses. It's not the smoke, though that's still there. There's something else, also. "Hey, do you smell…"

"Gasoline," Amber finishes for me. "It reeks."

I look around but can't see any fuel cans that could be the source. Then my gaze settles on the long rug below me. I crouch down and examine it.

It hits me. "I think I know why they couldn't run away," I mutter. "Look!"

Amber and Buffy turn to me in an instant, curious. I motion to the fabric and the peculiar burn pattern.

"What are we looking at?" Amber asks.

"Oh my gosh," Buffy says, suddenly catching on.

I nod. "It's hard to get away from the fire when the rug's been soaked with gasoline." I crouch closer and with one inhale my suspicions are confirmed. "Yep, that's gas."

Amber's hand finds a place on her chest. "Well, that's nasty. Let's just find this library and get out of here."

We peer into all the rooms that line the main upstairs hallway. No library.

I start to wonder if there even is one. I don't think I've seen it mentioned in any of the plans. Why would Robert – I'm assuming it was him – etch the word into his drawer if he didn't even have one? It doesn't make any sense. Unless our secret room theory is correct... Maybe the library is hidden.

Amber stops at the large floor-to-ceiling bay window that overlooks the front terrace. It's the same one where Cam said he saw something.

The room I peek into is another bust. Just a bedroom. I turn back, and see Amber is crouching down in a dark corner.

"Hey, there's something here," she calls. She picks up a black object from the floor, covering her hand with the sleeve of her jacket so as not to get fingerprints on it. *Smart*.

"What is it?" Buffy asks as we bound over.

Amber holds it out. "It's a camcorder."

"But the police have already swept the entire place..."

I'm stating the obvious but it can only mean one thing and I don't want to be the person to say it.

Amber gulps. "Someone was here. Someone was here after the police left."

"Or they're here now," Buffy suggests. Which is a mistake. Sure, it's a possibility, but I don't need that thought in my head. I think about the figure Cam saw at the window—

"I say we turn it on," Buffy says. "The camcorder, I mean."

I bite my lip. "I'm not sure—"

"Yeah, I don't know…" Amber adds.

"Hey," Buffy says, placing her hand on Amber's shoulder. "We *need* something. Otherwise … why are we here?"

"Fine," Amber says reluctantly. She tries to press the small buttons through the thick material, but it doesn't work.

"Here." Buffy pulls a bobby pin from the back of her hair and passes it to Amber. Carefully, she pokes at the "on" button. With a crackle at first, the camcorder switches on. The full battery symbol sends a shiver through my body. And that's when it hits me. *Someone was here and left a fully charged camcorder for someone to find.* It's a well-known fact that killers return to the scene of the crime.

A killer who was expecting someone to be stupid enough to come here, to be idiotic enough to look for clues and try to be a hero…

"Cam wasn't seeing things," I whisper, my eyes locked on the window in front of us. I glance at the others; their faces are a portrait of dread. I've seen a lot of horror movies in my time but *this* is what real fear looks like. No over-the-top crying or screaming, but terror that freezes someone in their place.

My blood runs cold. Has someone been watching us all this time? Suddenly it seems like madness to be here at all.

"I really think we should—"

And then a scream shatters the silence.

My feet are moving before I even realize what's happening. All I know is that was Cam screaming. And Cam wouldn't scream over nothing.

"Cam!" Amber yells.

We're stampeding back the way we came, dust and dirt and soot flying up around us as we go. I don't even care to look behind me, or into any of the rooms we pass. How could we have been so stupid?

I fly down the stairs, ahead of the others, skipping as many steps as possible.

"Cam—"

As soon as my feet hit the floor, I notice how much lighter it is down here than before. My confusion soon turns to panic when I notice the open door. Alabaster moonlight gleams in.

But there's no sign of Cam.

He's gone.

Taken.

And on the floor a note. Scribbled in block letters on aged paper. I crouch down and pick it up.

NO POLICE.

15

AMBER

"Cam!" Jonesy cries. "Cam, this isn't funny!" He bounds over to the door and stares out. We're quick to follow. But there's nothing. Outside, everything looks exactly the same as before. It's like Cam vanished into thin air.

"He's gone." Buffy states the obvious.

"That *bastard*—"

"Hey." My hand finds itself on Jonesy's shoulder. He's shaking, the note he showed us still crumpled in his hands. "We need to focus, or we won't find him."

We need to stay level-headed. I run outside and scan through the treeline. The cop car is still there. "We should tell someone."

"The note," Jonesy mumbles. He's standing in the door frame, tears in his eyes. "No police. They could be watching us now. Toying with us. We don't know what they'll do to him... God, this is all my fault."

"No," Buffy says. "If it's anyone's fault, it's mine."

"It's nobody's fault," I snap. "This isn't helping Cam. Let's focus on getting him back."

We stand by the front door, looking out at the lawn. *Think, Amber.* The killer wants us to think they've taken Cam outside, but I wonder. Mentally, I go back over the rooms we were in. There must be more to this house than we think. A big house like this, and no hidden rooms? Doesn't sit right with me.

"I don't know what to do," Jonesy says helplessly. "We should tell the police. But the note..."

Buffy's eyes meet mine. It's a risk. We all know it. But the sheriff is as scared as we are.

"If we want to save Cam, we need to do this ourselves," I say. "I think Cam is still in the house. We search it. Properly this time."

Jonesy halts his whimpers for a moment to look at me and Buffy. Then he nods. "For Cam."

"For Cam," I echo.

We head back inside. There are no signs of a scuffle. Slowly we circle the hall but everything is exactly as it was.

Buffy leans against the wall by the window where Cam was perched. Seeing her in the same place makes my stomach drop a little. He was right there. And now he's not.

Buffy continues. "The question is, where do we start? The study, maybe – see if there are any more clues?" She tips her head back in frustration, hitting it against the wall. "Unless it was a double bluff and he's really outside—"

"Wait." I hold up my hand. "Buffy, did you hear that?"

Her face goes white. "Hear what?"

"The wall." I stalk the little distance between us to where she's standing. "That did not sound like a solid wall."

I knock against the peeling wallpaper behind her and my suspicions are quickly confirmed. "It's hollow," I say in astonishment. I feel a flicker of excitement. *I knew there were hidden rooms.*

"A hollow wall could mean anything," Jonesy says, clearly not wanting to get his hopes up. But his face is alight.

"Worth a shot."

"You seriously think there's a hidden passage or something behind there?" Buffy knocks it for herself. An echoing sound greets her. "Yeah, there's something."

I nod. "If any house is going to have hidden passages, it's gonna be this one…" I start patting the walls, looking for hidden crevices, switches, buttons, anything. "There must be a trigger or lever somewhere."

Buffy and Jonesy soon join in, clawing at anything that we can find.

"What might it look like?"

Like I'm the expert in how to open secret passageways. "An indent, a button. Just anything … unassuming."

The three of us scour our surroundings.

I go over to the fireplace. It looks like a regular fireplace if ever I've seen one – old, with candles lining the top. There's a coal scuttle and a brass bucket full of pokers. Their points glimmer in the moonlight. *A poker would be a good weapon*, I think. And we could do with one.

I reach down and grab the tallest one … or try to. I yank it but it doesn't budge. "What the…" In frustration I hit the poker with the side of my hand and it finally moves. Not up but to the side, only slightly.

The lever! If I hadn't been staring directly at it, I never would've noticed.

"Hey," I say. "I think I have something."

The others hurry over. This better be something now. I don't want to have gotten everyone's hopes up for nothing. With steady fingers, I reach out to the poker and push it away from me. My breathing cuts out.

I don't know what I'm expecting to happen but … there's nothing. Nothing at all.

"Man!" Jonesy mutters. "Why can't—"

A grinding sound begins from behind us, like something's being dragged along a track. At once, our heads spin in the direction of the wall where Cam was sitting – or where the wall once was.

A passage has appeared.

*

We were right.

If any house is going to have hidden passages, it's gonna be this one.

"Holy shit," Jonesy says. His next words come with a sort of optimism that I don't expect from him. "Hey. Maybe Cam accidentally fell through. He could be in there, totally fine!"

As much as I'd like to believe that, I'm not too sure. If Cam had fallen through, he would've shouted for us. Tried to alert us to his presence. I can tell from her silence that Buffy is thinking the same. But we don't say it. It's not the time. I don't want Jonesy to lose hope.

"Let's arm ourselves," I suggest. The pokers are fixed in place – all decoys. I grab one of the candlesticks from above the fireplace. This could most certainly do some damage if it comes to it. Perfect. I grab two more and throw them to Buffy and Jonesy. At the end of the day, they'll be useless against *sharper* weapons, like, say, a butcher's blade – but they're all we've got. In reality, I don't think we'd stand a chance against a butcher's blade even if we did have a sharper weapon. Again, we're teenagers, not Batman and Robin.

"OK, we're ready."

Buffy goes through first, Jonesy follows, and then I'm stuck in the worst position of the bunch, at the back. Vulnerable to anyone coming from behind.

We press forward into the passage.

Every few steps, like an owl, I twist my head round to check behind me. I'm not having anyone stab me in the back, literally.

"Judging by the incline, we must be under the house," Jonesy says under his breath.

I think we've all made the subconscious decision to keep the noise down. Well, I definitely have. I didn't even realize I'm practically tiptoeing.

I let my fingers graze the cold stone walls as we venture further into the dark. The chill hits me like a gust of wind. Where are we? It's subtle but the passageway is sloping downwards. I think we're slowly going deeper underground.

"Upcoming," Buffy says, just loud enough so we both can hear.

"What is it?" I say. All I can see is the back of Jonesy's head. Thankfully, after a few more steps, the passage seems to be widening.

Into…

Three paths.

"You've got to be kidding me," I say, voicing what we're all thinking. They've clearly been made for a reason. But what?

"What do you two want to do?" Jonesy asks, one hand on his hip, the other at the back of his head. His flashlight skews from the openings, obscuring them. *Nu-uh.*

"Flashlights up at all times," I plead. The thought of the dark openings terrifies me.

Buffy raises hers. "Three tunnels, three of us. You're not going to like this … but I think we need to split up."

Almost in unison Jonesy and I retort with a big fat, "No."

Buffy gestures to the three tunnels. "We're gonna have to."

I step forward. "You know what happened last time."

Her lips tighten. "I know and I don't like it any more than you." In the harsh white light, her expression is determined. "But we don't have the time – Cam doesn't have the time – for all of us to go down the same path and hit a dead end. We don't know how far they go."

"Cam could be hurt," Jonesy's voice hitches. "He might not have a lot of time." It seems he has ditched the idea of Cam coming down here by accident. "Cam never would've trekked this far down without us. Sure, he had his flashlight but…"

I bite my lip. As much as I think it's a bad idea, splitting up is our only choice. Cam needs us. Plus, the longer we're down here… I don't exactly know what the oxygen supply is like this far underground.

"Fine." My heart is racing. I heft the candlestick in my hand.

"I'm taking left," Buffy says.

"Middle," I say.

Jonesy's left with the last option. "Right, I guess."

"Ground rules," I say to both of them as sternly as possible. "You shout, scream, if you see anything. And I mean *anything*. The sound should carry down here. Stay safe."

I watch as Jonesy's mouth opens but closes as quick. "That goes for you too," he says, pointing his finger at me.

I throw him a short smile and then peer at the looming dark. "Good luck," I offer under my breath.

But luck isn't what we need right now.

It's hope…

Hope that Cam is somewhere down here. Hope that we're not too late.

16

JONESY

I can't see a thing. All I can tell is that the path has curved, gone back on itself, and is subtly sloping down so that I'm even deeper underground. The air is thicker down here, harder to breathe in. My nerves trickle back as I realize how long it's going to take for me to retreat.

I'm not even certain I'll be able to hear the girls if they scream.

Will they hear me?

And then I hit a wall. It's a dead end.

I groan. It doesn't make sense. What are these passages even for? Did Robert Carrington dig them – or was it the killer? And why?

I imagine the killer watching me somehow. *What are you up to?*

I kick the wall in frustration. Some rubble falls to the ground. All this time wasted.

With a huff, I spin and begin my long ascent back.

17

AMBER

I'm gripping the flashlight so hard my hand starts to ache. Yet I still cling on for dear life. It's the only thing bringing me even a sliver of comfort down this path to God-knows-where.

I somehow haven't pissed myself out of fear but I won't count myself lucky just yet. With every step, I expect something – someone – to jump out at me. I stretch out a hand and let my fingers skim the walls that confine me. They're *so cold*. I pull away as quickly as possible.

I press on.

Find Cam. Find the others. Forget this all happened.

We're in over our heads. I realize that now. I'm sure Buffy and Jonesy do as well – Cam certainly does. My chest tightens at the thought of him. Alone and scared.

Who on earth is doing this? What do you get from killing and kidnapping random teenagers?

I increase my walking pace into a light jog. That's when I see something, finally. A light – it's only dull, but it's something. I burst into a run, my flashlight throwing beams all over.

I'm almost there. Almost—

I slam to the ground, a roaring pain spreading through my ankle. Typical. Just typical. Crossing my fingers, I raise my ankle and circle it tentatively. It's only a sprain. It might slow me down a bit, that's all.

But that's when I hear something.

Inching towards me.

Footsteps.

18

JONESY

Thump.

I stop in my tracks. Was that—

Thump.

The noise is coming from the dead end.

Slowly, I turn. I don't know whether I should be investigating or bolting in the opposite direction. But my feet take me to the wall.

Thump.

I bring the flashlight to the wall and my face closer.

Thump.

"OK, I get it," I snap, as if anyone can hear me. But someone seems to because the thumping stops. I feel hope flare in my chest. It can't be—

"If someone's there, make some noise." I hold my

breath, listening. *It's all in my head*, I think. It's my mind making things up to help deal with the stress of it all—

Thump.

I almost screech. "Cam?"

Thump. Thump. Thump.

I can feel myself beaming in the dark. It's him. It's him. It's really him. "Hold on, Cam! I've got to find a way in."

With a new-found sense of optimism, I scour the wall for anything. There must be another lever like before. Something inconspicuous… I bend down and scan the ground; I reach on to my tiptoes, bringing the flashlight closer and closer…

There. Right in the corner of the wall, a small crack is visible. I would have missed it under any other circumstance. Dismissed it as a chip. But it's too perfect, too neat. A normal crack wouldn't be so straight, it'd be rough and jagged. As I release a much-needed breath, I reach for the crevice and my finger fits perfectly inside. To my delight, I feel a button.

I press it before I can think twice. Instantly, the entire wall starts to recede. It's a door – and light is escaping from inside.

With a sudden rush of confidence, I barge in. It's a large room, completely lit by … camping lamps? And then I see him. I see—

"Cam!" I run over. He's tied up, his arms bound behind

him, a blindfold fastened across his face and tape on his mouth. No wonder he couldn't reply.

He wriggles around, trying to speak, trying to communicate. I remove his blindfold. The fear in his blue eyes is the first thing I see, and my heart instantly shatters. After a second, the terror starts to dissipate when he realizes I'm alone.

He tries to talk so I remove the tape next. "Jones," he cries then, "what are you doing here?"

"Saving you?" I say, while bending down to untie him. I ditch the useless candlestick and work fast, knowing whoever did this is most likely nearby.

"Alone?" His voice rises. "You shouldn't have come down here – how did you even—"

"The others are out there somewhere... Cam, who did this?"

The rope falls to the floor and Cam instantly stretches his legs out. "I don't know," is all he says. There's a wobble to his words.

"You've got to have seen something, heard something?"

"I was sitting where you left me, keeping watch. You'd all gone upstairs. And then ... I fell through the wall into complete darkness," he explains. "I felt a sharp pain on my head. I must have been knocked unconscious – I think I heard a sneeze but I'm not sure. Next thing I know I'm bound and blindfolded wherever *this* is..." His voice trails off. He doesn't want to relive it, that much is clear. I won't try to get anything else out of him now. The important thing is we get out of here.

"Come on," I say. "We need to be quick. Can you walk?"

He nods and stands, his legs buckling as soon as he puts weight on them. I can't help myself: my arms wrap around him so tight – probably too tight. He relaxes into my embrace. We stay there for longer than we should.

"Jones, I was so scared," he whispers into my ear. There's a sob in his voice. "I thought I was going to—"

"No," I interrupt. "You're safe now. We just need to get out of here, OK?" I'm not used to being the one in charge, the assertive one. I'm supposed to be the sensitive and scared-of-everything one. I'm not trained for this. Thankfully, it seems I'm doing a good enough job because Cam slowly pulls away. His face is damp and stained but I help wipe his cheeks.

"Where are the others?"

"We split up," I reply under my breath as I lead him out of the strange stone prison.

"Please tell me you're joking."

"I wish I was. We had to." My eyes meet his and I hold his gaze. "We had to find you."

Cam grabs my free hand tight. His own hand is deathly cold, distractingly so. We make our way along the tunnel.

I hear the door behind us close. It must be on a timer.

I've got Cam. Now we just need to find the others and get the hell out of here.

While we still can.

19

AMBER

The footsteps move closer. I swallow the ever-growing lump in my throat and tighten my grip on the flashlight as I shuffle backwards along the tunnel. My foot buckles every time I try to get up again. But the light is still getting closer.

The light blinds me. It stops me where I am. There's no point in trying to get away because it's only delaying the inevitable. I bare my teeth and look away. I can't—

"Amber?" A voice calls out. My panicked state fades as I recognize the familiar tone. Buffy. I look back and find her hurrying towards me, her flashlight lowered, exposing her face. "Oh, thank God it's you – what are you doing on the floor?"

I'm sure my face is still the horrified picture it was seconds ago but I can feel it begin to settle. "I twisted my ankle. Help me, would you?"

Buffy offers her hand and I grip it tight. I close my eyes in pain as she pulls me to my feet. I try to balance myself. I place my foot down and manage to do so without toppling. Maybe I can do this.

"Do you think you can walk?" she asks.

I nod. "Just about."

If you had told me yesterday that we'd go to Carrington Manor, I never would've believed you. And if you'd told me we'd go down a secret passageway to find our kidnapped friend, I'd have told you to quit fooling around. It feels like days have passed since we got here. I miss the light.

Buffy makes sure I'm steady before motioning to where she came from. "You're going to want to see this."

I follow her back into the dark without question, Buffy's arm keeping me upright. Best to see it for myself.

After a few minutes we're at the opening where I saw that original faint light. I can't believe what I'm seeing. "Holy…" I stray ahead, a slight limp to my step. It's a carved-out room, full of power tools, excavating equipment and a ton of industrial lights. Someone has been down here in the tunnels searching for … something. Clearly.

"Look," Buffy says, pulling me to the side. And then that's when I see the wall. One wall of the room is covered in papers and … newspaper clippings.

I limp to the wall and inspect everything I see. There's red string stretching over the entire thing, pinned to different articles, maps and plans. It must have some

170

significance. My eyes go wide. "These are all about Carrington Manor. Look. Sightings of the ghoul in the local paper… Plans of the house and grounds…" I look across and between the strings. They connect articles to blueprints of the manor, drawings, even a photo of a painting of Robert Carrington. What the…

Buffy is a few steps away to the right. She points at an article in front of her. "This is from yesterday's *Sanera Daily.* It's covering Brad and Shelley's deaths. What's the betting the article about Kenny's murder will be in here tomorrow…"

I gulp. "OK, officially freaked out," I say. "Someone is clearly down here a lot. Digging. Compiling a whole archive on Robert Carrington and his manor. But why? There's got to be hundreds of pieces on Carrington here." I wander off as I inspect even further. As I go further left, the clippings get older and older until—

"Buffy," I call, my eyes locked on to the newspaper cuttings in front of me. "These are the missing articles … from the library."

In the blink of an eye, Buffy is by my side, scanning them with me. And then I see it. The newspaper report from the day after Carrington died.

*LOCAL LANDOWNER ROBERT
CARRINGTON FOUND DEAD AT HIS
HOME, CARRINGTON MANOR*

"Why would they go to the trouble of stealing this?" I say, bewildered. "There must be some reason." I rip the page from the wall. The sound echoes for a long moment before we're cast into silence once again.

"Maybe this person is a completionist," Buffy suggests.

"Huh?"

"Look around. There's got to be every single think piece, article, news story on Carrington ever written here."

That much is correct. I scratch my head. "So you think the killer is obsessed with Robert Carrington?"

"I think they care a lot about him and his house, for some reason."

I think more about it. Why would anyone be a superfan of Robert Carrington? He was an asshole who everyone hated. The townspeople either abandoned him to the fire or lit it themselves. Why would someone dedicate this much time to *him*, of all people?

I look down at the article I've torn from the wall. The words blur in front of me as I read. So many words and not a lot of meaning. A lot of quotes from Sanera citizens who witnessed the fire and then—

"Hold on," I say. The words in front of me catch my eye. I have to read them over again a few times to check I'm reading this right. "'In spite of his vast lands, property and many tenants, it appears that Robert Carrington died penniless … or did he?'"

"Well, well." Buffy thinks for a minute. "Wait … it

172

might explain why whoever is hiding out here wanted this article. I think it's suggesting that Robert *did* have money when he died but it wasn't found. Which means…"

I finish her sentence: "He hid his money somewhere."

"Hold on," Buffy says. She's gazing at another article. "This one's an interview with Robert's lawyer, a Mr Smythe."

"And?" I press.

Buffy rips the article from the wall and recites what she reads. "'Robert and I were old friends and I have many fond memories of him. He was a kind man…'" She makes a face. "That seems debatable."

I look around at the carved-out room as she continues to skim the words. At the tools and equipment. And I think about the passageways. It makes sense.

"'I can assure you that Robert Carrington was a man of immense wealth who was a careful and astute investor. He did not die without money. Where that money went, I couldn't tell you. But it's somewhere out there.'" Buffy looks up at me. "Then this means…"

"There's no ghoul. Whoever is behind the killings is looking for the lost money," I say slowly. "It's why they've been coming here and digging these tunnels, searching for it. Why they've compiled all this information on Carrington and his manor. Brad and Shelley were sniffing around the manor – they were killed to warn people off. And Kenny … he threatened to come to the manor too.

So he had to die." I snap my fingers. "Someone is using the story of the ghoul to keep people away from the manor while they search for Robert Carrington's hidden fortune."

Buffy nods. "I mean, it's assuming a lot but … it's not a bad theory," she says.

I'd like to say we just made an important breakthrough. But some things still don't make sense. The "clue" etched into Robert's desk drawer: *Library*. Could that be where his wealth is hidden? Only we found no library. Maybe there isn't one at Carrington Manor. Maybe he was just bored and doodling. But having watched so many movies, I doubt it. I fear we're still in the middle of this mystery … with more work to do before we can close the book.

"Do you think we should try and find Jonesy?" Buffy asks.

We both peer down the path Jonesy took. We've made our way back up, our minds still reeling from our discovery. We put the articles back where we found them. Hopefully it looks the same as it did when we got there. It still doesn't feel real. Why have we never heard of this Carrington treasure before?

I hesitate. I don't even know how long we've been down here. It feels like hours. It's hard to tell when there's no sunlight, or light at all for that matter, as if time passes differently down here. I glance down at my phone. Zero bars. But my suspicions are confirmed: 5.34 a.m.

"I think we should," I reply. As much as the thought

terrifies me, it's the right thing to do. At the end of the day, Jonesy would try and find us. It also helps that I'm not alone any more.

"Can your ankle take it?"

"I'll survive if we—"

"Did you hear that?" Buffy is staring down the tunnel, eyes wide.

"What is it now?" I don't know if I can bear to look.

"Look!" She points, so I risk a glance. There's a light coming towards us. It's concentrated into a beam. Torchlight?

Goosebumps prickle my arms as the light bobs closer. Then a figure appears out of the passageway – no, two figures.

"Hey!" Jonesy's voice calls out. "I got him. I got him." And then my eyes go straight to Cam, who's just behind him. He looks worse for wear and thoroughly over this place. I can't blame him.

I whisper-scream and throw my arms around Cam. "I have never been so happy to see familiar faces," I say with a laugh. "And also, we're leaving this second."

No one argues. Appropriate reunions and questions can happen later. We hurry back up the passage. Jonesy and Buffy end up in front, and then Cam, and then me… Last again.

With a flashlight as my only weapon, I still look back every few steps.

That's when I spot a trickle at the back of Cam's head.

"Hold up," I call out. "Cam, you're bleeding."

He stops and turns and the others do too. I want to be out of here but it looks nasty; it needs to be covered at least. Stupidly, Cam touches the back of his head and winces in pain.

"How bad is it?"

"It's nothing," I lie. It definitely isn't nothing. There's a gash across the back of his head. He was probably knocked out from behind and doesn't even remember. "Just don't touch it." I can't think of anything else to use, so I pull my jacket off my shoulders and hear a clunk from inside – I'd almost forgotten that I'd swiped the camcorder – then take off my shirt. Luckily I'm wearing a tee underneath. I wad up the shirt and hold it against the wound. I didn't like this shirt anyway. How severe it is, I can't tell. This will have to do for now.

Cam takes over, holding it against his head. "I'll wash it and give it back…"

"Please don't."

"Yes, ma'am."

We're quick to start up again, and soon we're back in the hall. As we near the still open door, we walk closer and closer together, in near silence. Who knows what is around the corner…

Jonesy cranes his neck around the door. "Carefully."

The first thing I notice is how the night streaming in

from outside seems brighter than before. My eyes have adjusted to the pitch black. I'm no longer used to *actual* light from an organic source. And it'll be sunrise soon.

I guess time flies when you're trying to stay alive.

Jonesy takes the first step into the open, his flashlight held above his head. He shines it around before motioning us to follow. He doesn't have to tell me not to look back. None of us do. But, as we reach the bottom step, the front door slams shut.

"… Just the wind," Cam jokes.

We stay huddled together as close as physically possible as we make our descent, only breaking apart to escape through the broken fence. I catch a glimpse of the stationed car – the cop inside is still fast asleep. *This* is why we can't trust them to do what they're supposed to. Any guilt I had for sneaking around disappears. We've found out more in a single night than Sheriff Rogers has in a week. I bet he doesn't know about the underground shrine to Carrington, the tunnelling equipment or the lost money. The *rumoured* lost money, that is. This killer may be looking for something that doesn't exist.

Once past the manor's boundaries, I glance back, fully expecting the door to fly open and someone to come running after us. But no one comes. We follow the short grassy path and find Cam's car where we left it, still covered in branches.

Cam walks – well, stumbles – over to the driver's side.

"Whoa, whoa, whoa," I call out. "I'd rather be driven by someone without a head injury, thank you very much."

He scoffs and waves my concerns away with his free hand. "I'm fine."

"Absolutely not," Jonesy says firmly, holding his hand out for the keys. Cam sighs and hands them over, clearly annoyed. *Apologies that we don't want to end the night crashing into a ditch.*

"One ghoul attack and suddenly I'm not fit to drive," Cam complains.

"Not a ghoul," Buffy says.

Jonesy glances at her. "You've changed your tune."

"Amber and I found some pretty damning stuff down there. If the Carrington Ghoul *is* real ... he has a big obsession with himself."

Jonesy and Cam's faces wear identical expressions of anticipation. They've been spending way too much time together.

"We'll explain later," I say, then remember the camcorder. I unfold the jacket from my hands and pull out the last surprise. "Nabbed this as well."

"You still have it?" Buffy cries.

I laugh. "I thought it would come in handy."

Whatever is on this camera could be just what we need to find the killer. We should show the police – but I want to see what's on there myself first.

But then it gets me thinking ... why would the killer

leave it in the manor? The only reason they'd do that is if they *wanted* us to find it. The thought scratches at my insides. What could possibly be on there?

"Amber, you ready?" Jonesy's voice snaps me out of my thoughts. Everyone else is in the car waiting for me.

"Sure," I say and climb in. I'm relieved we survived the night, but I have a nagging feeling this is only just another beginning.

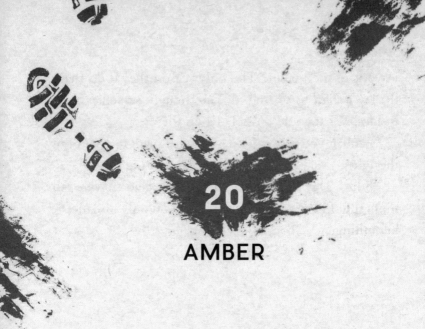

20

AMBER

After Jonesy drops me off, I grab the spare hidden key and quietly sneak into the garage. It's just before seven at this point and, thankfully, no one is awake yet. I hide my muddy sneakers behind Dad's old motorbike from before his risk-averse, overprotective-dad days. They can stay there until I have chance to clean them.

I manage to make it upstairs without waking anyone. I'm wholly expecting someone to be up waiting for me but my parents' bedroom door is closed so it seems I got away with it. They're pretty heavy sleepers. My room is cold – deathly cold, actually. It must be the anxiety from the night creeping into my subconscious. I shake it off and place the camcorder in my bedside drawer, then get ready for bed.

We've collectively decided to keep tonight a secret, for

now at least – until we've had time to talk it through and look at the footage on the camcorder. We'll tell people if we *have* to. Cam is more than happy to keep the true reason for his injury a secret because his mom would flip. He's going to say he fell down the stairs or something. Easy white lie … ish. From what I could tell, it's not a deep enough wound to cause any further trouble. I've watched enough medical dramas to know that.

By the time I'm under the sheets, it's way past seven a.m. We all decided to stay home from school. We need sleep. Mom and Dad will be more than all right with me ditching, especially after what happened with Kenny. For once in their lives, school isn't the priority.

But as I toss and turn in bed and the minutes pass, all I can think about is that damned camcorder. Every thought in and out of my head is—

I said I'd wait to look at it with the others … but what if there's incriminating evidence on there? Information that might actually kick the sheriff's office into gear? Maybe it has enough to get the FBI involved?

And there's the fact that it was seemingly left there *for* us. A message? A warning? Either way, shouldn't we look at it sooner rather than later?

I need to.

Against my better judgement, I get up and open the blinds, letting in serene morning sunlight. I take the camcorder out of my drawer, but Mom must have been listening out for me because as soon as I reach my bed again she barges through the door.

"Oh my gosh," I call out, thrusting the camcorder under my sheets. "What happened to knocking?" For some reason, I also cover up my body with a blanket like I'm naked.

I'm not.

"Sorry, baby. Um, have you decided if you're going into school?" Her tone is casual but her eyes are practically begging me not to. Today is her lucky day.

I shake my head. "I think I'm going to stay here and—"

She releases a sigh of joy and relief and happiness. "Great! Sorry, carry on."

I laugh silently before continuing, "I didn't sleep very well last night so I'm going to stay in bed and rest."

"Oh, honey, you do look dreadful. I'll make you some pancakes. You love pancakes, don't you – OK, I'll be right back." She hurries out. God, I do love her, even if she and Dad are difficult sometimes.

I end up staying in my pyjamas as I eat breakfast, which Mom brings to me in bed. The whole time the camcorder that I shoved under the sheets is on my mind.

"I'm going to the store," Mom says. "Your dad has already left for work. Will you be OK at home on your own?"

I nod, my mouth full of food.

"OK, see you soon. Get some rest!" She hesitates. "I'm going to lock the door after me. Just as a precaution."

I smile. "OK, Mom. Thanks."

When I hear the front door shut and her car pull off the driveway, I peel back my sheets. The camcorder has left my white sheets with nasty black stains. *Soot*, I think. I mutter an expletive and try to brush it off as much as I can. But it soon becomes clear that soot is impossible to wipe off. Typical.

I ignore it for now. Mom will notice, of course. Moms are so eagle-eyed. I'll have to come up with something later.

After a much-needed breath, I take the camcorder to my desktop computer and connect the cables. It only takes a few moments so I quickly realize there's only one video. From the thumbnail, I can discern a white boy wearing a letterman jacket…

Brad.

My heart pounds as I double click the video. It takes a moment to open up, and it is the longest moment of my life. The anticipation kills me. A bead of sweat even flows down the back of my neck before soaking into my pyjama top.

When the video finally does open, it plays instantly, and I find myself looking at Carrington Manor, in front of which stands a boy – Bradley Campbell. It almost makes me sick to see the house again so soon. Brad's voice, pitched low and ominous, sounds on the tape.

"A cursed manor. An age-old curse. And a murderous ghoul… Join us while we explore Carrington Manor and discover the secrets that lie inside its walls. I'm Bradley Campbell, and you're watching *Truly Haunted*."

I watch him intently. Like we suspected, Brad was at Carrington Manor to film his show, *Truly Haunted*. Were he and Shelley just in the wrong place at the wrong time, like Buffy and I thought? I carry on watching as Brad walks up the steps, continuing to set the scene and lay out the history of the manor. I have to say, he's great at presenting the show; I feel like I could enjoy this if I didn't know what was about to come.

Brad is followed into the house by the camera, or Shelley. She sounds scared when she speaks. They climb the stairs and edge along the hallway. Eventually, they end up right by where I found the camcorder. My heart beats faster.

"Let's make our way to Robert's bedroom…"

That was Robert's bedroom then. I had no idea. I was standing right by it when I found the camcorder. All these deaths have not only been in the same place but also right next to Robert's bedroom. I was practically on top of—

Shit.

Brad turns his back, and the door creaks open.

And my mouth drops. I see it.

I can hear Shelley stuttering. She's trying to tell Brad to run but he doesn't understand. He turns his head, and finally sees what I can see. The ghost – the ghoul. The Carrington Ghoul. He stands well over six foot and is surrounded by a spectral glow. He resembles every image I've seen of Robert Carrington, even the portrait in the manor, though the smart three-piece suit is now ripped and torn, singed in places. Underneath, his shirt, once a crisp, starched white, hangs limp and grey and covered in ash. But that's not what strikes me. It's his face, or lack thereof. A dark scarf is wrapped loosely around his features, covering everything bar two ghostly eyes. It's covering Robert's burns from that night.

The Carrington Ghoul, in plain sight!

And he looks real to me.

I watch as Brad crashes to the ground to avoid his ghostly grasp. Then the camera goes shaky in Shelley's hands. I think she helps him up and they run. The camcorder falls to the floor. I can hear their voices though. They plead and they plead. And then there's fire. So much fire. But the camcorder is seemingly fine; I can still see everything.

The fire spreads further and faster, a vortex of heat and flame. Brad and Shelley come into shot, huddled in the corner of the room by the bay window, the fire drawing nearer. Now only their legs are in shot, but I'm glad of that. Their screams stop and, soon after, the screen goes blank.

I sit back in my chair, my chest aching and my mouth dry. I barely knew Brad, but I knew Shelley, and I've just seen her die. Tears form and I let them fall. The salty water obscures my vision but then I hear something. Shuffling.

I quickly wipe my eyes just as the black screen turns a transparent shade of blue. Ghostly blue. What the—

The blue is moving, flowing. Almost like water, but spectral. Smoke, but not quite. My eyes can't fully comprehend it.

"Oh my God." My voice is panicked. The sicko wanted me to see this – wanted us to see this. To show what they're capable of. *To make us stay away.*

The camera shifts then angles upward. To Brad and Shelley's charred bodies.

I look away, the sight too much; the bile in my stomach threatens to make an appearance.

When I can stomach turning back, the footage has jumped. The fire is gone but the smoke remains. The ghoul steps in front of the dead couple, a large blade in hand. *His butcher's blade.* And I already know what's going to happen.

The figure raises the blade—

I jump towards the screen and pause the video before the blade makes impact. This is no longer something we can keep to ourselves. This needs to go to the sheriff. But I'm scared of what will happen if we do. I think of the note that was left for us at the manor.

NO POLICE.

But what choice do we have?

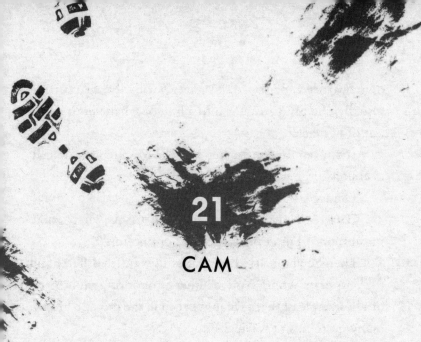

21

CAM

"Cam, I'm leaving now!

Mom's voice is barely audible through my headphones. "Hang on!"

I tug off my electronics and hurry out on to the landing. My head spins, reminding me of my wound. It makes me glad I took another day off school. There's no way I'd be able to make it through classes like this. Even before I reach the stairs, I catch the wave of Mom's perfume – her nice perfume.

"You only get that one out for special occasions," I comment suspiciously as I crest the first step and catch sight of her downstairs.

She's wearing a sly, red-lipped smirk which compliments her crisp white blouse and wine-coloured skirt. Her short bobbed blonde hair, the same shade as my own, is curled and styled. It's never normally so … tamed. Usually, she just throws it into a bun or whatever to get it out of her face.

A firm hand rests on her hip. "Well, this is a special occasion."

"You look like Michelle Pfeiffer."

"Flatterer," she replies. "I need to make a good impression if I'm going to get this promotion!"

"Then be yourself!" I plead, but I get it. It's different in the corporate world. You're either a robot or a nightmare of a boss. At least that's what I've seen in the movies. "How many more business trips?"

She sighs. Clearly she's had enough of them too. "The big-big boss isn't based in Sanera so we have to meet in the middle. Hopefully this is the last one for a while. I'll be back in the morning."

"Morning?" I echo but in a completely different tone. "This promotion better be worth it. I miss you."

"I know, my darling. But this saves me driving home in the dark. It's just easier to stay over." Mom clambers her way to me in the heels she clearly can't walk in. Her cold hand brushes my cheek. "You know we've struggled to make ends meet since your dad died. But this promotion … it could change everything."

I understand. And I've tried to help. But believe it or not, there's not a whole lot of job opportunities in Sanera, especially for kids my age. Which makes the fact that

Buffy's mom got a job here even stranger. I need to ask her what her mom does.

"Will you be OK on your own? I know this is bad timing with your fall."

I told her I fell down the stairs getting a glass of water in the night.

She examines my cut. "How are you feeling today?"

"I'll be fine. Don't worry."

"Well, make sure you lock the doors. My phone will be on if you need me. And turn on the security system. You remember how to use it, right? Please tell me you—"

"Mom," I interrupt and grab her hand. "I will be fine." The words roll off my tongue a little too easily considering a serial killer is picking off Sanera's teenagers. Not to mention that someone kidnapped me and stashed me in a basement.

"Why not ask Jonesy to sleep over? He might cheer you up."

"I might just do that," I say.

She raises her left hand and stares at the watch on her wrist. "I've got to go but I'll see you in the morning. Be safe." She opens the door before turning back to me once again. "Lock the door after me. Love you!"

"Love you—" The door slams. "… Too."

22

JONESY

I can't be mad at Amber; I would've watched the video too. And I would have probably turned it in to the police.

She told us she went to the sheriff's office and left the camcorder on the steps in a plastic bag. Anonymous. We could get into trouble for breaking and entering and tampering with a crime scene. I have a scholarship to work for and I don't mean to sound selfish but I don't want to be in Sanera my whole life. Like I told my dad, I just want to get through graduation.

We know the sheriff got the footage because he made another appearance on the news last night. He released the news of the footage but not the footage itself. At least he can do something right. There would have been mass hysteria if the town saw the Carrington Ghoul *in the flesh*.

I still find that part hard to believe. But Amber's insistent about how real Carrington looked…

What I do know is that what Buffy and Amber found under the manor implies that someone is conducting a serious search. Whether it's for Carrington's fortune, we can't be too sure. But if it is … well, it's not a ghoul doing that.

We've all stayed off school today. It was easy enough to convince Mom. She's actually been doing better – I think Kenny's death woke her up a bit. Even though it's only been a day or so, she's been a bit more present. I'm proud of her. She even told me Cam could stay again because his mom is going on another trip. I'm not ready to tell her about *us* yet though. It's something *I'm* still coming to terms with. Pining for your best friend for most of your life and then it actually happening … it's wild.

We agree to meet at Cam's to talk it all through. I'm nervous as I walk up his driveway. I knock on the door and before long Cam appears.

"Hello, hello, hello." His blonde hair is messy and his clothes un-ironed. So this is what a head injury and an absent parent do to a teenage boy.

"How's your head?" I pull him into a hug, still so relieved he's OK. It feels like an age has passed since I've embraced him. I've missed it.

Cam twists his neck to show me his wound. It's bandaged up so I can't really see anything. "A little sore but on the mend… I'll survive."

He ushers me in and locks the front door behind me. It's cosy in here; a darn sight warmer than outside. It feels like, since Brad and Shelley were killed, Sanera has lost its warmth; lost its life. It's silly but I can't help thinking it.

"Am I the first—"

It's an open plan entryway and Amber and Buffy's heads pop out from the living room. *Of course.* I would've liked a moment alone with Cam but that can wait. I'm sure we'll have alone time … soon enough.

"Hey," Buffy says. She knows I have my issues with her, I think. Cam says I just don't like being threatened by another smart person. But that's not it – not *all* of it, anyway. Something is off with Buffy. I can't quite put my finger on it.

Amber waves but she seems quieter than normal. In fact, a *lot* quieter than normal. She hangs her head while we get drinks and snacks. I think I know what's wrong.

"Amber, we're not angry with you, if that's what you think," I say, as we head over to the couch.

Her features unravel. "Are you sure?"

All of us nod.

"Oh, thank God," she says through a breath. "I was scared you'd all hate me for turning the camcorder in. Jeez, it was horrible watching it – I've never – I hoped the sheriff, even if useless, would make sense of it, but I don't—"

"Amber," Buffy says. She squeezes Amber's shoulder. "You. Did. Nothing. Wrong."

"What about the note though?" Amber gnaws on her lip.

"They're just trying to freak us out," Buffy says firmly, and Amber lets out another breath.

"Well, I'm glad you didn't have to see that."

"Can you tell us?" Cam asks cautiously. She's explained briefly over text but I think we need to know exactly what she saw. We're too far in to stop now. Even I know that.

Slowly, Amber closes her eyes and begins.

When she's finished, we're all silent. It makes me sick to my stomach thinking about it.

"That's so fucked," Cam says from the sofa where he's horizontal, cushions under his head.

Buffy juts in. "Cam," she says haphazardly, "when you were … taken…"

"You don't need to walk on eggshells," he retorts in a playful tone. "We were all there. We all know what happened. I was kidnapped by a likely serial killer and tied up in a basement. What is it?"

"Did you hear *anything*? Any clues?"

He shakes his head. "It's like I told Jonesy: I was sitting looking out the window, I heard a shuffling sound and then the next thing I know … *poof*, I'm tied up with a hell of a headache…" He hesitates, then adds, "I think he had plans for me. It's only fluke you found me at all."

He. It's funny, because we all slip up and resort to saying "he". Maybe it's because deep down we still think it is the

193

real ghost of Robert Carrington. No. The evidence under Carrington Manor indicates this is no ghost. The video footage … well, let's just say I'm confused.

"*Or,*" Amber emphasizes, "he *wanted* us to find you. For whatever sick reason… A warning? He wanted us to see that he can easily pick us off if he wants?"

There's a prolonged silence. Brad, Shelley and Kenny. We're all thinking it – the next victim could have been Cam – should have been Cam.

"What's next?" Cam finally says.

Buffy smiles faintly. "You really want more? After what happened to you?"

"Hey, I know I almost died, but I'm not letting that stop us from catching this freak."

Amber laughs. "I knew you weren't going to give in. What do you say?" She looks to me and Buffy to confirm but of course it's a unanimous "yes". We may be scared of what's to come. But we're in this now.

"Let's decide what's next in the morning," Buffy says.

We all give relieved nods.

"Thank you for saving me. Really." I watch Cam's face closely and quickly realize all his emotions are catching up with him. He pushes them back. Fear, worry, guilt, the whole nine yards. "Maybe we should watch a movie for now? Do something normal for once? Like, Buffy, we've never actually just hung out."

It's true. Since Buffy joined Sanera High, we haven't

had a moment to be teenagers. Sure, it's kind of her fault for initiating the mystery-solving thing. And I'm not one hundred per cent sure I trust her. But it would be nice to relax for once.

And maybe she'll let something slip about this mystery job she and her mom came all this way for.

"I'm down," I say. It's a win–win in my eyes.

Buffy sighs. "I'd love to but it's getting late and my mom is going to be here any—"

Like magic, a headlight flashes through the front blind.

"She's been very protective this week. I had to fight her to just come for the hour," she says, standing up. "Sorry, everyone."

Amber gets up too. "I've got to head home too." Now that I think of it, Amber's parents are probably a pair of nervous wrecks. I'm surprised they even let her out. "Do you think your mom could drop me home?"

"Of course." Buffy glances at me. "You need a ride?"

I shake my head and attempt to hide my blushing cheeks. "I think I'll keep Cam company."

I follow them both to the front door with Cam only a few steps behind.

"Lock up after us," Amber says sternly. We barely ever used to lock our doors in Sanera. Nothing ever happened here, after all. Now, every door is locked, blinds drawn.

"I always do," Cam replies with a smile.

*

After they leave, Cam vaults over the back of the couch and plops down beside me like his head wasn't bashed in a day ago. I really wish he'd calm down a little. Stop pretending to be a tough guy.

"Did you lock up?" I ask.

He laughs. "Yes. But you lot are paranoid."

"Says the guy who was kidnapped and tied up in a hidden underground tunnel. I would hope *you'd* be the paranoid one."

"You're such a doofus," he offers. He always has to have the last word. And then he's looking at me again. Well, *inspecting* me would be the better word for it.

I track his eyes as they flutter from my hair to my eyes to my nose to my lips. "Doofus, huh?"

He grins. "A very nice doofus."

His hand reaches my jaw. Slowly, I entwine my fingers with his like we're a puzzle. His hand is warm on my face and despite the situation all I can think about is the past few days. And how I so nearly lost them. How I so nearly lost *him*.

My thoughts must have translated to my face because Cam edges closer. "Tell me what's on your mind."

"I can't believe this is happening," I mutter in response. "The first time I met you – do you remember?"

He looks to the ceiling, trying to recall. "Was it the weird forest—"

I'm already nodding. "The day I started at school we

were doing a survival lesson in the forest. I couldn't tie a constrictor knot so you helped me."

He smiles. "My dad taught me," he offers, a smile cresting at the thought of his dad. "If you tie it well, it's difficult to get out of. If you tie it too loose … well, you might as well have not even tried." Cam moves closer, brushes his mouth against mine, pulls back again. "How does that make you feel?"

I don't know how it makes me feel – well, I don't know how to describe it, at least. But it does manage to make me smile, make me feel a sliver of calmness.

"Good," I manage.

Closer. "I'm glad it makes you feel … *good*."

At that, my mouth tilts upward. Cam is so good at defusing a situation; inserting comedy into a situation where it probably – definitely – isn't appropriate. Every time, it gets me.

I go to brush the hair from my eyes but Cam is already on the case. Gently, he pushes it behind my ear. His warm fingers graze my cheeks and I feel them combust under him. I'm sure they're embarrassingly rosy right now.

"Perfect again," he whispers.

I fake a pained expression. "Are you implying I wasn't perfect before?"

He grins. "OK. *More* perfect."

"Pretty cheesy. Was that the best you could come up with?"

"Yeah, it was pathetic," he admits.

I watch as his chest rises. Watch as his expression becomes serious.

"Jonesy," he mutters. The way he says it is almost like he says it by mistake, like it was meant to be a thought. Soft and unspoken. He looks into my eyes and this time I look back. A light blue mixed with a dash of … brown? I've never noticed that before, but I've also never stared this deep into his eyes before – anyone's eyes, for that matter.

"Can I…"

I don't even stop to register his words, nor do I think about what I'm saying before they leave my lips. "Yes … please."

Like fire on ice, he connects. I pull away at last, because I don't know what'll happen if I don't.

"That was…"

"Amazing?" he finishes for me.

He's grinning, like nothing bad will ever happen again. Like we're not actively pursuing a serial killer. But I don't mind. For one moment, I want to feel safe again. It feels good knowing that I've made someone feel like that too. Me. Jonesy. I smile to myself.

A few hours without the worry of the Carrington Ghoul and then we'll be back to solving this mystery.

23

CAM

The killer is in the house.

An emotionless white mask is pinned on to his face as he stalks his next victim. The carving knife in his hand leaves a bloody trail as he goes. He steps into the final doorway of the downstairs and peers in. The living room is empty but the television on. His head tilts to one side, thinking, before shooting his gaze to the ceiling.

Upstairs.

Quicker than before, he storms through the house and up the stairs. The floorboards creak heavily beneath his weight but it doesn't seem to bother him. The kill is calling him. And nothing will stop him now.

Upon reaching the landing, he kicks the doors off their hinges one by one. At the third door, a scream sounds. It's a guttural scream. Feminine.

He steps into the room. It's dark, but a street light illuminates it enough to make out the outline of a person. They are huddled into the corner of the room, whimpering. As the killer steps closer, he brings the knife up to his eyeline and wipes it clean with his gloved hand. The person screams and lunges for the door.

With a swift motion, the killer sticks out his hand and grabs them by the arm. He drags them towards the window to inspect his prey. A young woman squirms in the yellow street light and is only silenced when the knife is drawn to her neck. Her eyes widen in fear but all she can do is await her fate. The killer lets the blade explore her body, exposing her breasts—

Pause.

"Why does every eighties horror movie feel the need to show bare tits?" Jonesy says, TV remote in hand. "Like, how are you gonna be super forward-thinking and progressive with the final girl trope but then show other women's—

I grin at him. "You're so cute."

He's quick to roll his eyes. "I don't know why we're watching this, anyway. A horror movie, of all things."

I shrug. "Escapism?"

"Escapism? Dude, we're living this."

"I mean … I don't have my tits out." I laugh and, as much as Jonesy tries not to, he finally smiles. "I knew that would get you," I tell him.

"Let's turn it off," he says.

"We can do whatever you want." I put the popcorn bucket down on the table and turn to face him. His hair isn't as perfect as it was earlier, but I won't tell him that. I'm sure he'll see the state of it in due course.

"I would love to." He glances to the clock mounted on the wall. "But I should probably go. The curfew and all that… I didn't realize how late it was."

I shoot my eyes at the time. It's 11.12 p.m. "It's way too late for the curfew… Shouldn't you stay … if you want?"

"My mom will be worried if I don't show my face."

I nod, but Jonesy's mom doesn't notice whether he's there or not. "Let me drive you at least."

He grabs his phone. "I'll text Mom – she'll come and get me."

"Is that a good idea?" I ask, thinking that it's not smart for Jonesy's mom to drive anywhere.

"As far as I know she hasn't had a drink today," he says. "She's laying off it a bit, I think."

"Dude, that's … wow! That's good. Since when?" I say, trying not to sound sceptical. I don't think it's as easy as that, from what I've read.

"Since Kenny died – I think my dad spoke to her." Jonesy's fingers type away, then he looks up. "I've told her I'm ready – I know she'll be waiting up for me." He puts his phone down. "Which still leaves us a bit of time. Where were we?"

As much as I'd like to do whatever he's implying, I can't let him move on. "She's really not been drinking? You believe her?"

Jonesy runs a hand through his hair. "Look, all I know is that, right now, she's a lot more present. I haven't even seen a bottle."

"And how does that make you feel?"

He doesn't answer right away and then shrugs. "I don't want to talk about this," he says simply.

I nod and don't even attempt to continue the conversation. *In his own time.* "You're such a dweeb." I throw a random loving insult out to take his mind off it.

"Me?" He fakes a shocked face. "How am *I* the dweeb? Have you even finished the project for Ms Fletcher?"

My eyes widen. Actually, no I haven't. "When is it due?"

"In about —" he grabs my arm and inspects my watch — "eleven hours."

"Dammit!"

Jonesy stands up and laughs. "I'll take care of it."

I shake my head. "No — just because we're kissing now, doesn't mean I'm gonna let you do my work for me." Deep down, *yes please do all my work for me.* But it's not fair to Jonesy. He tries so hard in school and I just get by. Besides, it would be obvious if I suddenly started turning in well-researched work.

He sighs and pulls me to my feet. "After the week you've had … I *want* to do this … OK?" He kisses me and I give in.

"OK, fine. Thank you."

"I'll try and put in the adequate amount of spelling mistakes and misattributions."

I snort. "You're lucky I really like you."

The sound of gravel crunches. "I think that's my mom," Jonesy says. "See you tomorrow. Meet me at the corner in the morning and we can walk in together, if you want?"

"I'd love that."

I escort him to the door and watch as he heads down the driveway to the waiting car. After a few steps, he turns. "Hey, Cam?"

"Yeah?"

"I really like you too."

I head back to the den to clean up. Then I really should rest, with this injury. Unless … I finish the movie? My phone buzzes in my pocket. I pull it out to find a message from Jonesy.

Go to sleep.

I smile and I flick the lights on and turn the television off.

It's quiet now that I'm by myself. I take the bowl out to the kitchen and begin my nightly ritual. Each night this week I've turned the radio on so the house isn't deathly silent. Even when Mom's been here, it hasn't felt like it. Work has taken her full attention. I can't complain really, her career is important. But it's still weird.

When I turn the radio on tonight, "Total Eclipse of the Heart" plays. Of course, the most eighties song is on right now. It feels like an extension of the movie.

I speed through washing the dishes, wanting to get to bed but knowing this won't get done if I don't do it now. The house phone rings. I shut the faucet off and hesitate. It's late, but it might be Mom checking in on me. I shoot to the phone and pick up the landline.

"Hello? Mom?"

"Hello, Cameron," an unknown voice says into my ear.

"Who is this?"

Silence.

"Amber?" I ask. The voice is muffled and distorted. It doesn't sound like Amber, but it does sound familiar, somehow.

"This isn't Amber."

"Oh … Buffy?"

"Guess again."

My face scrunches. "You tell me."

"I'm an acquaintance," the voice replies.

That voice. I can't pinpoint it, but I think I've heard it before. I can't tell if it's a man or a woman. They've used a filter, maybe.

We don't have a fancy caller ID phone so there's no clue there. Some time-waster, winding people up, knowing we're all on edge after what's happened. I pick up one of the dishes and begin to dry it, the phone jammed between my shoulder and ear. "Well, if you *were* an acquaintance I'd know who you are… I'm ending the call now."

"END THE CALL AND I'LL GUT YOU."

I jump. The dish in my hands finds a new home on the tiled floor and shatters on impact. "Who is this?" I ask with a false confidence, attempting to hide the fear brewing inside.

The voice is lower now but still harsh. But it also seems forced, unnatural. "I told you … an acquaintance."

"Amber, this isn't fucking funny," I seethe, my words angry as they escape through clenched teeth. Not that I think Amber would do something like this. Of course she wouldn't.

"Amber went to bed *hours* ago."

The voice is calmer and slightly playful. I can tell they're smirking.

I peer through the kitchen window into the garden but it's way too dark to make out anything. "How do you know that?"

"Because I see everything," they say sweetly. "Nice job on the dishes, Cam. Your mom will be pleased. You've really kept the house in tip-top shape. I hope she gets to see it."

In an instant my blood runs cold; I end the call and switch the radio off. I run to the back door, unlock it, and throw on the back lights. An empty garden greets me. I lock the door again, and test the handle. The phone rings again.

Whoever was on the phone knows Mom is away. They know I'm alone.

It rings and rings.

In desperation, I snatch up the phone and shout, "What do you want?"

"Now, now," the unknown caller replies. "You should know not to speak to people like that."

"What do you want?" I repeat, but my nerves get the better of me and my voice quivers.

There's no answer. Just the sound of breathing.

No answer.

No answer.

Ding-dong.

The doorbell. I stare down the hallway, the front door in view. There are no shadows outside but that doesn't prove anything. It's easy to duck out of the way. I don't move a muscle or make even the slightest sound. I freeze, not out of choice but from fear, my body completely numb.

Seconds of excruciating silence pass with nothing but the distorted breaths through the phone. It takes everything in me not to scream. I can't make a wrong move here. My fingers reach for my mobile in my back pocket so I can call the sheriff—

The voice again. "You should answer that."

I don't move a muscle.

"You should answer that, Cameron," the voice says, louder.

I feel a trickle of sweat run down my forehead and on to my shirt.

"There's someone waiting for you. I think they need your help. It sounds a lot like … your mother?"

My heart drops. I listen, hard. I *can* hear something. A faint sound, coming from the front door.

I scream and slam down the house phone. I hear the plastic casing smash on the countertop. I've had enough of this. The block of knives catches my eye. I pull out the biggest one I can find and storm to the front door.

The frosted glass hinders my view of anything outside. I listen, trying to calm my breathing. That's until I hear something again – a cry, a whimper?

Mom?

In a panic, I raise the knife and it glints in the porch light. I raise it upward and place my free hand on the first bolt. If Mom is really out there… I slide it back.

What am I doing?

I slide the next one back.

I'm scared, but the thought of Mom being out there alone is worse. I unlock the door. Everything falls eerily quiet. I straighten the knife in my hand and step outside, searching for signs of anyone.

There's nothing. No one. Just an ordinary front yard and silent street. Very *Halloween*.

Now this is a horror movie scene if ever I've seen one.

I'm edging back inside when I spot something half hidden in the shrubbery out front. I dart over and grab the object.

A tape recorder.

A whimpering sound comes from it.

Time slows. It was never Mom. It's a trap and I fell for it.

I run inside and close the door behind me. Lock it fast. Then I remember. We have a security system on the right side of the door – a panic button that goes straight to the sheriff's office. Mom had it installed after Dad died. Never thought I'd have to use it.

I slam the button. Instantly, alarms go off all over the house and red lights flash on and off. More dramatic than I expected.

A message appears on the small screen.

911 called.

I sigh in relief.

But then I see it.

A shadow. Out of the corner of my eye. Behind me.

I spin to find the origin of the movement, but I see nothing. Everything is bathed in red light from the alarm, and then it's dark.

And then it's red again.

I turn slowly in a circle, knife raised. There—

Inside the house. A foot at the top of the stairs. The lights flash and everything is black. Red. Black.

I back myself into the corner, weapon still in hand. The lights flash red again – two feet.

Darkness.

In the next flash, I finally see the assailant in full. Robert Carrington.

No – someone dressed like him, I remind myself. A dark suit, white shirt. And the scarf Amber mentioned, coiled and masking the face. Hiding everything except those eyes. But there's something else, too. A light bluish ghostly shimmer surrounds them. An unearthly light.

All along, I never really believed in the ghoul. I thought Amber must have misunderstood what she saw on the video. Now that I see it for myself, though…

It's him.

Robert Carrington.

The Carrington Ghoul.

In his right hand, a large butcher's blade scrapes against the banister. It's the same blade Carrington was said to have threatened people with. The noise screeches as he makes his descent.

Yeah, fuck this.

I scream over the loud alarms but I soon realize it's a waste of breath. I run, scrabble with the lock. Red lights flash on, off, on, off.

When the red greets me again, I twist the lock and

pull on the handle. The door opens with a click and swings open.

I can hear sirens. The police are coming—

But everything goes quiet.

My gaze drops and I see the tip of a blade through the middle of my stomach. I try and claw at the knife but it's useless.

Blood pools over my fingers.

It's now I feel the presence behind me. I throw my arm out and I think it connects but the pain is too much for me to be sure. The presence gets even closer until I hear the slow breaths in my ear. I swear it's warm – ghosts shouldn't be warm, right?

Dark spots swarm my vision when I turn my head. My sight is cloudy and all I see are hazy shapes. But I can hear his laugh. Deep and harrowing. "Cameron, Cameron, Cameron … you should be more mindful who you let in your house."

I feel the knife twist inside me and I drop to the ground. I croak for Mom, Jonesy … but it's hopeless. I'm weak. Alone. I'm going to die.

Everything is sideways. My vision is blurred but I spot flashing blue and red lights drawing near.

And then … nothing.

24

AMBER

"I told you not to slam doors, Amber!"

Mom stands, arms crossed, in the doorway. Her leopard print blouse clashes with her floral pants but I would never say that to her face. I am not going to mess with her in the morning. She's already cranky that I'm going back to school. There's protective Mom and then there's *protective Mom*. Despite her unusual outfit, she still manages to look beautiful.

"It was the wind." Even I don't buy that.

She sighs. "Next time, just *close* the door. I like it on its hinges, thanks very much."

"OK, OK. Bye, Mom. I have a project due today. Can't be late!" We've had two days off school. Even with everything going on, it's still senior year.

She doesn't seem convinced but for once I'm telling the truth "Back by five," she warns me. "No later!"

There's a news van outside the school grounds when I arrive.

I make my way through the bustling crowds flooding through the gates. There's definitely more people than I expect in today but things can get boring after a week stuck at home and maybe people want the latest news. Maybe they think everything can go back to normal.

But not me. I can't unsee what I've seen. Two kids dying in the most horrible way.

I'm almost at the top of the front steps when I feel a hand on my arm. I jump, spin round.

"Mr Graham!" I cry. I give a small laugh. "I'm a bit on edge."

He looks tired, worried, with none of his usual good humour. "Amber, sorry to make you jump. Can you come with me please?"

"I have a project due in—"

"Amber, this is serious."

I swallow. I suddenly have a very bad feeling about this. "What is going on?"

"I'll explain. Come on." He jerks his head towards the door. Wordlessly, I trail after him. A few faces gawk at me as I pass. I'm aware of whispers following me.

I start to feel sick.

When I enter his classroom, two familiar faces stare back at me. Buffy. Jonesy. But—

"Where's Cam?"

Jonesy gives a shrug. His expression is tense. Buffy bites her lip.

"Please sit, Amber," Mr Graham says, closing the door behind him and pulling the window blind down.

I take a seat next to Buffy and glance in Jonesy's direction. We all look the same. Scared.

"OK, now that you're all here." He takes a seat behind his desk and rolls the chair until he's directly in front of us. His expression is gentle. "There's something I need to tell you."

"We should wait for Cam," Jonesy says.

Mr Graham glances to the floor, and back at us. He loosens the tie around his neck and swallows. "That's what I need to tell you. Cam isn't coming."

25

JONESY

I find myself shaking my head in disbelief. I was with Cam just hours ago. He's fine. He was fine. We were meant to walk into school together this morning but I was running late – when he wasn't at the corner, I assumed he'd gone on without me.

This can't be happening.

"Is he …" I breathe.

"He's in hospital," Mr Graham explains. He consults a scribbled piece of paper on his desk. "Currently in surgery for stab wounds to his stomach and back. He was attacked at his home shortly after midnight. when an alarm was activated." He looks up. "That's all I know, I'm afraid."

Amber and Buffy look as horrified as I feel.

"The principal thought it was best that I break the

214

news, but the police will want to talk to you," Mr Graham says. "For instance, they'll want to know what time you last saw Cam."

"I was with him until eleven thirty. I…" My words break off.

I was with him until eleven thirty.

And then I left. I left Cam alone and he was stabbed shortly afterwards. I think back. *They were watching us.* Holy shit, the killer was there, waiting until he was alone. Until I was gone and he was vulnerable.

Cam was right. He wasn't meant to escape Carrington Manor. The killer came back for him.

"Everyone, please breathe." Mr Graham rubs his forehead. He looks upset, his face swollen, maybe with tears. I guess even teachers have feelings. "We have every reason to hope that Cam will be OK. Sheriff Rogers wants to speak to all of you, so I'm going to ask you to stay put." He looks at me. "Especially you, Jonesy."

I nod – that makes total sense. But I feel another worry take root. What if the sheriff thinks I'm a suspect? No – I have an alibi. My mom picked me up. *My mom picked me up*, I repeat in my head. But will it be enough? What if they think she's lying for me? Or that I stabbed Cam before I left?

I can't believe I even need an alibi.

"Cam's mom was away for the night with work. Does

she know?" asks Buffy. Her expression is thoughtful now, like she's trying to piece all this together.

Mr Graham says, "The police are still trying to reach her. From what I gather they've called but had no answer and the hotel she's meant to be staying at have no one of that name registered. Which is … strange. She must have changed her mind. The school aren't sure there's anyone else to contact." He looks at me. "Unless there's anyone you can think of?"

I shake my head. "It was just Cam and his mom," I say. It's all too much.

"So you were there till eleven thirty, Jonesy," Amber says slowly, "and as soon as you leave, the killer moves in. That means they were watching you guys last night—"

"They wanted revenge," muses Buffy. "We weren't meant to rescue Cam."

I nudge her and glance up at Mr Graham; he looks bewildered.

"Rescue Cam?" he says. "Revenge?"

"It's nothing," says Amber, shooting Buffy a look. "She's in shock." She turns back to Mr Graham. "Buffy … bought into the ghoul idea. She thinks it was after Cam."

"Oh, Buffy." Mr Graham gives a sympathetic smile. "Ghosts and ghouls and goblins aren't real. But I can see this is a very scary time for you."

Buffy subsides.

"I think you kids should go home once you've spoken to the sheriff," Mr Graham says. "Try not to think about—"

"No. We're not burying our heads in the sand. We're going to find out who did this," I say firmly. Because this has changed everything. We thought we'd got away from Carrington Manor and the killer, but this asshole was waiting for the right moment, teasing us. No, we are not going to be played. Not again.

Mr Graham looks alarmed. "Find out who… No, Jonesy! I understand you're upset, but you should leave this to the adults—"

"I'm afraid we can't do that."

It's true. The sheriff has let the killer strike four times now.

We can't let it happen a fifth.

With Amber and Buffy close behind me, I hammer on the front door until Mom answers. Rooting through my bag for my key is the last thing I need right now. As soon as the door opens, I fall inside and she folds me into a fierce hug.

"Cam … Cam is…"

"I know, baby… The school rang to let me know. He's in surgery – we can check in later to see how he is. I'm sure he's going to be OK. But oh, I'm so happy to see you. Come here."

I let her hold me tight, in front of Buffy and Amber. I'd

217

be embarrassed any other time. Tears leak from my eyes and I can't stop them. Before I know it, I realize we're all crying, and Mom is passing out hugs left and right.

In spite of how terrible this has been, it's good to have her back. Eventually, Mom gets us inside and we wipe our faces. I gather myself.

"I think we're gonna go downstairs," I tell her. "Let me know if anyone calls. The hospital. Dad. The sheriff…"

"I know, I will." She nods as she lets us pass.

Stepping into my room, I'm hit by another wave of sadness. This was our hangout. I can't even begin to count how many times Cam has gone down these stairs and slept on the couch and petted Macey—

And then a horrible thought occurs to me. Cam wanted me to stay last night. And I didn't.

If I had stayed over like he asked me to, he might be OK.

"Don't even go there," Amber says suddenly.

I jump. "Where?"

"Blaming yourself for what happened."

"I'm not." I totally am.

"Jonesy, I know you."

Buffy nods in agreement. "I've known you for, what, a week and a half? That is so your MO."

I open my mouth to protest but end up giving a weak laugh. It's better than nothing.

"What's next?" Buffy says.

"I'm not letting him get away with it," I say. "Or her.

Because whoever is doing this is not Robert Carrington." I'm going to keep telling myself this, I think.

Amber considers. "The sheriff has the camcorder. Maybe it's given them a lead."

"Fuck that," I reply. "They've had it for nearly two days now and what have they done except let another innocent kid get stabbed?"

Her silence is deafening.

And telling.

Buffy nods. "We can't trust them to do this right. This killer won't stop, we know that much."

"You're right," says Amber sombrely. "They've killed three people."

"Four, if Cam doesn't survive the surgery," I mumble.

Amber shoots me another searching look. "Jonesy, don't think like that."

I nod rapidly. She's right. I don't even know why my mind went there. Cam's gonna be fine. The surgery will go perfectly and he'll be on his feet again within the week – well, maybe not the week. That's probably *too* optimistic, given he was stabbed in the stomach. But he's going to be fine. It's Cam. Of course he will be.

"OK, if we're not giving up, then what's the plan?" Buffy says, snipping the silence in half. "I think you two need to decide what we do next. My plan got us into this mess in the first place."

I let my thoughts simmer. Acting in a hurry will do us

no good. Buffy's right: the plan sucked last time. In fact, there wasn't really any plan. We weren't ready. This time we need to be prepared for what could happen.

"I think we should tell the police about the tunnels under Carrington," Amber says. "At the very least they'll shut that place down. It'll give us some breathing space to investigate."

Buffy opens her mouth to protest, then shuts it.

"Jonesy?" Amber says. "What about you?"

I think. I'm worried that if we tell Sheriff Rogers about the tunnels, he'll go barging in and spook the killer. I'm also worried we'll have to explain how we found them and get in trouble for trespassing on a crime scene, which could scupper my scholarship. And, even if we do, something tells me that this killer is several steps ahead of Sheriff Rogers.

No. I want to solve this by ourselves.

But if we're not involving the police – yet – we need to protect ourselves. We need to be one step ahead.

I lean forward and find Macey at my feet. She rolls on to her back and I scratch her tummy. Then I look up.

"I don't think we should tell the cops – not just yet. Before we do anything, I think we need to look for more clues, right here in Sanera."

26

AMBER

Sheriff Rogers arrives at Jonesy's house later in the morning and interviews us separately, with another officer present. He speaks briefly with me and Buffy, asking general questions about whether we'd seen anything suspicious in the run up to the attack. But he is with Jonesy for ages. They speak to his mom too. I wonder if it's all routine or if they suspect Jonesy. It's hard to believe they do — but he was the last person to see Cam before it all went down.

It worries me, because if the sheriff is focusing on Jonesy, they'll miss the real killer.

The sheriff tells us that Cam is in an induced coma. He assures us he's safe, with full security, which is something at least. But it still terrifies me that he's alone at the hospital. And his mom is still AWOL. The sheriff is cagey about it, but apparently she hasn't picked up any calls, mine included. Cam's not allowed visitors yet, but the sheriff promises to update us.

Cam will make it. I know he will.

And in the meantime, we're going to find his attacker.

"Oh, you're back," Mrs Adler says. She takes off her glasses and wipes her eyes. She's been crying. I'm about to ask if she's OK when I see the book on her desk. *Old Yeller*. That explains it. Nothing more depressing than a dead dog.

She clears her throat, which promptly snaps me back to this reality.

"Yes," I say. "I'm doing a project on—"

"You and your projects…" Her tone tells me that she doesn't trust me. Haven't been in the library for years and now I'm here twice in a week. Yeah, I'd be suspicious too.

"The school board is pushing us to cite more examples of library-based references in our work," I say smoothly, surprising myself. "There's a concern that, with the rise of computers, libraries may become obsolete. And we don't want that, do we?"

It comes a little too easy. But it seems to work.

"Goodness!" Mrs Adler says. "Well, we can't let the school board down!"

I smile. "I need whatever you have on the supernatural."

She frowns at me, accentuating her wrinkled forehead. I wonder how old she is. From what I hear, she's been here as long as anyone can remember ... maybe as long as Mr Carrington. I push the thought aside.

"The supernatural... Do I dare ask what subject this is for?"

"English," I answer. "We're studying *The Haunting of Hill House*."

Her expression softens. It seems I've sold it. "I love that one. Hmm, the supernatural. Well, we have a small section that might do the trick." She points through the stacks. "At the back, right between 'health' and 'cookery'."

Of course it is. Makes perfect sense. With one last smile, Mrs Adler places her glasses back on the bridge of her nose and picks up her novel.

I head towards the back.

The bookcases tower around me as I make my way down the furthest aisle; it's a good thing I'm not claustrophobic. The history of the place twists into my brain. Like, how old are some of these books?

I run my fingers over the spines and not even a lick of dust comes off on them. Wow, Mrs Adler really takes care of this place.

My overwhelmed eyes drift across the vast selection of literature: fiction, biographies, religion, and eventually cookbooks. I'm close.

Finally, my eyes settle on what I came here for. Right in the back corner, a little cue card is perched on the shelf.

I'm at the shelf in seconds, looking for anything that may be of use. Ghosts. Entities. Spectres. Poltergeists—

Carrington?

I stop at a giant deep-green tome with the all-too-familiar surname spelled out in block letters on the spine: CARRINGTON. Then, in smaller print: MYTH, MURDER AND MORE.

I pull it from its place and stagger back. This is no insignificant book. Managing, but only barely, I carry it to a table nearby. It makes a loud thud as I drop it; I almost expect Mrs Adler to tell me to keep it down. She doesn't, surprisingly.

"Give me something," I mutter to myself as I crank the book open.

It's *huge*. What could there possibly be in here to warrant this many pages? I turn to the contents, then stop.

There *are* no contents. No author's name or publisher. And the book … it's *handwritten*. Neatly, in a mixture of ink and ballpoint pen. Not typed at all. I flick through the book and find that it's an entire history of Robert Carrington and his manor. It begins:

For many years, Robert Carrington has been a misunderstood and maligned figure.

> His tragic death has overshadowed his
> many achievements. I will aim in this book
> to tell the true history of the man...

Sometimes the author has gone back and added extra notes and information. Queries about Robert Carrington's birthplace, the names and ages of his children when they died. How Carrington made his fortune — property, mainly. The layout of the manor, the grounds. Long paragraphs about how Carrington was misunderstood, that the people of Sanera turned against him. This person was *obsessed*.

I think of the wall of newspaper clippings in the hidden basement of the manor. A crazed fan would do that. Could they also be the author of this book? And someone who has written this big a tome would surely know about the treasure hidden somewhere in Carrington Manor.

The same person who kidnapped Cam?

The same person who murdered three people?

I scan through for clues. It's mostly stuff we already know, as well as lots of nitty gritty that isn't much use, except wait— On the last page, in what looks like new ink, is this line:

> After the manor lay empty for many
> years, it was finally bought in 1998.

I didn't know that. On the news, it said the manor was still abandoned. Certainly no one seems to be living there…

I think again of how clean and well-tended the manor appeared, in spite of the fire damage. The underground tunnels, the basement with lights and material. No one is officially living there – but someone *is* there, all the same. Could it be the same person who bought the manor?

There's something stapled into the back of the book. It's confirmation of a mortgage agreement on Carrington Manor, with thick black marker drawn through any of the identifying information. I squint, trying to make out any letters, but whoever redacted it has been thorough. But the date of sale is clearly typed – August 1998. So someone *did* buy the house. But why has that information been kept so quiet?

I stare at the paper. Someone got hold of the mortgage and stapled it into the book. Was it the buyer? The mysterious person tunnelling under Carrington Manor? Or are they one and the same?

But then why leave the book here? Like the camcorder we found with the footage of Brad and Shelley's murders, it's all too convenient.

One answer occurs to me – and I don't like it.

Whoever left the book here *wanted* us to find it. But why?

"Who wrote this?"

Because the book is so heavy I end up slamming it on

to Mrs Adler's desk. She jumps and her white curls shake.

"My goodness," she says, her hand on her heart.

"Sorry," I say. "I just … really need to know who wrote this."

Mrs Adler tuts and puts on her glasses. "The author will be on the title page, of course."

She spends a minute or so doing exactly what I did moments ago. Opens the book, looks for the author or contents, then flicks through in increasing concern.

"This is *handwritten*," she says, looking bewildered.

"Yup."

"That is truly odd."

"That's what I thought."

Perplexed, she sits back in her chair. "I'm trying to remember when we obtained this book. It does ring a bell. Maybe…"

And then she's swivelling the chair around to her computer. She types. And types. Slowly. *Very* slowly. "Ah. We recently added several new books to our database, there may be…"

Her eyes light up. "Aha!"

"You found it?"

"*Carrington: Myth, Murder and More*. The author is down here as R. M. Renfield – ah yes, I remember!" She nods at the computer screen. "It was an anonymous donation, along with a few other humanities titles. Less than a week ago, I believe. There was a Post-it note on the cover with the author's name. I didn't think to look inside." She sighs. "Remiss of me."

Less than a week ago? After Brad and Shelley were murdered, then.

"Do you know anything about who might have dropped it off?" I urge. "Is there CCTV?"

"Oh, goodness, no. We don't have the budget for that."

Great. "You don't have the Post-it note, do you? That was left with the donation?" I want to see if the handwriting is the same as the writing in the book.

"Honey, I'm sorry," she says apologetically. "I threw it out."

I bite back more questions. "Thank you anyway. Can I check this out?"

"I suppose so," she says, eyeing it curiously.

Clearly someone wants us to see this book, I think. If it's the killer, I don't want to play their game. But at the moment, we don't have much choice.

I saunter into Sanera Safe Mortgage Lenders, trying to look like I belong here. The nerves threaten to force me out of the building but I'm quickly greeted by a woman before I can leave.

"You're a little young for a mortgage, aren't you?" she asks, her grey eyes scanning me up and down. Her jet-black pin-straight hair is cut into a neat bob that ends at her pale chin. I've definitely seen her around town before.

You know almost everyone in Sanera. Maybe not by name, but it's hard to miss a face around here. *The way of a small town.* "Can't be more than ... sixteen?"

I chuckle. "Seventeen."

"Right... So, how can I help you, hon?" She motions me to follow her, so I do, closing the door behind me. I take a seat at her desk and the pure mess suddenly becomes apparent. There are mountains of files on almost every desk, which I'm sure is breaking all kinds of privacy laws. "I'm Abigail, by the way."

I smile at her. "Hi, I'm Amber. So, about that mortgage..."

Abigail's face is a mix of emotions, unsure of what to make of that. "Sorry?"

"Ha, only joking." I laugh nervously. "I'm actually doing a business and finance project and I'm struggling. I was wondering if you could explain how mortgages work a little bit – my teacher is useless, so I wanted to come direct to the source!" I flash her a toothy grin and hope to God it's convincing.

"Well, you've come to the right place," Abigail says, and in no time she's diving into a full explanation – quite a boring one, I might add. While she's talking, I glance around her office. This is the only mortgage lender's office in Sanera so whoever filled in the application surely would have come here. The information was redacted but it's worth a shot. I can't ask her about it directly because presumably it would all be confidential. Eventually, my eyes fall upon a filing cabinet in the corner of the room. It's massive – there must be a file in there on Carrington Manor.

Every so often I smile and laugh at Abigail's words to give the impression I'm listening. It seems to work because she carries on … and on. I just need to get to that cabinet—

The phone rings.

This might be my chance.

Abigail stops her spiel. "Sorry, I need to get this." She picks up the phone and answers cheerfully, then promptly walks into the next room.

Holy shit, I'm in luck.

I creep over to the filing cabinet.

There are three rows of files, all organized by zip code. Unluckily for me, I have no idea what Carrington's zip code is. With fast fingers, I flick through as many as I can, coming up blank, all the while listening out for Abigail's conversation. She still seems like she's in the middle of her call. I can't hear any goodbyes just yet.

Where are you?

Where are you?

Where are you?

I hear Abigail end her call and I frantically flip to the back of the cabinet. And then, just as the door handle turns, my fingers close on the file for "Carrington Manor: applications and sale".

I shove the file up my shirt and am back in my chair in seconds, ready to hear about mortgages when Abigail joins me again.

"Sorry about that. Where were we?"

I hesitate. I can't pass up the chance to ask her questions, even though she might shut me down. "Can I ask something a little strange?"

Abigail casts me an odd glance. "Depends…"

"I've been doing some research into local buildings as part of the project and … Carrington Manor isn't abandoned, is it? Someone bought it, a few years back?" The words leave my lips before I can even think it through. Instantly, her lips tighten, which tells me all I need to know. I press. "Why is it a secret?"

Abigail doesn't say anything but she looks like she's about to burst.

"Abigail?" I say. "You can tell me."

"I don't know what you're talking about, kid."

"I know everything, so you can stop with this clueless act," I bite, just slightly. The nice approach was going nowhere. Sometimes you have to snap.

"Look," Abigail whispers harshly as she looks over my shoulder to the front door, like someone might be listening. "I'm only telling you this because it's been eating away at me since those poor kids died there. It *was* sold. It was a private sale but clearly you know somehow so … whatever. No one has met the buyer. He bought it a few years back. He—" She breaks off. "That's all I know."

He. "Does the sheriff know about this?"

Abigail nods. "I told him as soon as those kids were found dead but they couldn't trace anything. It was a sketchy deal. Keys were posted to a random PO box out of state. We don't really have much documentation. It's bare bones, really."

"Do you know his real name?"

She shakes her head. "We shouldn't have approved the mortgage without the proper documentation, but look around. It's empty around here. We needed the money and he turned up at the right time."

"So you've no way of finding out who he is?" I ask, one last time.

Abigail shakes her head again, firmly. I excuse myself. The last thing I see is her frightened face watching me as I leave the room.

"R. M. Renfield?" Buffy blinks, clueless, her hands resting loosely on Jonesy's dining room table. "Nope. It doesn't ring any bells. But then again, I'm new here."

I sigh and turn to Jonesy. "Jones?"

"Nope." He thinks for a minute, then laughs. "Unless they're a relation of Dracula's deranged servant."

"Wait, what?"

"R. M. Renfield – same initials and last name. He's Dracula's devoted servant. Carries out his dark work…"

That's interesting, I think. Jonesy's smarts sometimes pay off. Maybe our mystery buyer is a vintage horror fan. Or maybe it's just a coincidence.

I tap my fingers on the file I stole from the mortgage advisor. "So we know Renfield is the new owner of Carrington Manor. They bought it in 1998 in a private deal. But I'm almost certain Renfield isn't their real name."

Jonesy nods, chuckling. "If they had the exact same name, down to the initials … I'd be even more creeped out than I already am. So the current owner of Carrington Manor is also the author of the biggest work of fan fiction ever to exist about a ghost. *And* probably the same person who constructed a shrine in the … basement." *Basement* is putting it nicely. If anything, that place is a dungeon. "*And* the same person who kidnapped Cam. Therefore, Renfield, whoever he is, is our killer. Right?"

"Right," I say. "Plus, it would make a sick sort of sense for them to dress up as Carrington if they're this obsessed with him. But why leave the book in the library for anyone to find?"

"Anyone to find?" Buffy asks, her brows raised. She's been leaning back and watching us. "Or … for *us* to find?"

It sends a chill through me. She's right. *We're* the ones sniffing around Carrington Manor. We're the ones digging into Carrington's death. The killer could have guessed we'd visit that section of the library and find that book…

I wonder, suddenly. Could Mrs Adler have put the book

there herself? But why? Let me add another person to my "do not trust" list.

"So, what? He's taunting us?" I say.

Jonesy shrugs. "Or trying to scare us off. Or distract us. We do keep getting in the way."

My mind keeps circling. There are so many puzzle pieces but none of them fit in the right place. There's still something we're missing.

"The way I see it," Jonesy says, "Renfield left the book there because he *wants* to keep us investigating. That's why he made sure the mortgage was in the book. He's feeding us the pieces. Because he's confident that we won't be a problem by the time we finally do fit them together."

My eye twitches. "So we're playing his messed-up game." I groan. "Brad, Shelley and Kenny. Cam. Why did he pick them as victims?"

Buffy snaps her fingers. "This is a Carrington superfan, remember. Whoever Renfield is, they know everything about Carrington. Including the fact there may be treasure buried somewhere in Carrington Manor or its grounds. So he buys the manor. Digs tunnels, brings in equipment. He doesn't want kids using the manor any more though, so he gets hold of enough props to deliver a convincing Carrington Ghoul. Makes sure a ghostly silhouette is glimpsed from a window from time to time, so that the kids who have been using the manor stop. And it seems to have worked because I don't know of anyone who goes there any more ... except us."

"But why go from scaring people to killing?" I say.

"Because he's close," says Buffy. "After all these years, he's close to finding the treasure. Then one night Brad comes snooping around, filming his show. So Renfield kills him and Shelley. He hopes that scares anyone else off. But Kenny threatens to come to the manor, so he has to die. And then *we* come, so he kidnaps Cam, the easiest target. But Cam escapes. Renfield is terrified Cam saw or heard something that night, something that might ruin all his plans ... so he has to silence him."

Shit.

If that's the case, Cam isn't the only one in trouble.

It's all of us.

27

AMBER

"OK, class," Mr Graham says weakly over the chatter. It takes a moment for the noise to die down, as well as an extra plea for quiet. "Please read from page hundred and two to hundred and four. Today we're looking at the fall of the Western Roman Empire."

Like automatons, the entire class do as we're told. Hardly anyone is in school today. In fact, so few people are here, they've combined the history classes. It feels weird having Jonesy by my side, but here he is, to my left. And then there's Buffy, sitting ahead and to the right.

It gives me comfort, having my friends with me.

The room is now filled with the flapping of pages and whispers. Whispers that quickly become normal conversations once again. Stick thirty kids in a small classroom while a serial killer stalks their town ... they're gonna talk. Mr Graham doggedly continues teaching, knowing that he won't be able to stop everyone.

Jonesy leans over to me. "Sheriff Rogers officially opened a missing person case for Cam's mom," he whispers. "They called her employer – the person she was travelling to meet – and she never showed up."

He speaks loud enough that Buffy hears too. Our mouths gape at the same time. *What?*

"You don't think…?" I ask, a little too loudly.

He shrugs. But the thought clearly has crossed his mind. Could she be another victim? "I'm hoping it's all a big misunderstanding and she lost her phone." He doesn't sound convinced.

Buffy cranes around a little more. "I don't like this at all—"

"Miss Allen," Mr Graham interrupts. Even our most affable teacher sounds exasperated. "Why don't you tell the class … what date did the Western Roman Empire fall?"

Every single eye shifts in Buffy's direction and I don't envy her in the slightest. I try and scour my brain for something to help her answer. The question gnaws at me. I've read about this. I've seen movies. The fall of the Roman Empire happened in…

Think.

Think.

Think.

"It's a trick question," Buffy says calmly. "There was

no one date. The fall of the Roman Empire happened over decades."

My brows rise. It's clear Buffy doesn't need my help. I can't confirm or deny her answer but, judging by the startled expression on Mr Graham's face, it must be right. Slowly his expression changes from surprise to delight.

"Well done, Buffy. Look, class, someone who actually pays attention to what I teach!" He beams at Buffy, then continues. "While the date of CE 476 is often cited, as Buffy points out, the situation is actually more complex…"

Everyone goes back to whispering. That's high school for you. People will gawk and root for your failure so they can make fun of you, but getting things right is boring.

Mr Graham raises his voice. "Can anyone tell me the factors that led to the fall?"

A handful of people scan the book.

"Without looking them up, please."

Everyone is clueless, including me. I look to Buffy again and I can tell she knows but doesn't want to stand out again.

"Anyone…?" Mr Graham sighs. "So that tells me nobody did the assigned reading. I know things have been tough, but you kids have tests coming up. I'm sorry, truly. If it were up to me, your exams would all be postponed, but it's *not* up to me. Anyways, the factors were—"

"Army numbers were dwindling," Buffy says clearly. She hasn't even bothered raising her hand. "The army was also no longer the effective machine it had once been at the height of the empire."

Mr Graham blinks. "Miss Allen, you're correct again. Very g—"

"Poor economy, poor emperors, poor health."

He nods. "Excellent! I think that's all of them. So, as Miss Allen has shared, there are many factors—"

"You forgot climatic changes," she adds.

Everyone is staring at her now, including Mr Graham. I always knew Buffy was smart – I didn't realize she was "show up the teacher" smart. I glance towards Jonesy, expecting to see a less-than-impressed face, but he's actually smiling. Maybe he's finally warming to Buffy. It's about time.

Mr Graham gathers himself. "Indeed, I, ah, missed that one. Miss Allen, you certainly know your stuff. But perhaps you can leave some for the rest of the class?"

I groan internally. Teachers don't like it when you show them up by being *too* smart. And this is why *I* don't speak up. All power to Buffy though. She killed it.

Mr Graham goes back to wrangling the class and Buffy goes back to taking notes. I glance at her. This mystery girl who showed up in Sanera just before the killings started. Whose mom relocated all this way for a job in a town with no prospects. Who somehow made herself at home in our gang. Who pushed for us to investigate. Who turns out to be wildly smart.

Suddenly, I wonder. I've always been quick to defend Buffy, to bring her into our group. I thought Jonesy was silly for questioning her, but it occurs to me now that he was right to be sceptical. She is so ridiculously smart and she really hasn't let on about it that much. But just now we saw the extent of her intellect. How easy it came to her.

The truth is, we don't know much about Buffy at all.

We take our usual spot in the cafeteria. It's weird being here. I haven't been absent from school so much in my life. I try to imagine for a minute that we're just ordinary students on an ordinary day. But I can't forget what has happened. To Shelley. To Brad. To Kenny. To Cam.

"Tell us everything you know about Cam's mom," I say to Jonesy.

Jonesy acknowledges me with his brows. "I couldn't get much out of the sheriff but it sounds like she set out in the car to the restaurant where she was meeting her boss and the rest of the team, just like she told Cam. A speed camera picked up the licence plate just outside of Sanera. She was meant to attend some important networking event for senior staff. She had a hotel room booked nearby. But it turns out, she never made the dinner. A colleague rang her when she failed to show, but there was no answer. It didn't occur to them to call the police." His eyes light up. "I forgot to say – Cam's awake and can have visitors. I say we ditch after lunch and go see him, if you're up for it."

"And you're only telling us now?"

In response, Jonesy takes a bite of his apple. "I was about to tell you before Buffy went and showed off in history," he jokes. "Way to embarrass the rest of us, Buffy."

Buffy shrugs, her dusty blonde hair falling into her face, and eats her yoghurt. "You could have done the reading," she says.

"This week has not been ideal for studying," Jonesy says, and I catch the defensive note in his voice. "Are you two coming to the hospital with me then?"

"Of course," I say. Like we'd miss seeing Cam. But I do have a question. "Are we telling him about the book we found?"

"No way," Jonesy blurts out. "We can't stress him out after what he's been through. We don't tell him about the book or Renfield or the mortgage file."

Buffy releases a less-convinced sound. "Maybe we should tell him. Talk it all through. Cam met the killer – twice. He came closer than any of us. He might have seen something we're missing."

I reluctantly nod. "It could jog his memory... Maybe he did see something ... or heard something."

I look to Jonesy for approval. He's not happy about it because he wants to keep Cam safe and he's still silently blaming himself for leaving that night. That's obvious.

"I don't think he's ready."

I throw him a short smile. "Why don't we leave this

up to Cam? If he doesn't want to know, we keep quiet. If he does, we include him." It feels like the fairest way. We don't want to piss Cam off by keeping him out of the loop.

Jonesy ends up sighing. "OK. I hope you're right."

28

CAM

"Good morning, Cameron."

My eyes flutter open to find Cathy, my favourite nurse, by my bed. As soon as she was assigned as my nurse, I knew I was in good hands. Some people just have kind faces and Cathy's features couldn't be softer-looking. She's in her scrubs but she doesn't let that drag down her personality. Already, she's shown off her rainbow lanyard a good twelve times.

She's checking my IV. What's in the IV, I couldn't tell you. I somehow find a way to zone out every time someone explains it to me. But the gist is, I'm doing well. Considering.

"How are you feeling?"

"Like I got stabbed."

Cathy looks at me, green eyes wide. "You got *stabbed*?

Why didn't you mention that?" Her tone is faux shock but then she gives a short snort. This is why she's my favourite nurse. Quickly able to match my energy and make me feel a little better about everything. "I can give you some more painkillers if you're uncomfortable."

I laugh and instantly regret it; my hand shoots to my stomach to combat the pain. As if that would help. "That was a bad idea," I mutter through clenched teeth.

"Don't touch the stitches!" She examines them, then straightens out my gown. I've only spent a short period of time with her, but you really get to know a person when there is quite literally nothing else to do. Cathy brought me a book from home to read but it didn't interest me. I'm not sure I'm the right market for a beach romcom.

"Any word on Mom?" When they told me she hadn't turned up at her work dinner, I was sure there was an explanation. She had a flat tyre. That car finally gave up and died. She lost her mobile phone. She always loses her phone. Something. But now … now I'm starting to worry.

She shakes her head. "Sorry, honey."

I don't hide my disappointment, then catch my breath. "You know what? I'll take those extra painkillers."

"You're too predictable."

And then Cathy is gone.

I'm alone again.

I watch as the IV drips. I'm glad it does. The constant hum of the machines stops me from losing it. If it were dead silent, I think I'd be more on edge. It also helps having two cops outside the hospital room at all times. It's reassuring, but it also can't last for ever. Eventually the sheriff will recall those cops and I'll be left to fend for myself again. I don't want to be prey, not again.

I haven't spoken to anyone much since that night. Of course, I was asleep for a lot of it but since then … it's been pretty lonely.

I want Jonesy. My phone has been taken by the sheriff as evidence, so I can't even text him. They're hoping there are prints on it, though I doubt it. I miss him. Amber and Buffy too. Being this scared and alone makes you appreciate your friends even more.

"Here you go," a voice calls out, lurching me from my inner turmoil. "Daydreaming again?" Cathy shoves three pills into my hand and passes me a glass of water. "Drink up, sunshine."

I do as I'm told. I do want the pills after all. They burn as they pass down my throat. Which has been constantly dry since that night. And I've found nothing will remedy it. I keep joking it's the fear lodged in there and it's too scared to come back out. But I don't think it's really a joke.

"Delicious," I say. "Um. Cathy?"

Her eyes float from a clipboard to me. "Yes, hon?"

"Has anyone … called for me?"

"Oh yeah. Your friend…" She stops, narrowing her eyes as she thinks.

"Jonesy?" I query.

"Yes, that's it."

Instantly, the tight knot around my chest unravels. "Really?"

"Yes, love." She smiles warmly. "He's been calling but you needed time to rest. I told him to come down later today with some other friends, if that's—"

"Yes, that's perfect," I interrupt excitedly.

Although seeing them will mean telling them what happened. It was hard enough recounting everything to the sheriff. I don't know what he thought about my story. He didn't say much, just looked worried. I mean, he's seen the camcorder footage.

I think it's safe to say he's still out of his depth.

The memory haunts me. That figure walking towards me, the lights flashing on and off, the knife in my stomach—

I flinch, but immediately regret it as pain tears through my abdomen. I hear the worry in Cathy's voice. "Cam, lie back please. Your—"

My gaze shoots down to my hospital gown. There's a splatter of red that's quickly spreading, staining the once-clean garment.

"You've ripped a stitch." Cathy hurries to a trolley, picking up supplies and returning with gauze, swabs and things I can't name. This is my first time in a hospital, so there's a lot I don't know.

"Shit," is all I think to say.

"It's OK." She returns to my side before lifting up my gown slightly to assess the damage. "Three stitches. Could be worse."

"I'm sorry."

"Don't be silly, it's my job," she reassures me. Her eyes are full of something. It's like she's sorry for me. I'm seventeen and alone here. "Just lie down, and I'll be back to patch you up. Do you need to see my rainbow lanyard again?"

I snort then she disappears and I'm back with my thoughts. And now sporting a new freshly open wound. The acute sting is another reminder of that night.

A very unwelcome one.

"Do you think he can hear us?"

Hushed voices. My vision is blurry at first. Figures are above me, looking down. I'm hearing things. I'm still groggy. But—

"Cam?" A gentle voice calls.

I mutter something indistinct back. Then blink a few times to wake myself up. When I do, I finally see them. It's still hazy but I can make out the familiar figures and I almost cry with happiness.

"Hey!" I say. My eyes dance over all three of them, taking them in. My friends. Amber, calm as ever. Jonesy, eyes intently locked on me. And Buffy, my newest friend, standing slightly apart. It's strange referring to her as a friend, but I think we're past the acquaintance part of our relationship – surviving a haunted house together will do that, I guess. I spot Cathy in the corner of the room; she throws me a thumbs up before exiting the room.

I don't remember anything after she left earlier. But I must be stitched up by now, though the gown is still stained.

"How are you feeling?" Amber asks first. She kneels so she's more on a level with me. Weirdly, it's the nicest thing ever. I finally feel like I'm not being looked down on. Makes me feel normal again.

"I've been better."

Jonesy lowers himself too. He's carrying a bag. "Your nurse got me to bring some clothes for when you can go home – she also said you'd had an *accident*."

"Well, that makes me sound like I pissed myself."

"Oh, she said you did that too…"

I move my arm to nudge him but quickly remember my situation. I glance at the bag of clothes. "They yours?"

Jonesy bites his lip. "Yeah, your house is still cordoned off, so…"

"Thank you," I say, cutting him off. "I shall wear them with pride." I smile at both of them, then over at Buffy. She's somewhat awkwardly standing back. "Hey, you."

"Hi, Cam," she says.

"Would you care to kneel down and destroy your

legs like the others?" I ask, trying to ease the tension. I'm not sure why she looks so on edge. Maybe she's blaming herself for getting us into this. But none of this is her fault.

She laughs and joins the others. "How is hospital life?"

"Oh," I say nonchalantly. "It's a real rager. Cathy is wild."

"Knew it." She looks over to the IV I've spent many an hour inspecting. "Looks like they've got you on the good stuff, too."

"It's almost worth getting stabbed," I say.

Amber groans. "Well, I'm glad the holes in your body didn't affect your humour... My knees, man." She stands and proceeds to comically wiggle her legs. Already, in the two minutes they've been here, my mood has somewhat lifted.

"Oh, you poor thing. I hope your *knees* are OK." My voice is laced with sorrow and a lot of sarcasm.

"Give me a break," she bites back.

And then we're all laughing. It makes me forget everything. I may be on a ridiculous amount of drugs right now but this is the only one I need. My pain is alleviated instantly and, even if it is for a short burst, it's truly amazing how much better I feel.

Eventually, all good things have to come to an end. Jonesy brings me back to reality. "We heard about your mom. I spoke to the sheriff again. They're doing everything they can to find her. They're in contact with the police departments in the neighbouring towns and they're keeping their eyes open."

I nod. "I guess. I'm worried about her." Jonesy squeezes my hand in response. It says a lot. *Sorry you got kidnapped; sorry you got stabbed; sorry your mom has gone AWOL.*

To change the conversation, I blurt out the first thing that comes to mind and secretly the thing that I've wanted to ask this whole time. "Have you found out anything more?"

There's a pause. I can see them all shooting looks at each other.

"Anything more?" Buffy asks at last. She's stalling, I can tell.

"You know. About the case."

I watch as Buffy looks again to the others. They both nod, and then her eyes are back on me. They're green. Bright green. I've never really noticed them until now. They're a stark contrast to her hair but so flattering. "We *have* got some things to tell you, but we have to make sure you *want* to—"

"Tell me," I interrupt.

Jonesy hesitates. "Cam, it's serious."

"You think I don't know that?" I don't blink. "We're catching this guy before he hurts anyone else."

"Guy?" Amber asks.

I nod. I don't particularly want to talk about what happened to me but if it can help move things forward, I'm down. "I couldn't believe what I was seeing at first but … it was Robert Carrington that night. And if it isn't, it's one hell of a costume." It sounds ridiculous coming out of my mouth but it's what I saw.

Weirdly, they don't seem taken aback. I guess Amber saw the video footage.

Buffy looks to the others before continuing. "The name R. M. Renfield. Does that ring any bells?"

R. M. Renfield. "Wait, wasn't he the dude in *Dracula*?" That's the only Renfield I'm aware of, and even that's a bit hazy. There's only so much one can recall from a Ms Carlton English class. She likes rambling. "Why?"

Amber pulls a large book out of her bag. Quickly they talk me through the facts: someone bought Carrington Manor … *that* someone was R. M. Renfield, Carrington's biggest fan.

"I thought it was abandoned," I say.

"So did everyone in Sanera," Jonesy says. "But we know for a fact that Renfield bought it. Amber may have had a chat with a mortgage lending company and stolen some records to confirm our suspicions."

I blink in disbelief, turning to Amber. Good girl gone bad. Well, almost. It's for the greater good or whatever. "Nice," I comment, making her chuckle. "So this *Renfield* is obsessed with Carrington – obsessed enough to buy the house in secret, to compile a book all about Carrington's life and death, create a board of related press clippings and dig a network of tunnels underneath the manor, all in search of treasure that may or may not exist? We're thinking he's also the killer?"

Jonesy shrugs. "People have killed for less. Considering how rich Carrington was, I can only assume the treasure is … a lot. It would make sense the person who kidnapped you and took you to the basement was Renfield. They were scared you saw or heard something that night. When you escaped, they came looking for you at home."

I frown, thinking. "I thought I heard those low grunts … but that could be anyone, anything."

"Maybe he doesn't want to take any chances."

I nod, slowly. "So Renfield kills Brad and Shelley for poking around the house. Kenny because he threatens to search the manor. He comes after us because we found the tunnels and got too close to foiling his plans. But kids have been going to the house for years. Why kill now?"

"We think he might have figured out where the treasure is," says Buffy. "He's been searching for years but he's on to something now. Too close to have a load of teenagers mess things up for him. So he starts appearing as the ghoul. It works. They stop coming to Carrington until…"

Jonesy nods. "Brad with his ghost show rocks up. Brad and Shelley were easy targets. Two kids alone. Maybe once he got a taste for killing, he didn't want to stop. He got carried away."

I feel like that's textbook for serial killers. They become addicted to the thrill, the power that comes from it.

There's a prolonged silence. I imagine this Renfield character, plotting his next move. Did he know we'd put this together? Did he *want* us to? Is he already five steps ahead, watching us walk into his trap?

I find myself watching Jonesy. I'm glad Amber and Buffy are here but, for a moment, I wish we could be alone together, just the two of us. I missed my friends, but him especially. I think how, after all these years, we've finally come together. Built something new and fragile.

And now, thanks to the killer, it's in jeopardy.

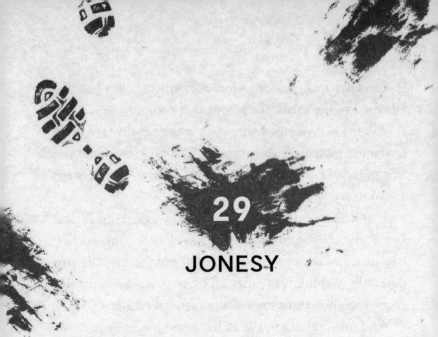

29

JONESY

"Jonesy, can you stay back for a second?"

Mr Graham's voice stops me before we leave the room. This isn't his class but he's here. For some reason. After finishing at the hospital, I came back for last period. Buffy and Amber weren't up for it. Understandably. But I needed the distraction.

"Yeah?"

"Close the door, please," is all he says. But I know something's up. Of course it is.

"What now?" I say, already anticipating the worst.

He pulls out a chair by the desk and sits heavily. His jaunty, brightly coloured tie clashes with his pale, grim face. "This isn't easy but I need to tell you that there's been another murder," he manages. My stomach drops. Another murder? "A body was found a few hours ago in the grounds of Carrington Manor. It'll be public soon, but the head agreed we should give you a heads up. I can imagine how scary this is for you. Given what happened to your friend, Cam..."

"Who?" is all I can muster, full of dread. Amber and Buffy are safe; I just saw them. But then again, I had *just seen* Cam.

"The body hasn't been identified yet. But Trevor Ward has been missing since this morning. He never showed up for homeroom..."

"I don't think I know him..."

Mr Graham shakes his head. His brown and purple chequered tie shakes with him. "I doubt it. He was a freshman."

"Why can't they identify the body?" I ask uneasily.

Mr Graham looks away. "The body had been ... burned."

And my heart sinks more. What. The. Fuck. "Why is this happening?"

It's a silly question to ask. As if my history teacher would know. But it's so *unlikely*. A serial killer in Sanera, of all places. Carrington was the only distinctive thing about the town. And now, everything is leading back to it. The root of everything. I say we just burn Carrington Manor to the ground. It would do everyone some good.

Mr Graham is frowning. "I don't know," he says helplessly. "And I don't *like* not knowing. In history, we're taught that the past will repeat itself unless we reckon with it. But that doesn't help here." He shakes his head. "The sheriff's office presumes Trevor was sneaking around the manor – we'll know more soon." He gives a wry smile. "I never thought I'd say this but there are more important things than school. The principal might disagree, but I think you kids should be allowed home while the police deal with this. Let's leave them the space to do their job."

The thing is, I'm not sure the police *will* deal with this. They haven't dealt with anything yet.

"I'm sorry I don't have more to share," Mr Graham says gently. "Go home, Jonesy."

I nod and leave the room. In the corridor. I pull out my phone and text everyone, minus Cam. I'll call the ward and speak to him later.

No need to scare him even more. And, after all, he's safe for now.

"I can't believe it," Buffy says.

"What, that the killer is still killing?" I say wearily.

She shakes her head impatiently. "No. I can't believe they didn't kill *us*. I really thought one of us would be the next target. That at least everyone else would be safe."

"It sounds like poor Trevor's curiosity got the best of him if he was snooping around the manor." I shrug as I fall back into the sofa. We're back in my basement. Macey bombards my face with her tongue as I close my eyes.

"Hey, girl, calm down," I say when I get a free breath. I free myself and tuck her under my arm.

Amber is pacing. "I can't believe, after all this, kids are still sneaking into the manor."

"As long as idiotic kids exist, that's going to happen," Buffy says. "Besides, we did exactly that. Although … I still think it's odd. Why this Trevor kid of all people? Brad and Shelley had a reason to go there. Kenny threatened to go. But everyone is scared now. What was some random freshman doing there?"

"Well, Trevor must be linked to everything. But how?" I say. "And don't you think the killer seems to have got bolder? It's not like he sticks to the manor. Kenny and Cam were attacked at home."

Amber swallows. "My parents are flying to DC tomorrow for my cousin's wedding. My grandma is meant to be staying to look after me, but…"

"You can stay at mine," Buffy says firmly. "Problem solved."

Amber nods slowly but she doesn't reply. She's got her thinking face on.

"Amber?"

"I have a better idea."

Buffy nudges her. "Is staying at my house *that* bad?"

Amber rolls her eyes. "No. But I think I've got a plan for how we can stop this asshole once and for all."

We both lean forward. "Say more."

"Let's say I call my grandma, tell her my parents changed their mind. I have a free house. We're all on Renfield's hit list, right?" We nod. "So let's make it clear I'm home all alone."

"You mean…"

"We set a trap."

Buffy's head juts forward. "You want to *Home Alone* your house? For a serial killer?"

I shudder. "With you as bait? No. Way."

"Jonesy! Think about it. If Renfield thinks I'm alone, he'll probably take a shot at me. But you'll both be waiting in the wings to intervene. We catch this scumbag, call the sheriff, put Renfield behind bars and we'll live happily ever after."

Right. Because things always work out the way they're supposed to. My head falls back and my hands plant themselves on to my face.

"Is that before or after we ride off in our pumpkin carriage?" I mumble through my fingers.

"I'm serious!"

I look through my fingers at Buffy, trying to communicate with my eyes. *Please talk her out of this.*

To my dismay, though, Buffy is nodding. "It could work…"

"OK," I say, deciding to entertain them and show them how stupid their idea is. I drag my dark curls out of my face so I can think properly. "Let's paint a picture. Killer waltzes into Amber's house, thinking she's home alone. We're lying in wait. Then what?"

Amber blinks. "I was thinking … lock him in a room?" she says, realizing how pathetic it sounds.

"We can go to the sheriff first," Buffy suggests. "Tell them our plan?"

"Yeah, the sheriff is going to be all over the idea," I say sarcastically. "Trapping a serial killer using human bait. It sounds totally legit."

As I think about Amber's idea more, though, I hate how tempting the plan sounds, if you can even call it that. It's ridiculously risky and there's a good chance someone will get hurt. But I can't keep living in fear like this. Every waking second of the day I'm checking there's no one behind me, or double-checking I didn't leave my window open, or triple-checking my phone to see if I've got any more messages about people I know dying. It's too much and soon it's going to send us over the edge.

Enough is enough.

I hate that I'm about to say this, but…

"If we do this…"

Amber leans forward. "Yes?"

"And that's an *if*," I say, "we need to plan it out right. We have to be ready for him. And *no splitting up*."

I'm met with only nods. But that's all I need.

"Then let's catch this dipshit."

30

AMBER

"Do you think we need duct tape?"

Buffy glances at me and the giant roll of grey tape in my hands. "I'd say so."

I put three rolls in the basket alongside a hammer and some tarp. This looks amazingly suspicious. But I'm a thorough person so, if I'm coming up with a plan, it's gonna be good. Now I've just got to live up to my own expectations, especially when another day has passed with no new leads from the sheriff. It's getting ridiculous.

Buffy looks around the nearly empty hardware store. She seems uncharacteristically nervous. "You need to breathe," I say as I scan the shelves for anything else we might need. "I can practically see the goosebumps on your arms from here."

Instinctively, she tries to rub them away. Buffy was the

person who suggested we investigate in the first place and now she's nervous. *That's what a serial killer will do to you.*

"I don't know how you're so calm," she mutters.

I gawk at her. "I'm not calm. I'm terrified."

"Well, you're doing a good ol' job at hiding it."

It's true. But somebody needs to bolster morale. And that someone always seems to be me. Not that I dislike it – I'm an empath after all. "Imagine how fishy it would look if I went up to that counter sweating my ass off. We're already risking enough buying this stuff. There's no need to seem even more suspicious than we do."

"I hate this." Buffy chews her nail. "At the start it seemed almost like a game. But now … I'm scared."

"Me too," I admit. I take a deep breath. "But it's going to work."

"Do you really believe that?"

At first I don't respond. I can almost see the apprehension radiating from her. I'm trying to convince myself as much as her. "I have to," I finally say. "Because I don't know what we're going to do if it doesn't."

"We could run," Buffy says foolishly. It's a joke, clearly, but also a stupid one. This won't just go away if we do.

I place another roll of tape into the basket. For good measure. "I've seen my fair share of horror movies, and those who run … they get their turn eventually."

"This isn't a horror movie."

"Isn't it?"

She blinks at me, and I continue. "Murders, haunted house, group of teens thinking they're smart enough to solve the mystery themselves, a bumbling sheriff, credulous public, the manipulative reporter? All the clichés are there."

Buffy breaks eye contact. As much as she doesn't want to admit it, I'm right. Of all the towns her mom could move to, of course she picked the one that was about to turn into *Friday the 13th*.

"If this is a horror film," she finally says, "doesn't the big bad man turn out to be someone we know?"

I give her a faint smile. "You're catching on. But that's act three. We're still in act two."

"Can I help you?" A voice cuts through. Raspy, hoarse.

I jump out of my skin and drop the basket. "Sorry," I offer. "Just a little skittish."

"My bad, I didn't mean to startle you girls," a woman says. She's fifty, maybe. It's just the cashier. Not the Carrington Ghoul or Renfield. That we know of, at least. But I highly doubt the person tormenting Sanera is the cashier at the local hardware store with lilac highlights. "You kids must be jumpy with everything that's going on."

"A bit," I say. "We're getting some supplies for school." I bend down and pick the basket up, raising my voice. "It's an, um, art project. No parents tonight, so we're going to have a big study session, just us girls."

Buffy eyes me incredulously. I wink at her. This is all

part of the plan. I don't know whether the killer is lurking in the hardware store, but you never know.

The woman smiles. "That's sweet. Is school not called off yet?"

"It's senior year. Can't afford to fall behind because of … everything."

"Oh yes, very true…" The lady's bright smile fades into something more pained. "It's awful what's happening. I've never seen the town like this. Gosh, we're one of the only stores still open. Sanera has always been so—" A sniffle interrupts her before she can finish.

"Peaceful," I finish for her. "Safe."

If we have anything to do with it, Sanera will be safe again.

We check out and the whole time my eyes are on the window, the cars passing and the brave souls who are walking around alone. Does nobody watch horror movies? It's not dark yet, but Kenny was murdered in daylight.

Buffy leads as we exit the store, toting the bags, and I immediately smack into someone coming the other way. "Shit." My bag crashes to the pavement and the contents spill out. Great, now we really look like murderers. Duct tape, tarp and tools. Couldn't look any more suspicious. Immediately I'm crouching, picking everything back up.

"We've really got to stop meeting like this," a familiar voice says. Brash and annoying. I think I might know who this is.

"Great," Buffy mutters as I stand up. I spot the red hair first, then the arrogant smile. Then the way-too-tight jeans. Rick Field.

"Nice to see you too. Haven't heard from you in a while. No news stories for you to misrepresent? Maybe a teenage boy to go do your dirty work?" It's sudden and I don't expect to say it aloud, but alas.

He rolls his eyes. "I never forced the kid to stand up in front of the entire town. I spoke to him once and he came to the conclusion of going to Carrington. I didn't think he'd freaking die because of it—" I catch him peeping into my bag. Confusion spreads across his features. "What are you doing with a hammer?"

"None of your business," I snap, then remember our plan. "Night in, crafting," I tell him loudly. "Alone. Solo."

"Where are you going?" Buffy asks.

Rick casts her an unenthused look. "And why should I tell you?"

"I don't know," she replies, crossing her arms as best as she can with a bag in one. "I thought you might be off to cause more trouble. Hurt some more grieving families' feelings."

"You two are ridiculous. I'm *on a walk*."

"On a walk," I echo. "On. A. Walk."

"Nice to know the murders haven't affected your hearing. Yes, on a walk. Now if you'd excuse me—"

"Wait," Buffy says, jutting her leg out. It stops him

before he can go anywhere. "Have you found out anything else?"

Rick tightens his lips. "You mean apart from the charred corpse found in the grounds of Carrington Manor? Apart from that, nothing."

"Robert's secret fortune," I blurt out. "Is it real?"

I watch as he clearly tries to decide what to tell us. He releases a heavy breath. "I believe so. But it's all rumours. Besides, I can't reveal my sources." Before he walks off, he turns back to us once more. "All I'm going to say is old people love to talk about the past."

And then he's gone. He looked pleased with himself, as well he might. These murders have done wonders for his career.

Old people love to talk about the past.

There's only one person who comes to mind.

"To what do I owe the pleasure?" Mrs Adler calls out as she spots Buffy and me. She reaches down and unbolts the library door, her glasses hanging from the wire as she does so. "I'm afraid I was just closing up, girls. I have a meeting across town."

"We only need a minute of your time," I say, still clutching my bag. We didn't have time to drop anything off because we knew she'd be closing up soon. "It's important."

Mrs Adler doesn't seem happy about it but nods and ushers us inside. The door closes behind us. "Another *school project*?" she asks as she takes a seat behind her desk. No longer can we hide behind the guise of a school project. We really did test our luck.

"No," I say. "We need to know anything you know about Robert Carrington."

Calling Mrs Adler's expression perplexed would be an understatement. Her brows are raised, and her mouth open in confusion. After a moment or so, I can see it all falling into place in her head. "Your friend. Cameron. He was one of the victims, wasn't he?"

I nod. "He's doing OK, but we can't let anyone else get hurt. We thought you might know something."

Mrs Adler sighs and sits back. "I'm not quite sure what you want from me, girls."

Buffy says, "Robert Carrington amassed a huge fortune during his lifetime. Then he died and it just … disappeared. Do you know what happened to it?"

"The state and the bank took all his properties. Most of them were demolished some years back now for new builds. The library was actually one of the few original buildings left untouched. It's protected by a preservation act for buildings historic to the town. I'm just happy that it kept me my job! This place is *never* going anywhere."

"But what about his money?" I persist. "We found articles saying he died penniless."

Buffy joins in. "Which makes no sense for a wealthy landowner."

Mrs Adler nods and places her glasses on to the bridge of her nose. They're a turtleshell style and clash with the floral cardigan she has perched on her shoulders. "It doesn't," she admits. "And of course there were rumours. I heard stories about him hiding his riches, even some that he converted it to gold!"

"Why would he do that?" I question. *Gold?*

"Well, you should know if you've done as much research as I think you have. Robert hated Sanera, or the people at least. He had no next of kin so, along with the property and land, his money would have eventually gone to…"

"The state," I finish for her. Holy shit. It is true. It's all true. "He hid it out of spite, so that the town wouldn't profit from his death." Robert hated the town for the way they resented him. He hid his money rather than let the town have it. It makes perfect sense. If you're bitter and twisted, that is.

"But the question is … where?" Buffy adds.

The treasure, maybe gold, is hidden somewhere in Carrington Manor. It explains the tunnels. Renfield's been digging them, searching for Robert's riches. The house was bought three years ago and he must have been searching this whole time.

And maybe he's finally close.

Jonesy is where we left him when we get back to my house, and that's still working on fitting a tripwire to the back door. He hasn't got the time to go back to the library for books on the matter, so alas, his two classes of electrical engineering will have to suffice. It was an extracurricular in sophomore year.

"Glad to see you're still alive," I call out as we walk through to the kitchen. "We have a lot to tell you."

He's focused on the work, hair in front of his eyes as he replies, "What now?"

We fill Jonesy in on everything. Our encounter with Rick Field and his tip that sent us to Mrs Adler. It seems the treasure is one thousand per cent real now.

"Wow. So our suspicions were correct," he says. "It explains the motive. This is no ghoul – it's someone greedy for a fortune."

Buffy walks closer to Jonesy as he fiddles with the door. "How is it going?" she asks, trying not to get too close. Whatever he's doing doesn't look safe.

"Terribly." A spark flies and he steps back, startled. Finally, he brushes the hair out of his eyes and we get a look at his face. It's covered in dust and God knows what else. What the hell has he been doing?

"I've electrocuted myself twice. But I think I've – there. I think I did it!"

We wait. A few seconds pass where he doesn't move a muscle. Nothing happens.

"Yes!" Jonesy beams. "It actually worked!"

"Good job," Buffy says warmly.

"Not bad," I say. I don't want his ego getting too big. "So what will it do exactly?"

Jonesy begins rubbing his hands together, as though he's been waiting for this question. Oh, a guy and his toys. "I thought you'd never ask… So, upon triggering the mechanism on the front door, the trespasser will set off a dormant timer. The mechanism can *only* be triggered by the front door. As long as the attacker enters through the *front* door and not the back, we're good." He frowns. "We just need to make sure they do that."

"*Front* door. Got it. We leave the front door unlocked," I say. "Let them come in in plain sight but we need to be ready. Then what?"

"Well, let's just say it's crucial they leave by the back," Jonesy says.

"Why?" I ask.

He smirks. "You'll see."

"That's risky," Buffy says.

"All of this is risky." I cross my arms. "But it's no riskier than waiting around for the killer to show up and murder us."

Buffy gnaws her lip again. "I don't like the idea of using you as bait."

"You're bait too." I grin at her. "If they're as smart as they clearly think they are, they're probably expecting you to sleep over."

Jonesy steps in. "What's to say they haven't already caught on to all this?"

We fall silent. Jonesy is right.

We could be falling into another trap.

31

JONESY

"OK, so we have this sorted, right?" I ask. We're all perched around the kitchen table with a sketch of Amber's house. It's covered in scribbles from the past thirty minutes of planning.

Amber nods.

Buffy too. "I'll go call my mom to bring me some clothes. Makes it look believable."

"Good idea," I say as she gets up and steps out of the room. My eyes drift over to Amber, who's staring at the sketch, lost in thought. "You good?"

My words seem to startle her. "Not really." She forces a laugh.

"I'd be shocked if you were." I smile and wrap my right arm around her. She leans into me. "It's gonna work."

"How do you know?"

I shrug. Because I don't. It's all hope but that's all we have right now. "Excuse me, but my trap is foolproof."

She cackles. "So optimistic. Cam is rubbing off on you." Her words are warm. "I like you two together. I really do."

"I—" I stop myself. There's no point in hiding it any more. We haven't exactly done a great job at keeping it a secret. "Thank you," is what I finally settle on. "I like us together too ... not like we've had much time to experience it."

"You will have the time," Amber assures me. She stands. "I need the bathroom. I'll be right back ... oh. Forget I said that. Big horror movie no-no."

I laugh as she heads out.

I stand and begin cleaning up our mess, taking some scrap paper to the bin. It's then that I realize I can hear Buffy talking on her cell phone, out in the hall.

"I can't," she whispers. "Amber and Cam are fine. But Jonesy still doesn't trust me. I've tried everything but I can't crack him. He's a tricky one."

My stomach turns.

"Not yet," she continues. "I don't want them to suspect me."

I falter back, suddenly dizzy. This whole time Amber and Cam called me paranoid but I wasn't. Buffy is hiding something and I knew it. So much for trusting your gut.

"I'd better go." Buffy's voice whispers. "Yeah, don't worry. I'll handle it."

She's coming back.

Quickly, I retreat back to the table just as she re-enters the kitchen. I try to act as normal as possible but it's hard. Who was Buffy talking to? An accomplice? Does this have something to do with Carrington? With Renfield? ... With the murders?

The murders that only started when she arrived here in Sanera.

"Mom's on her way," Buffy calls out. She tucks her phone into her back pocket.

"Great!" I gabble. "So great. Can't wait for tonight."

Can't wait for tonight? What is wrong with me?

Thankfully, Buffy laughs. "I know. We're all tense." She crosses the room and sits again. The whole time my eyes are on her. I don't think I can physically look away. I have a feeling I need to be careful around this girl.

And I'm listening to my gut this time.

32

AMBER

I stare out of the back window of the house. Nothing. No sign of an intruder. God, if Mom and Dad knew what we were doing... Setting a trap for a serial killer in their house? They would lose it. Even if *Home Alone* is their favourite Christmas movie.

Normally, I'd sit back here to relax. Watch the sunset disappear behind the hills. But there's no time for relaxation now. We were waiting until dark – but the killer didn't wait till dark to kill Kenny. He could be here in five minutes or five hours. There's no way to tell. But he'll come, I can feel it.

I try and stay calm, like I did with Buffy in the store.

"Are we still certain about this?" Jonesy says, pacing nervously up and down.

"Too late now, buddy," I say breezily.

He glances towards the living room, where Buffy is waiting. "Amber, I need to tell you about—"

There's a ring on the doorbell. Jonesy will have to wait.

"It's Mom – I'll grab it!" Buffy shouts from the living room. I hurry to join her – it'll be her mom, but better safe than sorry. Family photos surround me and all I can think is how much all my ancestors are judging me hard right now. And even more so when she unlocks the front door. It's 5.40 p.m. Her mom, right on time.

Buffy's mom stands on the doorstep, wearing comfy clothes and carrying a duffel bag. She's blonde and pretty like her daughter, though her hair is cut just above the shoulder. "Hi, darling," she says. "I can't stay – I have a flan in the oven. All ready for your girls' night in?"

The only sign we have other plans is the haunted look in Buffy's eyes.

"So excited," I say with faux excitement. "Thanks so much for bringing Buffy's stuff."

"All right, you two have fun. Let me know if you need anything."

Once Buffy has hugged her mom, I quickly usher her into the house, closing the door behind her and "*forgetting*" to lock it. This is either the best idea I've ever had, or the beginning of the end. Time will tell.

Once Buffy's inside again, we drop the act. Buffy pulls

her hair out of her face, then claims her agreed position on the couch, with her back to the front door. And I'll be sitting beside her – or so the killer will think.

I carefully reposition the mannequin beside her and step behind to see how it looks. It looks real enough to my eyes. From the back, there's no way to tell it isn't me – especially in the darkness, lit only by the flickering light from the TV. One of my old wigs came in handy. And this mannequin? My mom's a tailor. She makes a lot of my clothes so we have a ton lying around.

I'll actually be in the corner of the living room, hidden behind the curtains, right in line with Buffy. The curtains cover enough of my body that I'm hidden but I still don't feel great about it. The important thing is that I can see Buffy and I can see the front door. Jonesy waits in the opposite corner, hidden by the piano. I can just about make out his silhouette, but, from the door, he's invisible – with a good view of his surroundings.

"Hey, this is intense," Buffy admits. The television plays on low because it would be extremely unbelievable if we were sitting there in silence. It can't be too loud, otherwise we could miss any noises. It's a back and forth until we decide on a sensible volume: twenty-two.

I watch as Buffy's legs bounce up and down from the nerves. Over and over. I don't blame her. She's bait. I'm poised to lure the killer towards the back door, then Jonesy will pounce from behind. On paper, it's perfect. But now it must stand the test of practicality. This could go extremely well or … deadly wrong.

"We're right here with you," Jonesy says in the dark, his voice low.

"If it gets too much, just let us know and I'll trade places with you," I reassure her, then grip my metal baseball bat. Jonesy has one too.

"It's fine," Buffy says tightly. "Just stick to the plan and we'll be fine."

Hours pass.

Jonesy insists we remain still and silent. But after so long, Buffy and I get antsy and start whispering. My legs are practically screaming in pain. Jonesy takes no part in our conversation; he stays silent in his corner. I glance at my phone, that I made sure was on silent. 11.43 p.m.

"I'm getting tired," I admit.

Gravel crunches on the driveway.

My heart feels like it stops. Instantly, my hand tightens into a fist around the bat and I hear Jonesy shift. From here, I can only make out Buffy's outline, but she's quickly gotten into place, her head rested on "my" shoulder, watching the TV. It needs to look as natural as possible and I think we've nailed it.

There's another crunch.

And then another.

Between each disturbance, it's pure silence, bar the loud

beats in my chest and the faint ticking of the clock on the mantelpiece.

The door creaks open. An all-too-familiar blue hue cascades into the house.

I make out a silhouette in the doorway. It hovers for a moment. Like they're surveying the room, scanning for life before stepping forward. Slowly but surely, the figure makes their way to Buffy's still frame.

Something glimmers in the dark by their side. There's only one thing it can be.

The blade.

Any moment now.

One last step sees the figure lit by the moonlight streaming in through the window. I can't believe my eyes, even though Cam's seen it in the flesh and I saw the video. The Carrington Ghoul.

It's not every day a ghoul is in your living room. Pale and ghastly. The glowing blue aura. A butcher's blade in hand. The same blade he stabbed Cam with. He takes another step—

Now.

Jonesy hurtles forward, a raw, uncharacteristic sound erupting from him as he does so. He twists the bat in his hand so the butt of it connects with the figure's shoulder; we hear a crack.

That sound snaps me back to reality. This is no ghost – they're a killer and we're going to take them down. It's my turn. With all the courage I can muster, which isn't a lot, I pounce from my hiding spot, bat raised above my head. I swing. It connects with the other shoulder. It emits a similar sound. The ghoul doesn't fight back. Instead, they stagger, seemingly disorientated. They raise a hand … in pain?

The blade wobbles in their hand. Jonesy grabs it from him, reaches to the wall and flicks the light on. The room is suddenly cast in a harsh yellow hue.

"They're not glowing any more," Jonesy notes.

Buffy is standing, her hand on her chest. We stare at the Carrington Ghoul, who isn't glowing at all.

But I *saw* the glow. "Jonesy, turn off the light again."

He frowns, but does it. The light flickers off and suddenly we can see the ghostly aura once again. "Huh?" He flicks the overhead lighting back on and it fades.

"It's a fix," Buffy says.

I nod. "Glow in the dark material if I had to guess. None of this is real."

Jonesy approaches the intruder. They're still stunned, head swaying and barely standing up. "Why don't we ask them ourselves?"

"May I?" I ask – but the intruder bolts.

It all happens so quick it takes me by surprise. We run after them. Jonesy is just ahead. As we hurry into the main hall, we find the ghost lying on the floor by the back door, trapped under a net of some sort.

Jonesy turns to us, a little bit too smug. *So that's what his mechanism does.*

"It worked!" he says, pointing at the limp figure. I swear I can almost make out short mumblings coming from the culprit. Do ghosts mumble?

"I had no doubts at all," I reply with a nervous chuckle. "Where was I?" I hurry over. I can't believe we caught the ghoul without any help from the sheriff. Maybe we have a knack for mystery-solving.

I squat by the figure. They've stopped struggling now. *This is a little disappointing*, I think. But who cares? We have them. I tug at the bottom of the head garment; it comes loose with ease.

"Let's see who you" – I pull it off – "are…"

A fog of silence draws around, suffocating us. You could cut it with a knife.

"And who the hell *is* he?" Buffy says first.

I have no idea. It's just a kid, with his mouth taped shut. He has short brown hair plastered in sweat. He makes muffled sounds, clearly trying to communicate with us. I rip off the tape and he starts talking, fast – too fast to understand.

"Whoa, slow down," Jonesy says, as he joins me in a squat. "Who are you and *why* are you trying to kill us?"

The kid stares back at us. He's got to be younger than us by a few years at least. "I … was…" He struggles to breathe.

Shit.

He *really* can't breathe—

I jump up and run to the kitchen cupboard, rummaging around until I find my dad's spare inhaler. The kid accepts it and takes a few puffs. Instantly his breathing steadies but now he's shaking. A horrible feeling washes over me. Something has gone very wrong.

"OK. Now talk. Why are you trying to kill us?"

"I am not trying to kill you," he offers between short and pained breaths. I hate to admit it but already I can tell it's the truth. He's not our guy. But he knows something. There's no way he doesn't. He's wearing a Robert Carrington costume.

"Then explain. How did you get here?" I fight back disappointment. Of course we couldn't trap Renfield. He figured it out. Of course he did.

"The last thing I remember is walking to school yesterday morning. I'd just gone through the alley by Katrina's – it's a shortcut – and then … nothing."

We all look at each other. The alley is secluded; I've always thought it looks a bit eerie. "But how did you get *here*?"

The boy shudders. "When I came to, I was in a car or truck. I was blindfolded. Whoever it was dragged me out. I could hear a door handle turning – and then they shoved me from behind, put a knife in my hand and told me to walk – that's all I know. My God, my shoulders – I think they're broken."

The desperation in his voice rings true. But I still have so many questions. "You were trying to kill us. You attacked us!"

Instantly, he shakes his head. "I walked in and you pounced!"

I blink. He's right. He never did anything to attack us. All he did was walk like he was told to. Shit. "Do you remember *anything* about this person?" I press, leaning closer.

But all I get in return is a shake of his head. "I was blindfolded until the very last moment. I didn't even recognize the voice. It sounded weird, distorted."

"Great." I seethe, unable to hide my annoyance.

Jonesy joins me, kneeling. "What's your name?" he asks calmly.

The boy blinks. "My name's Trevor. Trevor Ward."

Trevor Ward. I think I mishear him at first. Now, that makes no sense. Actually, it *can't* make sense. Buffy, Jonesy and I stare at each other.

"What?" He looks around at us. Confusion is practically etched into every single crease on his face. "Why did you all go weird when I said my name?"

"Because…" I blink. "You're supposed to be dead."

33

JONESY

I close the kitchen door behind me, leaving Mr Not-So-Dead tied up on the floor. I'm ninety-five per cent sure he's telling the truth but we can't be certain, not just yet. Buffy, Amber and I stare at each other.

There's a moment of shared silence that's laced with a ridiculous amount of confusion. We can't make sense of any of this.

"He's supposed to be dead," I mumble.

Amber sighs. "Well, he looks very much alive to me. The charred body outside the manor clearly wasn't Trevor Ward. So who was it?"

Just another question to add to our ever-growing list.

"Renfield knew we had set a trap," Buffy says, staring at the floor. Her left foot is crossed tightly behind her right. Nerves. "He was never going to come."

That much we've gathered.

"But why send the kid?" I eventually ask.

"He likes playing games, that's clear," Amber says. "Maybe he wanted us to think, just for a moment, that we were ahead."

"Then rip it away at the last second," I continue. "But all the same – faking Trevor's death? Why?"

Silence. None of us can think of an explanation because what logical one could there be? Is Renfield just messing with us? Or is there something else going on?

"We need to take him to the sheriff." My hand reaches for the kitchen door handle but just as I press down, Buffy's hand stops me. "What is it?"

"Can we trust him?" she asks.

And I want to scream at her. *Can we trust you?*

"We can," Amber answers. "Go on, Jonesy."

I finally grip the handle and push it forward. The cold white overhead lights creep through until the door is open fully. I don't remember them being so cold. I swear—

Amber screams. Trevor's eyes are closed and he's limp. Lifeless.

Amber runs to the body and checks his pulse, puts her head to his chest. She gives a sigh of relief. "He's alive. Freaking passed out, that's all."

My heart beats out of my chest. "Way to give us a heart attack. The stress clearly got too much for him. Poor kid."

"So what now, then?" Buffy demands, ushering us on.

"Do we still call the police? An ambulance?" I stare at the slumped body and ponder. And then I see something, hidden in the folds of Trevor's costume.

A piece of paper.

I cross the short distance and pick it up. The others stop bickering and pay attention.

"What is that?"

"I don't know," I respond truthfully. "But I think it's for us." *He* left it for us.

Hesitantly, I unfold the paper. At first, the words swim before my eyes. And then they make sense.

Neat block capitals, in ink. I read aloud.

DO YOU STILL THINK YOU CAN BEST ME?
OUR FINAL DANCE DRAWS NEAR. I REQUEST
YOUR PRESENCE WHERE THE FIRST TWO
TOOK THEIR LAST BREATH. YOU WANTED
TO FIND OUT MORE, DIDN'T YOU? WELL,
YOU'RE ABOUT TO GET YOUR WISH.

MAKE HASTE, FOR TWO OF YOUR OWN ARE
RUNNING OUT OF TIME. WITHIN THE HOUR.

AND I WOULDN'T TELL THE POLICE. NOT IF
YOU WANT TO SEE YOUR FRIENDS AGAIN.
DON'T THINK YOU CAN OUTSMART ME,
BECAUSE I'LL KNOW. I'M WATCHING.

ALWAYS.

I stare at Buffy and Amber. *Two of your own.*

He can't mean Cam, surely. He's protected. He has police outside his hospital room, doctors and nurses.

"He's taken two more victims," says Amber tersely.

I scratch my head. "*Two of your own.* That means we know them. Who else is there—"

"There's something else here," Buffy says, her voice flat. She's crouching by Trevor's body and stands up with... "Another camcorder."

This time we don't dawdle. Buffy flicks the device on. The screen is dark at first, black almost. But then a video plays.

The camera pans across a room, lit by flickering candles. To a terrified woman, bound and gagged, eyes wide. She's in a muddied white blouse and a reddish skirt that's been ripped down the side. Light hair is also dishevelled and partly covering her features. But I know that hair, those eyes.

Our questions are answered.

Cam's mom. Renfield has Cam's mom. But does that mean...

"We need to check on Cam now," Amber announces. "Call the hospital."

The landline falls from my hands and I drop to my knees.

I'm sure my reaction tells the others everything

286

they need to know. The terrified receptionist told me everything.

Cam's been taken.

When his nurse went to check on him an hour ago, his bed was empty. They sounded the alarm. The police have already searched Carrington Manor and there's no sign of Cam.

I know he's there, of course.

He's under their noses, somewhere the police wouldn't know to look. And he needs us. We have no choice but to return. We need to save our friend before it's too late.

There's also Trevor to deal with. He's most likely at least dislocated both shoulders. He needs professional help.

Amber grips my arm. "We're going to get Cam back, I promise," she says. It's almost like she's got to convince herself as much as me.

She wipes my cheek. I didn't even realize I was crying.

I compose myself. "I'm done with this," I say, with sudden anger. "I'm going to *destroy* him."

Buffy bows her head. "This is exactly what he wants."

I look at her, less than impressed. She's the last person I need advice from right now; after that phone call, I know she's hiding something. I want to tell Amber what I overheard but it's not the time. We need to get to Carrington Manor. "What do you mean?" I challenge.

"If we go rushing into that house unfocused, angry,

we will die. If we let our feelings outweigh our common sense, we will die."

I stare at her. She's telling the truth. And truth hurts. Even more so when you can't trust the person for shit.

I take a deep breath.

Buffy rests her hand on my back. It makes me shudder. "Jonesy, I know you're hurting, but we need to be smart about this. And we need to be fast," she announces. "We need to work together. We need to think one step ahead."

Not that they'll believe you anyway. I look at Trevor's unconscious form and draw a shaky breath and nod. "You're right. He's going to try and pin this on us, isn't he?" *Within the hour.*

Buffy nods. "For Cam."

Amber forces a weak smile. "For Cam."

For the first time in a while, my heart lifts with something other than fear. Tonight, this will end. Then I hear a faint police siren sound in the distance. It's brash. They're coming. And when they do, they'll find Trevor's unconscious body.

It's now or never.

"For Cam."

34

CAM

One Hour Earlier

The hospital room is dark except for the stationed cop's reading light. It emits barely any light, but it's enough to keep me up. The idea of asking him to turn it off is a no go though. He's been here all day, keeping me alive; he deserves this time for himself. So I ditch sleep for now – it'll come eventually.

I reach for my phone and scroll through the multiple messages I've sent Jonesy today. At first I was glad the sheriff gave me my phone back but now all it does is plague me. Jonesy's last response was yesterday, about the latest murder. Some kid called Trevor. Since then, it's been crickets. I haven't heard from Buffy or Amber either. I asked the cops about my mom but again, no news.

Appalling thoughts seep into my mind. What if one of my friends has been attacked? No. I'd have found out about it. Cathy wouldn't have kept that from me. Maybe they're doing more research. Maybe they've found something out – something big…

Thoughts whirl around my tired mind. It doesn't help that the silence is deafening now I'm no longer hooked up to anything; I don't have the joys of constant white noise. It feels all wrong. Quiet noises that would once go unnoticed now seem loud. Small creaks, that are most definitely just the noises of the building, are terrifying. My ears are suddenly more sensitive.

That's when I pick up on what I can only guess is a radio. It's only faint. I look around and see the cop pull his radio to his ear to listen.

"Urgent assistance required. Dispatch, please relay: Code 10-66 to all nearby units."

His chair sends a loud shriek across the room as he rises to his feet.

Code 10-66. Whatever it means, it cannot be good. Quicker than I've ever seen him move, the man collects his things and hurries to the door. Officer Prescott, I'm pretty sure. I haven't spoken to him but I've overheard his conversations. I had to do something to pass the time.

The door creaks open. "Hi," Officer Prescott offers. "I've gotta go – emergency."

"What's going on?"

"It's nothing to be worried about." He doesn't sound so sure. Another murder? My throat tightens. He can't leave.

"Are you sending anyone else?" I pour hope into the words.

"I'll get them to send someone up," is all he says before turning on his heel and exiting the room; the silence returns in full force. And now, on top of it, complete darkness.

I miss his annoying-ass reading light. The thought of falling asleep alone now terrifies me. I try to fight the fear but it's futile. Sometimes it's OK to be a baby. And now is one of those times.

I decide I need to turn on the big light.

Feigning confidence, I tug the sheet from myself until my legs are free to swing off the side of the bed. My feet hover over the cold hospital floor as I prepare myself for the run to the switch. It's not far at all but, in the dark, it feels like a marathon. I'm sure it stems from when, as a little kid, I was convinced being under the sheets would keep me safe from monsters. It's a silly thought, but I'd be lying if I said I didn't still slightly believe it.

I brace myself, ready to push myself from the bed. My legs have gone slightly dead from being bedridden.

"Here we go," I whisper to only myself.

And then that's when I feel it.

A hand grabs me from under the bed.

35

JONESY

Composing myself is the hardest part.

Then I do it. I crawl once again through the gap in the shredded iron fence.

As I stand, the dreaded manor peeks through the treeline. It feels bigger than before. Grander. More intimidating, knowing what we do now. We're walking right into a trap, but the price is too high not to. But we have to try. We've got our flashlights, a kitchen knife and a couple of bats. And it's going to have to be enough.

So much for making a plan.

I grab Amber's hand as she passes through the gap and haul her to her feet; Buffy is close behind. They look up at Carrington Manor with similar expressions of dread. We really were naïve enough to think we'd caught him. Of course it wasn't going to be that easy.

We make our ascent.

"We're doing this," Buffy says. Her voice shakes a bit, but I'm glad she's talking. I've had enough of the silence and the waiting.

"Whatever happens in there," Amber says, "I'm proud of us."

I nod. "Why's that? Wait, let me guess. Is it because if we were in a horror movie, we've made it to the final act?" It's a joke, clearly. Inside, I'm trembling. But as Cam's not here to lighten the mood, someone needs to. We'll get nowhere if we're all scared shitless without any relief.

"No," Amber says. "Though that is true. I was referring to how badass we are."

"Are we?" Buffy says, with a nervous laugh. "I don't feel very badass."

Amber is forced to explain. "Come on, you two. We took it upon ourselves, against our best judgement, to try and solve a murder – murders! Plural! And we got closer than the police ever did. We're here. We're going to try and save our friend."

I'm glad she's being positive but I can't feel the same way. The key word there is "try". Like we *tried* to trap Renfield – but we failed. Now Cam, and his mom, have been taken again and the Carrington Ghoul is still at large. My gaze drifts from the girls to the house that is looming ever closer. It seems like it's growing with each step we take, more so than it should. Its presence is astounding and terrifying all at once.

And suddenly I can't go one step further. Not without knowing if I can trust the people by my side.

I stop. The girls notice immediately and they turn to me. Buffy's green eyes meet mine.

"Buffy, I overheard your phone call," I mutter. My hand tightens around the weapon in my hand.

Amber steps towards me. "Whoa, Jones," she says. "What are you talking about?" Her eyes drop to my trembling hand. "Calm down…"

"Ask Buffy," I say, eyes fixed. "Buffy, tell Amber about what you're hiding. I knew I couldn't trust you. I knew you were keeping something from us. I heard you say as much on the phone. You said: 'Amber and Cam are fine. But Jonesy still doesn't trust me. I've tried everything but I can't crack him. He's a tricky one.' And that you didn't want us to suspect you."

Buffy's mouth falls open. "I…" She stutters on her words. She's been caught out. She looks incredibly guilty.

"Buffy?" Amber says. She steps away from her. "What is he talking about?"

"It's not what he thinks, I promise!"

"Then what should he think?" Amber combats, her voice slightly raised.

Buffy sighs, looks towards the manor, to us, and to the floor. "Fine," she offers as she wipes her hand across her eyes. "I *have* been lying to you about something. But it's not what you think, Jonesy."

I wait.

"I didn't move here because my mom got a job she couldn't pass up. I moved here to … get away from my old town. From my old school."

There's a beat. I can see her struggling to say more. "Come on, out with it!" I snap. It's not like me but I've had enough. My best friend, my everything, is inside that manor and we can't waste time. But I can't go in if I can't trust Buffy.

Amber presses. "Buffy. Please."

Buffy releases a sharp breath. "At my old school my best friend died." I see a tear form. It glints in the moonlight as it crests and falls down her face. "She fell down a flight of stairs at school, when it was just the two of us. She'd had a heart condition all her life and the doctors said she must have had a heart attack. But I was with her at the time so everyone's heads turned towards me. There was an investigation. We had our problems, argued quite a bit, so it looked suspicious. I know that. In the end, I was cleared, but school was never the same. Everyone thought I was a killer, that I murdered my best friend…" Her words trail out as more tears fall.

I look at Amber and back to Buffy. "Why did you not tell us? Why keep it a secret all this time?"

"I … I was too scared. At first."

Amber goes to Buffy, puts out a hand, wipes away the wetness.

She continues. "I would have told you all eventually, but then Brad and Shelley happened. I thought it would make me look guilty, if I told you when you knew there was a killer on the loose." She sniffles. Her gaze is wide and utterly sincere. "I told my mom I was scared you wouldn't trust me if I did. She encouraged me to be honest. That's the phone call you overheard, Jonesy."

Shit. She's telling the truth.

Amber wipes her face again. "That's why you wanted to help so much," she says gently. "You wanted to help Brad and Shelley because you couldn't help your friend."

Buffy slowly nods. "I'm sorry. I'm so sorry. I just—"

Amber pulls her into an embrace, cutting her off. "You have nothing to be sorry about. It's a complicated situation, we see that now. What was her name?"

"Nancy." She lets out a shaky breath. "I really miss her."

"Buffy," I say. "I'm sorry for attacking you like that. I didn't know."

Carefully, she untangles herself from Amber until she's looking directly at me. "It's fine, really. I shouldn't have hidden it from you for so long – because now isn't the best time to be having this real talk." There's strain in her voice. "But in case anything happens to me in there…" She gulps. "I just want to say that these past two weeks, while truly awful, have been at least bearable because of all of you…"

My heart warms. "Buffy—"

"Let me finish, please. You didn't need to take me into your gang, but you did, and I'm grateful. I'm sorry for convincing you to start all this in the first place. And, Jonesy, good job on listening to your gut. You knew something was up with me from the start." She throws the last sentence in there quickly, clearly a little more nervous to say it, but it makes me laugh. I needed that. "I'm sorry I lied to you. I really want to be your friend, if you'll let me."

"I wouldn't have it any other way," Amber says first. She loops her arm through Buffy's.

We stand in silence for a moment, and I feel warm inside. Probably the warmest I've felt for days. I'm not sure where my next words come from. "Time and time again, life proves that, through the darkest of times, light can pass through the cracks."

Amber snorts. "Calm down, Aristotle." Through the dark, I see her nudge Buffy. "Pretentious, much? He's still annoyed that you're smarter than him, Buffy."

I tut. "Love you too. But I was never *that* jealous."

Buffy grins. "I thought it was beautifully put, thank you."

We're smiling as we turn to face the manor. If we stand any chance of doing this, it's together.

Eventually, our ascent is complete. We stand, side by side, in front of Carrington Manor, just like we did a few days ago. Except this time, we're missing a person.

Last time Buffy took the first step and led the pack. This time, it's different. Without even assessing the situation, we all step forward together. As one. United.

"We stick together this time," I remind them.

"Yeah. *No* splitting up," Amber says in a stern voice.

I think that is definitely something we can all agree on.

And with that, we bound up the rest of the front steps, knowing that if we stop for any longer the fear will crescendo and become unmanageable.

No more stalling. No more waiting. Only action.

The stone stairs are once again silent beneath our feet. But the silence is loud, somehow. Renfield knows we're here – I'm sure of it. He's probably watching. That much is clear now. All the times we thought we were being inconspicuous … we were wrong.

The aged door creaks open as we reach the top, but no one is there to greet us. Thank God.

"Well, isn't that inviting," Amber says.

"It's just the wind," I suggest, smiling knowingly. I don't think it was *ever* just the wind. The house is alive or something – if not, our minds are.

It's quiet. A little too quiet. Where is he hiding? We know of one secret passageway. And one secret passageway suggests that there's more. Could Renfield be in the walls this minute, waiting?

We all stop outside, expecting something to jump out, but no one comes. Instead, my gaze lifts upward. The bay window above is in view and – for now – clear. Only the reflection of the moon shows itself in the glass. Even that freaks me out.

"I'm going in," I finally force out. I push ahead. My steps are hesitant at first but they quicken as a cool chill whips the back of me, as if Mother Nature is ushering me to my demise. *Dark.* I don't turn but I can hear the girls' footsteps behind me. It's comforting.

Inside the hall, we stop and look around.

Every door is closed this time, proving that someone – Renfield – has been here since. And something tells me it's not to keep out a draft. Is Renfield behind one of them, ready to pounce? Or, more importantly, are Cam and his mom?

Slowly, we form a tight circle. It's not even something we have to discuss. We can't have a single corner of the room unwatched. It's a death sentence otherwise. We move cautiously into the room and, as we pass the fireplace with the poker lever, Amber grabs a candlestick and shoves it in her back pocket. Not the most dangerous weapon but the more weapons the better.

"Where would he be?" Buffy whispers as we reach the centre of the room. Around us, we can see everything. The crest of the stairs, every door, and … the exit. It is all cast in a cold light, only lit by the moon like before.

"Upstairs?" Amber suggests. "Or … down there."

She doesn't need to specify where she means by

"down there" because it's obvious. I hope to all gods that Cam's not down there. The number of hidden rooms underground is probably endless. We could be trapped.

"I say we go up—"

A loud, roaring guffaw rips through the house. The room shakes and the doors rattle from the pure volume. *Renfield*. I hear a tinkling mixed in with the echoing laugh from … above. My gaze rips upward, just in time—

I push Buffy to the floor just as a chandelier comes crashing to the ground. We hit the floor with a hard thud and glass rains down. Our screams combine with the sounds of shattering crystals. Amber is at our side in seconds, hauling us to our feet one by one. Buffy holds her shoulder, wincing. She must've hit it as I pushed her aside. Better a sore shoulder than being crushed to death.

I didn't go unscathed either. My eyes catch a sparkle in my arm – a chunk of glass embedded deep, through the sleeve. I breathe slowly, grip the shard with precise fingers and, clenching my teeth, pull it out. It hurts like hell but it's necessary. Blood runs down my arm as I push up the sleeve.

"You need that covered," Buffy says, eyeing the wound.

I nod, looking around for anything I can use. It's less than ideal but I end up taking off a shoe, pulling my sock off my foot, and wrapping it around my arm; Buffy passes me a hair tie to keep it in place. It'll have to do.

We retrieve our weapons and return to our huddle,

now even more shaken up as we gaze up at the stairs. The knife is cold in my hand. The thought of having to use it terrifies me. Amber clutches her bat. Buffy hers too. But that terrible laugh still echoes in my ears.

I notice something then; a warm light is mixed in with the cold. It comes from behind us. As one, we all turn.

"What the…"

A candelabra affixed to the wall is lit. It flickers as the draught from the front door hits it. And then—

The next candelabra lights.

And then the next.

Our heads whip from candle to candle until every single wick is alight and the room is filled with candlelight. My stomach turns at the strangeness. Even if the Carrington Ghoul is a fake, how do we explain this?

"Hey, everyone," Amber says softly.

I'm too busy inspecting the room to reply. I can't help but think we're missing something obvious. The flames must be fake or maybe—

"Hey!"

I whip my head around to Amber. "What is it?"

She's looking in the direction of the main staircase. Nothing is different at the base of the stairs, so I trace them up, one by one, the anticipation brewing like a kettle on an open flame. It's when my gaze reaches the top of the stairs that my breath hitches. Through the banisters, I see … legs.

Without even thinking, I falter back, my hands instinctively bringing the girls with me. *No kid left behind.*

At the top of the stairs waits a figure, watching us. A dark silhouette.

Carrington. Renfield. One and the same? The time has come. The final showdown. The third act. It's all led up to this.

"We're here," I shout. "We came, just like you wanted. Now show us Cam!" My voice strains as the possibilities cross my mind. I force myself to focus. While we're distracted, someone could take us out. Who's to say Renfield's working alone? The thought of a second Renfield never even crossed my mind … until now. On that thought, I band closer to the others. They seem to get the memo.

Renfield angles his head at our words. He's wearing the same rusty black suit. He glows with the same eerie blue light. *But it's fake,* I tell myself. All an act. What Cam saw, the video Amber saw – it was never a real ghost.

"You're right on time," Renfield finally says, his voice reverberating throughout the room. His words come softly but leave an impression.

Amber takes a step forward. "Give us Cam and his mom and we'll leave you alone. We won't tell anyone what we found here." It's true. At this point, I would take Cam and leave without saying a word if it meant he got out of here safe. Selfish, I know.

But something tells me we're in too deep for that.

Instead of answering Amber, Renfield does the unexpected. He takes a step forward.

He walks down the stairs slowly, as if floating. My hand tightens on the knife. I know it's time. Everything becomes certain. My hairs stand on end.

"I have to say," his words echo as he slowly makes his descent, still in the shadows, "I was impressed by your deductions. And your tenacity."

My blood runs cold. His voice is low, chilling, yet forced. *With something familiar about it too*, I think. I know it from somewhere.

"Don't give me this Carrington crap. We know you're a fake, *Renfield*," says Buffy firmly. "Lovely home you have here. Been looking for anything?"

A pause and then he chuckles again. It's horrible and raw. "Oh, you already know the answer to that one… I had always heard stories of Robert Carrington's hidden treasure. I suspected those stories were true, if the right person were to look. Lovely Mrs Adler likes talking about the past, but you know that." Through the dark, his eyes penetrate.

Always one step ahead.

"So, what?" Amber presses. "You bought the house and started tunnelling? Killed kids just for some treasure that may or may not exist?"

"Oh, it exists," he coos.

I blink. Did he find it?

But Amber's not finished. "You're obsessed with Carrington. Compiled a whole book of notes on him. Which is weird. You're, what, Robert Carrington's biggest fan?"

"*Fan* is the wrong word, Amber." Hearing her name on his lips terrifies me. My eyes dart past Carrington into the gloom beyond. Cam and his mom must be hidden here somewhere. *Where. Are. They?*

"Is it?"

"Yes. So imprecise. I think … *sympathizer* is a more suitable descriptor."

"Sympathizer?" I say, wanting to keep him talking while I listen for any sound, scan for any clue that Cam and his mom are nearby. Try to keep Renfield onside. He holds Cam's life in the palm of his hand. I can't risk that.

"Yes. You see, Robert Carrington, he was a wronged man." Another step. "He grew resentful of Sanera, and for good reason. The townsfolk let his sick family die. And they hated Robert. He was their landlord and they despised him for it. I believe they set the fire that killed him. Let him burn to death. I wanted to avenge him. But then I learned of the treasure. No one else was clever enough to look. To wonder where his vast wealth went. It was only fitting that it should be mine. The only person in this ridiculous town who really understood Carrington and his legacy."

All three of us exchange glances.

"So you are killing people to get back at—"

Another step, but it lands with heft. Angrily. "I am making it right. An eye for an eye. Robert's family deserves justice, too. The treasure is just a bonus, a reward for avenging him, if you will," Renfield bites, now halfway down the stairs. A few more steps, he'll be in view.

"I used to come here when I was a kid – about your age. I was fascinated by the Carrington Ghoul, like all the other fools in this town. It opened my eyes to who the real villains in the world are."

"Who are the real villains?" Amber asks.

"The imbecilic townsfolk of Sanera," says Renfield.

"That fire was said to be an accident," Buffy says.

"It simply does not matter what they said!" Renfield screams. And something clicks. His voice. The tone, the cadence, I've heard it before. I hear it daily. "You must pay attention! They were selfish. An innocent person died."

"Do you even hear yourself?" I say, forgetting about appeasing him. "'An innocent person died', you say. How about the innocents *you* killed?"

He releases a short gruff noise in response before taking another step down. He's so close it aches. The tip of his chin goes in and out of the light, teasing us.

"All those kids, using the manor for their own ends. Drinking. Worse. For years I didn't mind – it suited me for people to think Carrington Manor was a joke, while

I conducted my research. But then I realized the treasure was not just a theory. It had to exist and I could feel I was close. So I let people see me in windows, in the shadows, and eventually they stopped coming. Then I found the first secret passage, though it was nothing like they are now. Robert sure liked to play games. When Brad and Shelley turned up, playing at being ghost hunters, I knew they'd investigate the whole house. I'd had enough. I couldn't risk them foiling my plan when I was so close to my prize. The first two were easy enough; they didn't even fight it. It was so easy that I put out my fire and … what do you kids say? *Went to town?*

"I hoped their deaths would serve as a warning and it would end there. But then there was Kenny. Oh, pathetic Kenny. Couldn't risk him storming up here with a bunch of other youths." He laughs. "He wasn't so confident in the end, I can tell you."

"And why Cam?" I ask. "And his mom?"

He laughs again, causing me to grit my teeth. "I was waiting for you to bring them up… They were the most fun. Cam's mother was passing and she saw me drive up to the manor. I couldn't have her putting two and two together. No, no, no. Too risky. As for Cam, he may have heard my allergies that first night, cursed Sanera pollen! I couldn't be certain, but it wasn't worth the chance. Also, I couldn't have him telling the foolish sheriff's office about the entrance to my tunnels. He didn't even put up a fight at the hospital. Some guards *they* were, too. It's actually quite humorous how incompetent they are."

"Get his name out of your mouth!" I scream. At my words, I feel Buffy's hand fall on to my shoulder. She's telling me to keep it together. To stay calm. But this is *Cam*. I don't think I can be calm.

Amber takes over for me. "What about Trevor? Why fake his death? And how?"

Renfield waves his hand airily. "You'll be surprised what cops will fall for if they're presented with a charred body and a missing kid. The rumour mill does it all for you. But sending Trevor to you was merely a distraction to keep you at bay while I took Cam. I called a fake Code 10-66 to get his "guards" away. It was just so easy, it's laughable. I *did* laugh, watching you come up with your silly trap. Thinking you could capture me – when, all along, you were always coming here tonight. I sent the police to Amber's, away from Cam all at once, to get you here even quicker. Just. So. Easy."

"Trevor will tell Sheriff Rogers about you. He knows. We talked to him!"

A slow maniacal trickle leaves his throat. "The boy is terrified. He won't say anything as long as I'm alive."

What the fuck? Did Trevor know more than he let on? I don't know what to believe any more. But the charred body— "Who else did you kill?"

Another laugh. "Amber, I heard about your little visit

to Sanera's mortgage lender's. Abigail told you everything, didn't she? Or she *thought* she did. If she'd followed the paper trail, she'd have realized who really bought this house. I couldn't have that now, could I?"

I swallow.

"You killed Abigail because she could prove who you are?" asks Amber, trembling.

"I wouldn't have bothered with her if you hadn't gone sniffing around, making her wonder about the house sale. After you left her, she started digging again, and I couldn't have that. It seemed she was having some guilty thoughts. Poor Abigail! So you can blame yourself for Abigail's death, Amber."

No, I think. This isn't Amber's fault. It's all on Renfield. Everything is *his* fault.

"How does this end for you? For us?" Buffy hides her tremor well.

"I think you know. I'm not going to let you leave. It's going to be so easy to pin this all on you, Buffy. Did you really think you'd get away from your old secret?" He glances at me. "Besides, Jonesy would never leave without his love."

I'm going to kill him.

Buffy tightens her grip on my shoulder again and I force a breath.

"Where are they?" I ask with a sudden new-found sense of calm. Buffy's right: I have to bury my fury. For now.

A step down. "How about I take you to him?" Another step. "But first … why don't we introduce ourselves properly? It's only polite, after all."

He steps forward and pulls down the scarf that covers his face.

It takes a moment for my eyes to adjust, the moonlight an unreliable light source. But when they do, Renfield's face comes into focus. My heart stops and my knees almost buckle beneath me. I trace back through the past fortnight, replaying every moment and discovery in disbelief. This whole time, he's been right under our noses.

Mr Graham stares back at us. "Surprised to see me?"

36

AMBER

"Mr Graham?" I say, my voice raspy. "If that even is your name."

His mouth upturns into a wide grin I've not seen from him before. It seems I didn't know a lot about my history teacher.

"Oh, it's my real name. Renfield was just a cover. I couldn't have my name tied to this house, could I? You can only make so much of a mortgage private. And Dracula's biggest follower and believer seemed like the perfect alias. As he served his master, so I serve mine."

Master? He really is messed up.

"How did you do it?" Buffy asks. Her tone is admiring and I know she's playing for time. "The ghoul was so believable. So real."

"You'd be surprised by the fun things you can find in

the drama department. Glow in the dark paint really goes a long way." He points to the candles that lit by themselves. "And those? Simple electric candles, on a timer. We use them all the time on stage. But you really should have seen your faces."

"You're sick," I fire back.

"Ah, ah, ah –" he wags his finger – "remember I have your friend. If you want to see him again—"

"She didn't mean that," Jonesy interrupts. Our eyes meet. I did mean that. Obviously. But we'd better not anger the serial killer. Not until we have Cam and his mom back.

"We want to see them," I force out. "Please."

"Very good, Amber," Mr Graham says approvingly, like I've just nailed a tricky question in a history quiz. "Manners *are* important."

"Why?" Jonesy says quietly. "Why?"

"I told you. Robert Carrington was misunderstood. The people around here hated him. I believe the townsfolk set the fire that killed him themselves. Half the people in this town are their descendants. They should be punished." He smiles. "And then there's the treasure. Do you think I like being a poorly paid history teacher in this miserable town? Teaching you idiotic kids? No. I've spent my whole life in Sanera. This was my ticket out of here. I wanted to go out with a bang, though. Make sure no one ever returned to Carrington Manor again – and they won't. Not after tonight. Not after another tragic fire in which more foolish children die. Why do you think I sent you all those clues, the camcorder, the book? I wanted to make sure you were here tonight. To witness the Carrington Ghoul's final showdown."

I swallow. *Final showdown*. Something tells me we're going to have a front seat.

"Now, enough conversation. Why don't you follow me?"

"To where?" Buffy asks, voice just about level.

"Ah, you're not so smart any more, are you?" he taunts. "You're not as clever as you think, Miss Allen."

"Is he in the tunnels?" I ask.

"They're handy, aren't they?" he says. "Instantly, I knew the treasure was down there somewhere, buried. Where else would you hide your riches if not hidden away from the naked eye?"

Mr Graham steps forward to where an ornate box stands on a shelf. I hadn't noticed it when we first walked in but it's heavy, inlaid with gold. It's not exactly big. Mrs Adler suggested Robert's money was now in the form of gold… I don't think you could fit much gold in there. So what *does* he have?

"I found it, at last. Hidden in one of the secret false walls. I waited, though. I want to see your reaction when I finally get what is rightfully mine, what I have worked for so many years for. And it's finally time to…"

Mr Graham approaches the box, his expression hungry. We could probably run and he'd be too caught in the moment to realize. But Cam and his mom are still here. Somewhere.

"My entire life has led to this," he mutters, his fingers on the clasp.

It pops. He lifts up the lid.

His face freezes.

"What?" All of a sudden, he's panicked. He tips the box upside down, holds it up against the light, clearly perplexed. "It was supposed to – where is it?!"

Buffy, Jonesy and I catch each other's glances. There we go. Maybe that theory of Mrs Adler's about the gold really is true. But that means it's still out there somewhere. What happens now?

For a moment, Mr Graham simply stares, aghast. Then his gaze snaps back to us and roars, "We're going upstairs."

I open my mouth to snap a witty remark but I see it for the first time – the glint of the butcher's blade tucked into his belt. I'm not taking that risk.

"Don't try anything," he says. "You won't make it – and your friend Cam definitely won't."

Jonesy nods. "We won't try anything," he promises.

Mr Graham jerks his head and, slowly, we start to climb the stairs, with him walking behind us. I glance back at the half-open front door. It's so tempting. We could run and get help. But it's useless. Cam would be dead before the police even got here. We have to stick it out now. *For Cam*, I remind myself.

At the top of the stairs, he gestures to us to walk on, all the way to the end of the hall, right by where we found the camcorder – the camcorder he left for us – and to the final door on the left.

"Robert Carrington's bedroom," Buffy says quietly.

His voice behind us is gloating. "That's right. I thought it only fitting that it would end here. Treasure or not."

The final showdown.

Another blaze, claiming four more children's lives – only, this time, Carrington Manor will be razed to the ground. For once and for all. And we'll be to blame.

But if he burns down the manor, his chance of finding the treasure might be lost for ever. Maybe he's slipped up and overlooked that detail. Or maybe, though, he just wants us to suffer in agony even more than he wants Carrington's gold. One thing is certain: he is one sick teacher.

Jonesy looks back to us and then to Mr Graham. "Is Cam in there?"

Mr Graham smiles coldly as he pulls a long, rusted bronze key from his pocket. A slight scrape on the keyhole makes me cringe. "Why don't you see for yourselves?"

Of course, Jonesy takes the handle in his grip and slowly opens the door.

And we follow.

For Cam.

We walk into the dark room together, like we promised before we entered the manor. It's vast. I can just about make out two chairs in the centre of the room, a four-poster bed, thick swathes of curtains, a wardrobe.

A light flickers and the room is cast in a weak yellow glow. Most of the room, however, is still in darkness, but the chairs, where I expect us to find Cam and his mom ... are empty.

Two loosely coiled lengths of unravelled rope lie abandoned, one on one of the chairs, the other on the floor.

I glance at Mr Graham, whose expression is as shocked as ours. Hope flares in my chest. Did Cam get away?

Jonesy laughs. "Someone never learned how to tie a *good* constrictor knot," he says, voice laced with the same sarcasm that was dished out by Mr Graham. Let's see how he likes it.

"Huh?" Mr Graham storms in, glances at the empty chairs and begins scanning the room. "That little shit..." From here, I practically witness the cogs in his mind whirring. But then his expression changes and, before I can move, he has Buffy in an iron grip, butcher's blade to her throat. That freaking blade!

A gasp escapes my lips.

She struggles but it's no use. A seventeen-year-old girl is no match for a full-grown adult male, especially one with a blade. She tries to let out a yelp but nothing comes. He's crushing her windpipe. She won't have long.

"Cameron! Come out or your little friend gets it!" he calls out, eyes scanning every corner of the room. His voice is disgusting to the ear, pure evil-sounding. The bedroom is lit by just one tall candelabra in the centre of the room, so the outer edges remain gloomy and the wardrobes and thick curtains create shadows. Another one of his stupid magic tricks. Him and his theatrics. It's worked against him this time. The shadows are a great place to hide.

I realize Jonesy is staring directly at me. His eyes dart briefly behind me, and back to me. He's seen something. *Cam.* I nod at Jonesy and we begin to piece together our silent plan.

"Come on, Cameron!" Mr Graham seethes, his teeth bared. "You wouldn't want me to hurt her, would you?" The blade presses against Buffy's throat and she lets out a little cry. A drop of blood forms and trickles down. The treasure still eludes him and he's killed four people. He has nothing left to lose. We don't have long…

I watch as Mr Graham turns slowly in a circle. One last step and I'll be close enough—

"There!" Jonesy points to the other side of the room. Mr Graham whips round, turning away from me, and I take the risk. Buffy twists, just as I smash my foot on to the candelabra and the room succumbs to the darkness. I hear the door slam shut. Cam?

I wish I could say it was an even playing field but

Mr Graham still has a knife. I'd say it's more like a battlefield.. But it's four against one; I prefer our odds. Maybe even five if Cam's mom is able.

Thuds commence. What they are and who they belong to are a mystery. I hear Buffy scream, which tells me she's free from Mr Graham's grasp. I hope.

I hurry in what I hope is the direction of the door and grope around until I find the cool metal of the handle. I fling it open. Faint moonlight filters into the room. Buffy is in the corner, clutching at her neck and breathing hard, but there's no more blood. She'll be fine. Jonesy stumbles to his feet, his gaze on two people wrestling on the floor. Mr Graham and Cam, locked in a furious fight.

I scan the room for the blade and see it's been thrown across the room. Mr Graham has resorted to punching Cam, who fights back with as much force as he possibly can. I can see red trickling through his hospital gown. *It's just broken stitches*, I try to convince myself. But Cam's not strong enough for this and I don't know how much longer he can last.

I run for the blade, but Jonesy is there first. He grips it and turns. I've never seen his eyes so focused, so devoid of emotion, and they only look more steely when he holds the blade above Mr Graham. It shakes in his grip, probably from holding it so tight. With a swift motion, the blade comes roaring down—

It flies across the room.

Mr Graham kicks Jonesy again and he falls to the floor. Shit. Shit. Shit.

I look back and Cam is groaning on the floor, trying to get up but unable to move. But Mr Graham has shifted his focus now. To Jonesy.

He doesn't even look for the blade, just leaps on Jonesy and closes his hands around my friend's throat. Slowly, he begins to squeeze.

I need to do something.

So I do.

I grab the abandoned butcher's blade. The blade that killed four people. It is wet in my hand. It feels wrong. It's covered in blood – someone must've been cut in the commotion.

But I can't think about that right now. With swift steps, I reach a struggling Jonesy. Large hands are wrapped around his neck, the pressure beginning to turn him purple.

I breathe in. Slow and steady. After this, I can't go back.

"Do it!" Buffy yells, her voice hoarse.

And then I plunge the blade down, right towards the small of Mr Graham's back – when a hand shoots up and catches my wrist.

It seems our dorky teacher is a lot stronger and more determined than we thought. He wrenches the blade from my hand and I cry out at the pain in my wrist, stumble back. He still has Jonesy pinned beneath him and Cam is still whimpering on the floor.

Think, Amber, think.

Wait—

I reach behind me, into the pocket of my jeans, and my fingers close around the cold metal of the candlestick. And I've never been so happy to have this stupid-ass weapon. Without even thinking, I lift it high above my head and bring it down with as much force as I can muster. A *crack* sounds as it makes contact with Mr Graham's head.

He keels over, and Jonesy wriggles out from under him, so that Mr Graham sprawls on his back. We watch as a pool of red spreads around the top part of his body.

"We need the blade," I whisper.

"What?" Jonesy croaks.

"Every horror movie ever," I say, edging over to the butcher's blade. It's slick in my hands. "The villain comes back for one last scare." It sounds ridiculous to still be comparing this to every horror movie ever. But when it turns out our mild-mannered history teacher is behind all the killings? If you had told me this last week, I would have told you to come up with something better. But here we are, and I'm not taking any chances. I kneel down next to Mr Graham's limp body—

His eyes shoot open, rage swirling inside.

Everything slows down. I realize two things.

I have to save my friends.

And, after this, I can't go back.

I don't let him get up.

I fall on to all fours, hyperventilating. "I killed him," I mutter between breaths.

Cam groans and coughs. I find Buffy at my side, holding my head up. "It was self-defence," she whispers. "Amber? You did what you had to do. You saved us."

I saved them. It was self-defence. But it doesn't matter. I still killed someone.

"Amber, breathe." Jonesy appears by my side. He holds my hand in his. "It's all over. We're safe." His voice is still hoarse.

"You," Cam says through short breaths. "You came for me." He sounds barely conscious. We need to get help, fast.

Jonesy goes to lift him up but Cam calls out, "Mom!" In all the commotion, I've almost forgotten Cam's mom is here somewhere. "She's…" His voice trails out but he raises his hand and points towards the back wall.

My eyes follow his trembling finger to find an aged fireplace, and beside it a coal scuttle and a brass bucket full of pokers.

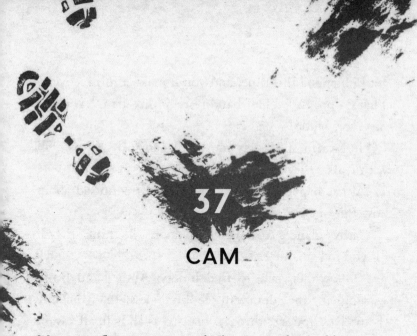

37

CAM

My eyes flutter open and I'm instantly grabbing my stomach in pain. A firm hand swats me away.

"Stop touching the stitches!"

The familiar voice confuses me. And it's now I realize where I am. The hospital. I remember suddenly – Mr Graham.

I try to sit up and again am batted down. "Cathy, is that you?" I say as I squint, my eyes still adjusting to the harsh fluorescent lights. Eventually, it becomes easier to make out the shapes and I recognize the small woman ahead of me. My shoulders relax at the sight of her.

"Reunited with my favourite patient. You look awful," she comments.

I laugh. "I feel it too."

"Well, I've upped your doses. Just stay in bed, don't

get kidnapped this time, and you'll make a full recovery. That's a promise." Her hand rests on my arm. "You're a survivor, kiddo."

Her warm smile sets me off. I can feel my eyes fill with tears.

"What happened?" I finally ask, still confused about how I got here. "Where's my mom?"

Cathy glances towards the door. "I think they'll fill you in."

I follow her gaze to find Jonesy, Amber and Buffy waiting in the doorway, looking less than healthy themselves. Jonesy's throat is bruised as all hell; all I want to do is hold him. But that'll have to wait. Buffy has a small bandage on her own throat.

And then … Amber. Physically, she looks fine, but there's something off. Amber has always been the moral compass for the group. She's a good person and she was forced to do a terrible thing.

They all filter in. Buffy's hand rests on the door, ready to close it, when someone else puts a hand out to stop it.

Mom. I don't believe my own eyes at first. She's here. Finally.

She steps into the room and I melt. I've never seen her so dishevelled, so torn up. She has bandages on her head and neck and her right arm is in a cast. As soon as our eyes meet, the crying begins. "Oh, Cam. I am so sorry," she says through wails, wrapping me in her arms.

She has nothing to be sorry about. But that's a mother's guilt talking.

The next four hours speed past.

We talk and talk. Talk about how Mr Graham became so obsessed with finding the treasure and avenging Robert Carrington's death that he murdered four innocent people and destroyed their families.

Brad.

Shelley.

Kenny.

Abigail.

Mom sits silent through all this until, at last, she says, "You did this all on your own? You kids are incredible."

"But the treasure is still missing," I say.

"Good," Jonesy adds quickly. "It's caused nothing but pain."

He's right, but the thought of it, all that money hidden away somewhere so close by … it would be silly to say I wasn't tempted to go and look for it. But that's for another day. Right now I need to heal. Physically and mentally.

A knock comes at the door. Everyone's head shoots to the origin of the noise, all clearly still on high alert.

Sheriff Rogers pokes his head through. "Hope you don't mind," he offers, stepping inside. "I wanted to come and see how you were all getting on. You've had a … wild night." *A wild night.* Like we haven't just taken down a serial killer? Like we haven't saved Sanera from losing even more people?

"Yeah, you're welcome," I say. "By the way, I guess someone had to stop this and it wasn't going to be you." It's a little rude, sure, but whatever.

The sheriff freezes and begins to chew on his bottom lip. Then he says, "You're right."

I blink. "Sorry?"

Sheriff Rogers comes further into the hospital room until he's only a few feet away from all of us. His eyes are bloodshot and sunken. He's clearly having a rough time. "We weren't ready for this," he says truthfully.

"Four teenagers did your job better than you," Mom snaps. "You should apologize." She glares at the sheriff.

He chuckles nervously. "I mean, we did our best. It's been a hell of a couple of weeks. But you kids should be proud. Sometimes it's under your nose the entire time."

A hell of a couple of weeks? I lose it then. I tell the sheriff exactly what I think of him. I use colourful words and Mom doesn't even tell me to watch my language. In the end, he doesn't offer an apology. It would be useless anyway. We don't want it. He leaves the room with his tail between his legs.

Mom swallows. "I'll never forgive them for not protecting you, Cam."

I'm not sure I will either.

Jonesy grabs my hand then. "Hey, it's all over now."

A door bangs and we all jump again. Then Amber says, seriously, "It's just the wind." We laugh and I watch as Mom looks down at Jonesy's hand on mine. A small gesture, but it tells her everything. The smallest actions can have the loudest messages. She looks between us, a faint smile on her lips.

"Why are you looking so corny?" I say.

"You don't realize it do you?" she murmurs. "What you kids have is special. Not many adults, let alone teenagers, could do what you've accomplished these past weeks. You've saved so many lives. You saved *me*."

I scoff in relief ... and disbelief. Did we seriously just get applauded by my mom for risking our lives? Praise is not exactly what I was expecting. "I thought you were going to be furious with us."

"Oh, I am," she says, suddenly sterner. "But you can't deny the service you've done for Sanera. I don't even want to think about what would've happened if that *teacher* had got away with it."

Mom puts her warm hand in mine. Now both of them are occupied by the people I care for most. It makes me smile. Truly. For the first time in weeks, I don't feel like I have to watch everything I do, everywhere I go. I can breathe again ... even if it does currently hurt to do so. Metaphorically, maybe.

"I think you should do something with what you have," Mom suggests, motioning to the four of us.

Buffy frowns. "What we have?"

"Together you took down a serial killer when the entire sheriff's office couldn't. There's something there for you guys and I don't think you should pass it up. You'd be silly not to do it."

I blink at Mom's suggestion. "Are you saying we *should* put ourselves in danger again?" I ask uncertainly. Because surely I'm hearing her wrong.

"Not every case you take on has to be a serial killer. Maybe you could find a missing artefact or – oh, I don't know," she says, flustered, "solve cases. But I think you could do great things. Together."

We're laughing again then, at the absurdity of it all. I don't know how easy it'll be to find *cases*. But whatever way life dares take us, I'm willing to follow it – with these guys by my side.

EPILOGUE

BUFFY

Three Months Later

Macey snores in my lap; I watch intently as her chest rises up and down. Never have I ever seen her this calm. Normally, it's all go, go, go. I think she's getting used to me.

I glance up from the gorgeous dog to Amber on the couch opposite. Her eyes are focused on the new laptop her parents bought for her. After the whole ordeal last year, they were less than impressed, as was my mom. But everyone else in town was singing our praises and holding celebrations in our names. Our parents came around to it eventually. Amber's parents gave her a laptop to apologize. Her own laptop. Let's just say we all have borrowed it at some point.

"What are you doing on there?" I ask, unable to see the screen.

"Trying to think of our mission statement." She throws her hands out when saying the words, like she's painting it for me. It's not necessary. I *do* know what a mission statement is.

"Why do we need one?" I ask. "Everyone in Sanera knows us. They know what we're capable of."

She sighs. "We can't limit ourselves to Sanera! Do you not want to help people in other places? Not everyone is going to have heard of us."

I chuckle at her words. Amber has made a lot of progress over the last few months. Being on the other end of the knife and dealing the killing blow really messed her up. It would anybody, but Amber especially. She's a gentle person. Her parents got her into therapy, and it seems to be really helping. As is our new endeavour. And if it's working, I can't fault it.

Besides, she has me to help her now.

"I love your optimism," I say.

I catch her rolling her eyes before diving back into the typing. The keys emit a pleasant noise. "What about something like this—"

The basement door opens, followed by the sound of quick feet descending in succession. Jonesy and Cam appear manoeuvring a giant board down the stairs, so big it takes both of them to carry it.

"Do I dare ask?"

Amber sits forward. "Is it what I think it is—"

Cam nods his head furiously before she can finish her sentence. "Yep!"

Before I know it, Amber pushes her laptop to the other side of the couch and clambers over, dropping on to the arm beside me.

"OK, I'm ready," she says. Somehow, she hasn't woken up Macey. This dog, I swear, sleeps through anything.

"What is this?" I say. "Did I miss the memo or something?" I don't like the idea of them leaving me out.

Jonesy raises his eyebrows at me and grins. I feel a flicker of unease. *Seriously … what did I miss?* I know I'm the new girl but it's been nearly four months now. I feel like I have a right to be kept in the loop.

Cam clears his throat. "Ladies and gentlemen." He pauses… "And Macey…"

At the sound of her name, she wakes up and bounds towards Cam.

Seriously?

Forced to fuss her, he reaches down and rubs at her head for a long moment. I have no idea what's going on, but I'm invested now. I love Macey but that's enough fuss. This is killing me – wrong choice of words. I *need* to know.

Eventually, Macey saunters off into her bed. In the next second, she's asleep again. Oh, to be a dog. Life would be so simple. I wouldn't be stressed about what I'm doing after high school. Sure, I can go to college. But after what we've done, that sounds kind of tame.

Well, that question may be answered now. All thanks to us solving the case. It turns out, we are pretty good at solving mysteries. And other people think so too, because, after it all went down, we started getting attention from people in Sanera. People wanting us to solve their problems. Only small ones, like missing jewellery and pets, but it's been fun using our skills. And, honestly, it's nice spending time with friends and it still being considered "work". The best of both worlds, really.

"Where were we?" Cam says, raising the board up again. He and Jonesy exchange a warm look. Their relationship got off to a rocky start, to put it mildly, but finally they're safe, they're free, and more importantly, they're happy.

"I present to you…" He and Jonesy swiftly tug the board around, unveiling the big secret. "The official logo for our mystery-solving service!"

For a moment, all I can take in are the colours – bright lilac and yellow, and a pinch of green. Then, the image takes shape. A paw print that's also a magnifying glass. The perfect logo for our business.

Ours. Mine and my friends'.

"It's incredible!" Amber calls out.

I finally understand their excitement. "I love it," I say truthfully. "Bright, striking and effective."

For the first time, I realize how serious they are about the venture. School finishes for good in a few months. I have college offers, of course. Jonesy and Amber have scholarships lined up. Cam ended up receiving a great sports scholarship at a decent college, even if he was trying to convince us he was a screw-up. Eventually, we'll probably have to go our separate ways. But until then ... we have this.

I go back to what Cam's mom told us when he was still recovering: "There's something there for you guys and I don't think you should pass it up. You'd be silly not to do it."

I smile to myself at the memory. That promotion she almost died for – she got it. Cam drove her to the rescheduled meeting. She's now a senior managing consultant, which will most likely come in handy for us at some point. The rest of our parents are supportive but nowhere near as hands-on. And things are looking up for everyone. Amber's parents have chilled out about her being friends with Cam and Jonesy, and her therapist encouraged her to talk to them about her bisexuality too. They've been way cooler than she expected. Jonesy's mom has stayed clean this last four months and built bridges with his dad so they can be better parents together. Sanera High has recovered from having a serial killer in the history department and the teachers have bent over backwards trying to help. Everyone is worried for us, of course, especially as we're putting ourselves out there and fighting crime – but they're hopeful for our future too. They agree it's worth the risk. Our last risk saved the town. The next one could be … well, who knows what that could be!

I smile. I can't believe that I have this life, with friends who accept me and my past. I can finally put what happened with Nancy behind me.

She really did fall, by the way. In case you were wondering.

I'd like to say we have no secrets from each other any more. But that's not quite true.

It's better for everyone that I keep this one. Jonesy had every right to be jealous of my smarts, even if he insists he never was, because he never found out where the treasure really was.

I did though.

Something always niggled at me, from that first visit to Carrington Manor. The word "library", scratched into the desk drawer. Robert had clearly left that clue for a reason. But there wasn't a library in Carrington Manor. Even when Sheriff Rogers raided the place, with the knowledge of the secret passages, they never found a library. I consulted all the plans, even found some floor plans hidden away. Nothing. It perplexed me for a while – until I really sat down and thought about it.

Robert Carrington hid his wealth somewhere no one would ever suspect.

Somewhere that would never be torn apart.

Somewhere *too historic to the town*.

Sanera Public Library.

It was under our noses the entire time. It's really quite funny, because I don't think even Mr Graham, who dedicated his life to the mystery, ever realized that. He was adamant it was somewhere in the house, somewhere in those tunnels, when it turned out he couldn't have been further from the truth. Isn't that poetic justice? Robert knew people would eventually come sniffing for his treasure, so he built the tunnels to send them down the wrong track. How hilarious, that the man Mr Graham *idolized* fucked him over. Planted fake treasure to top it off.

I know keeping this secret is the best thing to do. At this point, the treasure has done more damage than good. I don't want it falling into the wrong hands because I saw first-hand what greed can do to a person.

Of course, I'm not sure exactly where in the library it's hidden, and I don't *want* to know, although I think Mrs Adler might have wondered about it too. I think back to the old creaky floorboards when we first set out on this whole enterprise. That would be a good hiding spot.

But, as I say, it's better that it stays buried.

"Buffy?" Cam pulls me from my thoughts. "What do you think?"

As I sit here, smiling with my friends, I realize I'm truly happy. For the first time since Nancy died, I feel happy again. With my new friends who I've been to hell and back with.

"Listen, I like it," I say. Then I make my voice serious. "But there's just one thing you haven't considered … something pretty important."

I wait for their smiles to falter, for the worry to set in, before I continue.

"If we're going to solve mysteries, then we're going to need a name."

ACKNOWLEDGEMENTS

So the time has come to write the acknowledgements for *Let's Split Up*, something I never thought I'd get the chance to do. This has been my dream book since its inception in 2021, a novel where I could blend all the media I grew up with and I'm still obsessed with today. It all started when I asked myself the question 'What if *Scooby-Doo* was a little scarier?' ... and the rest is history.

First off, I want to thank my editor, Polly Lyall Grant, who took a chance on this story. My publishing journey has been unconventional, to say the least, so I can't fully put into words how grateful I am that you saw my vision for this wacky book. I got the offer for my book deal while I was serving customers at my old bookselling job – a moment I will never forget. And, yes, I barely did any work for the rest of the day.

I have a screenshot of a conversation from two years ago saying how Scholastic would be the perfect home for *Let's Split Up*. I couldn't have been more correct. It's been the greatest time working with the team. Ellen and Eleanor, thank you for being as excited about this book as I am. Your ideas have been invaluable.

Genevieve, Wendy, Judith and Sarah – your editorial advice made this book the best it could be and taught me that maybe there is such a thing as too many em-dashes. Thank you.

Tina, my superstar publicist, I am so lucky to have you on my team. The moment I had my first conversation with you, your enthusiasm shone through, and I knew this book, and myself, were in expert hands. Thank you so much.

A huge thank you to Jamie Gregory for the epic book cover. It's so striking and encapsulates the story so well. Legend.

Thank you to my agent, Alice Caprio. I know our relationship is still in its early stages, but your support has been so helpful. I can't wait to see what we do next!

To my former Waterstones team – Meg, Jenny, Marie, Yas, Jo, Matt, Sarah, Lindsay and anyone else I've had the pleasure of working with. Your support while I was drowning in deadlines means the world to me; you guys know how much I miss you. You're more than just colleagues to me.

Joe Hall, your friendship is so special. I can't wait to see you conquer the world with your stories. P.S. how much longer do I have to wait to read your WIP?

Emma Finnerty, I don't think I could've done this without your encouragement and friendship. Your knowledge and general awesomeness made this journey so much easier.

Ben Alderson, you've been my biggest supporter and I'm so privileged to call you a friend. I am so bloody proud of what you've accomplished in the past year. It's just going to get better.

Rosie Talbot, I think back to our trip to York with El when *Sixteen Souls* came out. I never in a million years thought I'd get to say that we share a publisher! Your advice changed my life. Thank you.

Jasmine, my oldest author friend. Thank you for always having my back. You guys are not ready for her gorgeous romances.

Thank you to my online friends and author icons. Char Hesslewood, Andy Darcy Theo, Beth (@readbybeth), David Kang, Frances Wren, Lucy Rose, Joel Rochester, Kat McKenna and so many others. Your kind words mean more than you realize.

Suraka, your video was the first thing I saw when I opened TikTok after announcing my book deal. I cried. Thank you for being such an incredible champion for this book.

Mom and Dad, I love you so much. Never once have you doubted me. Now look where we are. Thank you for buying me the *Scooby-Doo on Zombie Island* VHS and kick-starting this whole thing.

To Ted, the best little brother I could ask for. Thank you for letting me project my love of mystery-solving teens on to you. You're the Scooby to my Shaggy.

And Charl, my not-so-little sister, I guess you can be Scrappy. Love you too.

My gorgeous dog, Macey, who became a character in this book. Originally, book Macey had a different name, but it just didn't feel right.

Weasel, Nan, Grandad, other Nan and everyone in between – I love you all so much.

Thank you to my friends Wiki, Abby, Rhea, Charlie, Jessie, Greta and anyone else along the way. You're the best.

Finally, all of you. Whether you've been following me on TikTok since the start, or you found me last week, or you just saw this in the bookshop and it caught your eye, thank you so much. Being an author has always been a dream of mine and that dream is finally coming true.

Bill Wood is a former Waterstones bookseller with a growing online platform. In less than three years, he has amassed a following of over 120,000 bookworms and ten million likes on his TikTok. Bill has a BA with honours in film and screenwriting from Birmingham City University. He currently lives with his family and Staffordshire bull terrier, Macey. *Let's Split Up* is his debut traditionally published YA novel.

**LOOK OUT FOR
MORE NAIL-BITING
YA HORROR FROM
BILL WOOD IN
AUTUMN 2025**